Praise for New York
bestselling auth
and her Hope

"A sometimes heartbreaking tale of love and relationships in a small Colorado town…. Poignant and sweet, this tale of second chances will appeal to fans of military-flavored sweet romance."
—*Publishers Weekly* on *Christmas in Snowflake Canyon*

"Once again, Thayne proves she has a knack for capturing those emotions that come from the heart…. Crisp storytelling and many amusing moments make for a delightful read."
—*RT Book Reviews* on *Willowleaf Lane*

"RaeAnne Thayne has continued her tradition of creating believable, flawed characters that reflect our lives."
—*Idaho Statesman* on *Currant Creek Valley*

"Hope's Crossing is a charming series that lives up to its name. Reading these stories of small-town life engage the reader's heart and emotions, inspiring hope and the belief miracles are possible."
—Debbie Macomber, #1 *New York Times* bestselling author, on *Sweet Laurel Falls*

"Plenty of tenderness and Colorado sunshine flavor this pleasant escape."
—*Publishers Weekly* on *Woodrose Mountain*

"Thayne, once again, delivers a heartfelt story of a caring community and a caring romance between adults who have triumphed over tragedies."
—*Booklist* on *Woodrose Mountain*

"Readers will love this novel for the cast of characters and its endearing plotline…. A thoroughly enjoyable read."
—*RT Book Reviews* on *Woodrose Mountain*

"Thayne's series starter introduces the Colorado town of Hope's Crossing in what can be described as a cozy romance… [a] gentle, easy read."
—*Publishers Weekly* on *Blackberry Summer*

"Thayne's depiction of a small Colorado mountain town is subtle but evocative. Readers who love romance but not explicit sexual details will delight in this heartfelt tale of healing and hope."
—*Booklist* on *Blackberry Summer*

RaeAnne Thayne

Wild Iris Ridge

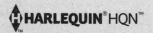

Recycling programs
for this product may
not exist in your area.

ISBN-13: 978-0-373-77859-1

WILD IRIS RIDGE

Copyright © 2014 by RaeAnne Thayne

All rights reserved. Except for use in any review, the reproduction or utilization of this work in whole or in part in any form by any electronic, mechanical or other means, now known or hereinafter invented, including xerography, photocopying and recording, or in any information storage or retrieval system, is forbidden without the written permission of the publisher, Harlequin HQN, 225 Duncan Mill Road, Don Mills, Ontario M3B 3K9, Canada.

This is a work of fiction. Names, characters, places and incidents are either the product of the author's imagination or are used fictitiously, and any resemblance to actual persons, living or dead, business establishments, events or locales is entirely coincidental.

This edition published by arrangement with Harlequin Books S.A.

For questions and comments about the quality of this book, please contact us at CustomerService@Harlequin.com.

® and TM are trademarks of Harlequin Enterprises Limited or its corporate affiliates. Trademarks indicated with ® are registered in the United States Patent and Trademark Office, the Canadian Intellectual Property Office and in other countries.

Printed in U.S.A.

To my siblings, Brad, Maureen, Chris, Mike, Jennie and Carrie, who have set a wonderful example to me of caring, compassion and strength. I love you and I'm incredibly grateful for our big, noisy, crazy family.

CHAPTER ONE

THIS WAS, WITHOUT question, the craziest thing she had ever done.

Lucy Drake stood on the front porch of her great-aunt's house, shivering at the cold, damp breeze that slid under her jacket.

She ought to just find a hotel somewhere in Hope's Crossing to spend the night, instead of standing here on the dark and rather creepy-under-the-circumstances doorstep of a massive Victorian mansion after midnight in the middle of an April rainstorm.

If she had an ounce of brains or sense, that is exactly what she would do—climb back into her BMW and head for the nearest hotel. Hope's Crossing was overflowing with them, and on a shoulder-season April night when the ski tourists were gone, she could probably find hundreds of empty rooms.

Then again, if she had either of those things—brains *or* sense—she wouldn't be in this situation. Right now, she would probably be at the end of an eighteen-hour workday, heading back to her quiet condo on Lake Washington with another few hours of work ahead of her before she finally crashed.

Another gust of freezing wind whined fitfully under the eaves and sent the branches of the red maple beside the porch clawing across the roof like skeletal fingers.

She zipped up her coat and reached for the doorknob of the house. Crazy, she might be, but she didn't need to be cold and crazy, too.

The door was locked, of course. What else had she expected, when Iris House had been empty since December and Annabelle's shocking death? Even though she had known it would be locked, she still felt a hard kernel of panic in her gut at one more obstacle.

What if she couldn't get in tonight? What if she could *never* get in? Where would she go? She had come all this way, two days of driving from Seattle. She had subleased her condo, packed all her belongings, brought everything with her. She would be stranded without a home, without shelter, in a town where the two people she cared most about in the world were both gone.

The lateness of the hour and her own exhaustion from the stress of the past week pressed in on her, macerating her control. She felt it slipping through her fingers like fine-grained sand but she forced herself to take a deep breath.

Okay. Calm. She could handle this. She had fully expected the door to be locked. No one had lived here for months. If she had showed up on the doorstep of the old house and found it wasn't secure, *then* she would have cause to worry.

This wasn't a problem. She knew right where her great-aunt always hid the spare key—assuming no one had changed the locks, of course....

She wasn't going to go there yet. Instead, she turned on the flashlight app of her phone and used the small glow it provided to guide her way around the corner of the wraparound porch.

The chains of the old wood porch swing clanked and rattled as she sat down, a familiar and oddly comforting sound. She reached for the armrest closest to the front door with one hand, aiming the light from her phone with the other.

After a little fumbling, her fingers found the catch and she opened the tiny, clever hidden compartment Annabelle had created herself inside the armrest.

Only someone who knew the magic secret of the porch swing could ever find the hollowed-out hiding place. She reached inside and felt around until her fingers encountered the ice-cold metal of the key to Iris House.

"Thank you, Annabelle," she murmured.

She discovered that no one had changed the locks when she inserted the key and turned it. See, there was a bright spot. Next hurdle: What if the security code had been changed since her last visit?

Knowing she didn't have a moment to spare, she didn't take time to savor the scents of rosemary and lemon wood polish and *home* that greeted her inside.

Instead, she bolted to the keypad for the state-of-the-art security system Annabelle had installed several years ago. Her fingers fumbled on the keypad but she managed to type in the numbers that corresponded with the letters *H-O-P-E*.

The system announced it was now disarmed. Only then did she let herself sigh with relief, trying not to notice how the small sound echoed through the empty space.

She flipped the light switch in the entryway, with its parquet floor and the magnificent curving staircase made up of dozens of intricately turned balusters.

How many times had she rushed into this entryway during the two years she'd lived here during her teen years and called to Annabelle she was home before dropping her books on the bottom step to take up to her room later?

Suddenly she had an image of when she'd first arrived at fifteen, her heart angry and battered, showing up at a distant relative's home with everything she owned in bags at her feet.

Apparently, things hadn't changed that much in seventeen years—except this time her bags were still out in the car.

She turned around, half expecting Annabelle to come bustling through the doorway from the kitchen in one of those zip-up half aprons she always wore that had a hundred pockets, arms outstretched and ready to wrap her into a soft, sweet-smelling embrace.

That familiar sense of disorienting loss gnawed through her as she remembered Annabelle wouldn't bustle through that door ever again.

She felt something dig into her palm and realized she was still clutching the key from the front porch. She slid it onto the table, making a mental note to return it to its hiding place later then took another of her cleansing breaths.

Right now she needed to focus. She desperately needed sleep and a chance to regroup and regain a little perspective.

The air inside Iris House was stale, cold. She walked through turning on lights as she headed for the thermostat outside the main-floor bedroom Annabelle had used the past few years when it became harder for her to reach the second or third floors.

The heating system thermostat was set for sixty-two degrees, probably to keep the pipes from freezing during the winter, but the actual temperature read in the mid-fifties.

She tried turning the heating system off and then on again—about the sum total of her HVAC expertise. When no answering whoosh of warm air responded through the vents, she frowned. Annabelle used to complain the pilot light in the furnace could be tricky at times. Apparently this was one of those times.

Lucy was torn between laughter and tears. What did a girl have to do to catch a break around here? She had walked away from everything and packed up her life to come here, seeking the security and safety she had always found at Iris House.

With all the possible complications that could have ensnarled her journey here from Seattle, she had finally made it and now a stupid pilot light would be the one thing keeping her from reaching her goal of staying here.

It didn't have to be a stumbling block. Last time she counted, the old house had nine fireplaces and she had seen a pile of seasoned firewood against the garage when she pulled up. She didn't have to heat the whole house, just one room. She could pick one and spend a perfectly comfortable night in front of the fire then have a furnace technician come in the next day.

And wasn't that some kind of metaphor for her life right now? Who ever said she had to fix every disaster she had created right this moment? She only had to focus on making it through tonight then she could sort the rest of it out later.

Considering none of the beds likely had linens at

all—and certainly not fresh ones—for tonight she would bunk on the sofa in the room Annabelle had used as a TV room, she decided, and deal with the rest of the mess in the morning.

"You can do this," she said aloud.

Hearing her own voice helped push away some of the ghosts that wandered through the house. Annabelle. Jess. Even her younger self, angry and wounded.

Energized by having a viable plan of action, she quickly headed out into the rain again and grabbed an armload of wood from the pile, enough to keep the cold at bay for several hours, at least. Trust Annabelle to keep her woodpile covered and protected so the wood was dry and ready to burn. Her great-aunt had probably cut it all herself.

Back inside, she dropped the pile of wood on the hearth in the cozy little den and found matches and kindling sticks in a canister on the mantel.

She was *so* not a Girl Scout, but Annabelle had insisted both she and Jessica learn the proper way to light a fire. Those long-ago lessons bubbled back to the surface, and in moments she had a tidy little blaze going.

Perfect. In no time, the room would be cozy and comfortable.

She added a larger split log and watched the flames dance around it for a moment before they caught hold. Already the house felt a little warmer, not quite as empty and lonely.

She yawned, tempted to curl up right this instant on the sofa and drop off. No. She would sleep better in a nightgown, with her teeth brushed and her face washed. Closing the door to the room behind her to hold on to the heat, she headed out for one more bone-chilling trip to the car for the suitcase that held her essentials.

She carried the case straight to the bathroom just off the kitchen and made it through her ablutions with bleary eyes. After grabbing a couple of blankets out of the linen chest in the downstairs guest room, she opened the door to the den—and was greeted by thick, choking black smoke.

For an instant, her exhausted brain couldn't quite process this latest disaster in a depressingly long line of them. Then in a wild burst of panic, her synapses started blasting messages, one after the other, and she had the presence of mind to slam the door shut.

Smoke. Blaze. Iris House was on fire.

"No! No, no no!"

It was probably just the chimney not drawing correctly. That's all. *Calm down.* She would just put the fire out and air out the room and all would be fine.

Fire extinguisher! Where was the bloody fire extinguisher? Annabelle always kept one under the kitchen sink, she remembered. She raced back and yanked open the cabinets then blessed her great-aunt's independent, self-reliant mindset. The fire extinguisher was attached right to the inside door.

Lucy yanked it off and quickly scanned the instructions, then stopped long enough to grab a dishcloth out of a drawer to cover her mouth before charging back to the den.

She couldn't see any flames through the smoke, which further reinforced the idea that a chimney draw issue was to blame. She hoped, anyway. At the same time, she wasn't completely stupid. If she couldn't deal with the problem on her own, she would call the fire department.

Coughing, eyes burning from the smoke, she activated the fire extinguisher and sprayed toward the logs.

The fire sizzled and spat at coming into contact with the chemical as the extinguisher did its job.

Okay. Crisis averted.

She hurried and unlatched the window to let some of the smoke out. Just as she turned around, she heard an ominous crackling and a loud, angry roar from overhead.

Her stomach turned over. She had heard that sound once before, in one of the upstairs bedrooms one memorable wintry January day when she was seventeen. This was more than a problem with a poorly drawing flue. This was a chimney fire.

In that previous fire when she was living here, that had been a case of an old bird's nest falling and igniting. This could be another one or perhaps creosote buildup had ignited.

Whatever the reason, this was a nightmare. Chimney fires burned hot and fierce and could burn through the masonry, the walls. Everything. In addition, flying debris could ignite the roof and take down the entire hundred-twenty-year-old historic mansion.

She couldn't burn down Iris House. She had nothing else left.

Though she knew it was risky, in one last desperate effort, she aimed the fire extinguisher up the chimney, adrenaline shooting through her as fast and fierce as those flames, until the chemical ran out then she scooped up her purse and raced for the door with her phone in hand, already dialing 911.

Apparently, someone beat her to it. She ran out onto the porch just as a couple of guys in full uniforms were running out of a fire truck parked behind her car, lights flashing. Another engine was just pulling up behind it.

Somebody must have seen the smoke pouring out the window and called it in. Yay for nosy neighbors.

"Is there anybody else inside?" one of the firefighters asked her.

"No. Just me. It's a chimney fire, centered in the den. Go to the end of the hall, last door on the right."

"Thanks."

"Oh, am I so glad to see you guys," she called to the third firefighter she encountered as she headed down the steps of the porch.

This one wasn't in turnout gear, only a coat and helmet that shielded his features in the smoke and the gloomy night. She had only an impression of height and impressive bulk before he spoke in a voice as hard and terrifying as the fire.

"You won't be so glad to see us when we have you arrested for trespassing, arson and criminal mischief."

Lucy screwed her eyes shut as recognition flooded through her.

Oh, joy.

She should have known. Brendan Caine. He was probably the reason she hadn't wanted to call the fire department in the first place. Her subconscious probably had been gearing up for this encounter since she saw that first puff of smoke.

It would have been nice if she could have spent at least an hour or two in Hope's Crossing before she had to face this man who just happened to despise her. Not the way her luck was going these days, apparently.

She lifted her chin. "How can I be trespassing in my own house, Chief Caine?"

He jerked his head up as if she had lobbed a fireball at him. In the glow from the porch light, she saw his rugged features go slack with shock. "Lucy? What the hell?"

She tried for a nonchalant shrug. "Apparently, having the chimneys cleaned is now at the top of my to-do list."

"You did this?"

"The furnace wouldn't kick on so I thought I would warm the place up with a fire"

"The pilot light has been dicey all winter. I've been meaning to have somebody in to look at it. I've had to relight it a couple times a week."

Of course. He only lived about four houses down the street—and since Annabelle had been Jessica's great-aunt, too, Brendan would naturally feel responsible for looking after Iris House.

"I didn't know how to light it and I was freezing," she said. "I just figured I would stay warm with a fire tonight and deal with the furnace in the morning."

"And you never thought to go to a hotel?"

"Why go to a hotel when I happen to own a twenty-room mansion?"

Before he could answer, the two firefighters who had first charged into the house came out. "Chimney fire," one said. "Looks like some creosote ignited. It's mostly extinguished but we'll need to head up to the roof to put out any hot spots."

She wanted to sit right down on the porch steps and sob with relief—but she would never do that in front of Brendan Caine, of course.

He pulled out a radio and issued instructions in it that were completely beyond her understanding, something about a ladder truck.

"I want my paramedics to take a look at you," he said to her after he finished.

"That's not necessary. I'm fine."

"It wasn't a request," he said, his tone hard. "We need to be sure your lungs are okay after breathing all that smoke."

He spoke to a couple other guys who had just pulled up. "Redmond. Chen. Run vitals on Ms. Drake here. Let me know if you think we need to transport her to the E.R."

"I'm perfectly fine. I don't need to be checked out, and I certainly don't need to go to any E.R!"

One of the paramedics, a big, burly bald guy with a mustache and incongruously sweet features gave her an apologetic smile. "It won't take long, ma'am."

They led her over to a waiting ambulance. Had Brendan called out *every* truck in his entire department? For the next ten minutes she sat mortified on a stretcher while they checked everything. Oxygen levels, normal. Blood pressure, slightly high—no big surprise there. Temperature and reflexes, all as they should be.

"Everything checks out," the bald guy said.

"I told you it would."

"Sorry, ma'am. We have to follow procedure. The chief can be a stickler about that."

"Am I free to go?"

"As far as we're concerned."

Not knowing what else to do, she retreated to the safety of her car and for the next hour watched as the

Hope's Crossing volunteer fire department scrambled across the various roof levels, climbed up and down ladders and peeked through windows, checking out every inch of Iris House.

Finally, they seemed to be certain the fire was completely out. The ambulance peeled away first then one engine after another until only the first ladder truck and the SUV that said Fire Chief on the side were left.

When Brendan walked onto the porch, speaking into his radio, she finally gathered the courage to climb out of her vehicle and approach him.

The rain had stopped, but the April night was still cold, with a damp wind that seemed to burrow beneath her coat.

He looked surprised to see her again, as if he had just remembered her existence—and probably would have preferred to forget it.

"I guess you're okay or the paramedics would have taken you to the hospital."

"I'm fine. Just like I told you. What are the damages to the house?"

"Too soon to say. You've got smoke damage, definitely, though it seems to be isolated to the TV room. We've got the windows open, airing things out."

"That's a relief."

"It could have been a lot worse."

She shivered as all the nightmare images that had been parading through her mind seemed to march a little faster. "I really do appreciate everyone. Please tell your department thank you for me. I'm sorry to call them out of their beds in the middle of the night."

"It's part of the job," he said, his tone dismissive. He tilted his head. "Now, you want to tell me what the hell you're doing here? Why didn't you tell anyone you were coming?"

She shrugged. She couldn't tell him everything, the personal and professional humiliation she had left behind. "Spur-of-the-moment decision."

"You're lucky you didn't end up fried to a crisp."

What would have happened if the creosote hadn't ignited so quickly? If it had smoldered for an hour or so, until she was sound asleep just a few feet away from the fire? She would have died of smoke inhalation first and *then* been fried to a crisp.

Cold panic dripped down her spine, but she clamped down on the nerves before they could flood her completely.

"I know."

He gave her one of those dark looks that could mean anything. "You can't stay here tonight. You understand that, right? We need to make sure the house is safe tonight, with no lingering hot spots. You'll have to find a hotel."

If she had only done that in the first place, they wouldn't be having this conversation right now.

"I can do that," she said.

Of course, he didn't invite her to stay at his house. They didn't have that kind of amicable relationship, despite the fact that she was godmother to his children or that his late wife had been not only her cousin but her dearest friend in the world.

"I still can't quite wrap my head around you showing up in the middle of the night like this. You should have let me know you were coming. I could have made sure the pilot light was turned on for you, and none of this would have happened."

She was tempted to remind him caustically that she didn't need his permission to visit her own house. He might be watching over it, but *she* had been Annabelle's only surviving heir.

Iris House should have been Jessica's. She had adored the place, and she and Annabelle had always talked about turning it into a bed and breakfast one day after the children were grown, with Jess running the day-to-day details.

But Annabelle and Jess were both gone. Lucy was the only one left, the sole owner of this rambling old Victorian mining mansion she had never wanted in a town she had once been so eager to leave. Since her own dreams had just burned up hotter than any creosote fire, she had decided to borrow Jessica's for a while.

"Like I said, spur-of-the-moment decision. I didn't think things through."

"How very unlike you," he said, his voice dry enough to make her bristle.

She was too tired to fight with him tonight. Instead, she changed the subject. "How much damage do you think the fire caused?"

"We won't know until we inspect things in the morning. From what I could see, the fire seemed to be contained to the chimney. I doubt you'll see any structural damage but we can't be certain until at least tomorrow. It might be Monday or Tuesday by the time we know anything." He paused. "Are you planning to stick around that long?"

She glanced at the house, feeling that steady, relentless dribble of panic again. "Yes," she said, lips tight.

She had no reason to tell this man who disliked her

so intently that she would be here for the immediate future, that she had nothing left but this smoke-damaged house that sat in the rain like a graceful grande dame.

"You can call the fire station and leave the name of your hotel once you figure it out. I'll get in touch with you as soon as I know whether the house is safe to inhabit."

She could afford a night or two in a hotel, but she would have to come up with another solution if this dragged on longer than that—especially if she was going to pour all her resources into pursuing Jess's dream. Again, nothing she was willing to share with Fire Chief Caine.

"Thanks," she murmured.

He studied her for a minute longer and she knew she must be a mess—bedraggled and sooty and smelling of smoke and fire extinguisher chemicals.

"Welcome back. I guess."

SOMETHING WAS UP.

Brendan frowned as he watched Lucy Drake slide back behind the wheel of her fancy BMW. She sat for a moment gazing out the front windshield into the darkness as if she couldn't quite remember how to put the car in gear.

He was aware of a tiny, wriggling concern, like a slippery earthworm in the garden he couldn't quite grasp.

Usually, she was brash and confident, striding through the world with her designer suits and leather briefcases.

On her rare visits to Hope's Crossing before Jess had died, Lucy would blow in with a backseat full of expensive gifts for the kids and for Jess and story after story about her exciting life in Seattle as the marketing director at a hugely successful and rapidly expanding software company.

Yeah, the circumstances were rough tonight. It had to be a rude welcome for her to come back to Iris House and end up with a chimney fire five minutes later.

That didn't completely explain the way she had been acting. The woman who had just headed away looking lost and alone didn't seem at all like the fiercely driven go-getter who usually made no secret of her disdain for him.

Don't you think you can do better than a washed-up jock with more muscles than brains?

He pushed away the bitter memory he hadn't realized still haunted him somewhere deep inside to find he wasn't alone in his contemplation of Lucy's little red BMW.

Pete Valentine, one of his volunteer firefighters who ran a successful plumbing business the rest of the time, stood at his elbow. The other man licked his bottom lip with a greedy sort of look as his gaze followed her taillights. "Lucy Drake. She's still as hot as ever. Man, she used to make my balls ache in high school."

He glowered at the locker room talk which, unfortunately, wasn't all that uncommon among his crew at times.

Pete was married to a nurse at the hospital. If she heard him talking like this, Janet would probably give him a whole new definition of aching balls.

Pete seemed to take his silence as tacit permission. "Something about that whole badass-Goth-girl thing just did it for me, you know? Especially because she was so smart on top of all that attitude. Honor roll, the whole thing. I sat behind her in Mrs. McKnight's English class senior year, and I spent the whole semester trying to get a peek beneath all that black leather, if you know what I mean."

He had always thought he liked Pete, but right now he wanted to take one of the attack fire hoses to him, for reasons he didn't quite understand.

"Yeah, well, how about we don't take any more visits down your horny teenage memory lane while we have a job to finish?" he growled.

Pete blinked at his tone and his glare. "Uh, sure, Chief. Sorry. I didn't mean anything by it. I was just surprised to see her, that's all."

Yeah. Join the club, Brendan thought as Pete hurried away.

He never would have guessed when he tucked the kids in at home with Mrs. Madison and drove past this very house on his way to his shift that evening that he would be back here—and facing Lucy in the process.

Though her car was long gone, he still couldn't help gazing down the road where she had traveled.

He hadn't missed how evasive she had been when he'd asked how long she was staying. He had to hope it was only a day or two.

Some people just tended to shake things up wherever they went, to spawn chaos and tumult without even trying. Lucy had that particular gift in spades—as tonight clearly indicated.

He and Carter and Faith were finally digging their way out of the deep, inky chasm Jess's death had tossed them all into. They were finally settling back into a routine, moving forward with one steady foot in front of the other. His kids didn't need Lucy to aim all that chaos in their direction and shake up the world that was finally feeling calm for the first time in two years.

No sense in worrying about it, he thought as he turned back to the fire and all the details he needed to do in order to clear the scene and send his engines back to the house.

One thing about Lucy. She never stayed long in Hope's Crossing. In a few days, no doubt she would be packing up her little red car and heading back into the fray, to Seattle and her high-powered career and the world where she belonged.

CHAPTER TWO

A MAN WHO had reached the ripe old age of thirty-six ought to have picked up a little sense along the way.

The next morning, Brendan sipped at his coffee at the counter of his father's café, The Center of Hope, waiting for some of Pop's delectable French toast. Though his cup was still half-full, Pop topped him off without asking the minute he set it back down.

"Lucy Drake! That darling girl." Dermot's weathered features creased into a concerned frown. "You're certain, are you, that she came to no harm, then? Did you give her an examination?"

"I had a couple of the EMTs check her out. They reported all her vital statistics were normal. She was only exposed to the smoke for a few moments."

"You didn't check her out yourself?"

"No, Pop. I relied on the word of a couple guys who have a combined twenty years as emergency medical technicians. Maybe I shouldn't have been so trusting."

"She's a family friend. Godmother to your children. You can't be too careful with people who are that important."

Did Pop mean it was okay for Brendan to provide subpar care to the various strangers he encountered in the course of his job every day? "You can put your mind at ease. She was fine when she left Iris House last night, I promise."

"That's a relief. And you're sure she had no burns?"

"Positive."

He should have expected this interrogation. By his very nature, Dermot was concerned about everybody in Hope's Crossing, but he especially fretted over those he had taken under his wing. For reasons known only to him, Dermot had developed a soft spot for Lucy from the moment she showed up in town to live with her great-aunt, all black clothes and pale makeup and a truckload full of attitude.

Brendan sighed and sipped his coffee. When he'd decided on the spur of the moment to grab a quick bite of breakfast at the Center of Hope Café before he headed home, he had hoped he could avoid thinking about Lucy for five minutes—something he had found impossible throughout the night as he worked the rest of his shift.

Dermot wasn't making that task particularly easy by bringing the woman up the moment Brendan walked into the café. He should have known his father would have heard about the fire the night before, that it would be a central topic of discussion in town.

Dermot knew *everything* that went on in Hope's Crossing, from the precipitation level for the month to the color of Mayor Beaumont's new suit. Owning the town's most popular gathering spot meant he was usually privy to the best gossip and the most interesting tidbits.

Flashing lights and an assortment of ladder and pumper trucks showing up in the middle of the night to one of the town's historic silver baron mansions would certainly have set tongues wagging.

The minute Brendan walked into the café, Dermot had demanded all the details about the chimney fire excitement at Iris House—and particularly about the juicy rumors that Lucy Drake had been the cause of it.

"Where did she spend the night, do you know?"

He sighed. "Can't tell you that, Pop. Sorry I didn't think to press her for more details about her lodging arrangements. I was a little busy. You know, putting out the fire and all."

Dermot was unfazed by his dry response. With six strapping sons and a daughter, very little *could* faze his father, especially not a bit of mild sarcasm.

"I hadn't heard she was coming back to town, had you?"

"No. She didn't tell me." A little warning would have been nice. Air-raid sirens, at the very least.

"How long is she planning to stay?"

"No idea," he answered.

"Well, have you told the children yet?" Dermot persisted. "Carter and Faith will be thrilled to see her, won't they? Why, Faith is always talking about her aunt Lucy sending her this or that, video-conferencing with her on the computer, emailing her a special note."

He picked up his coffee cup with another sigh. So much for hoping he could eat a hearty breakfast without having to think about the woman for five minutes.

"I haven't seen them yet. I had a meeting first thing when my shift ended and didn't catch them before they left for school this morning. Mrs. Madison took them. My plan was to grab some breakfast here and then head home and crash for a few hours until school is out. I'm sure I'll have the chance to tell them later."

They *would* be over the moon at the unexpected treat of a visit from their favorite aunt. Lucy wasn't truly their aunt. She and Jess had been cousins, linked mostly through their relationship with Annabelle, but his late wife had adored Lucy like a sister.

She had been the maid of honor at their wedding. In typical Lucy fashion, she had been too busy to come back for any of the pre-matrimonial events until the weekend of the wedding, where she had appeared late to the rehearsal dinner with apologies about a last-minute meeting she couldn't miss and then had left early from the reception to catch a flight.

"They do love her," Dermot said. "She's been good to them, hasn't she? As busy as they keep her at that outfit where she works, she still somehow found time to fly down for Faith's birthday last year, remember? Just to take her to Denver. Faith didn't stop talking about the ballet and the shopping for weeks."

Right. Lucy was a saint.

"Faith didn't make some plans with Lucy again to bring her to town, did she?"

"Not that I know about," he answered. He only knew she had been in Hope's Crossing less than eight hours and he was already tired of her.

"Pop, can we talk about something else?"

"Something else?"

"I don't know why Lucy Drake is back in town, and to be honest with you, I don't care much. I only want the little idiot to stay out of my way and to do her best not to burn down Iris House again."

"Darn. I guess that means I'll have to return all the

cans of gasoline and the jumbo box of matches I just bought at the hardware store."

If he hadn't been distracted by the tantalizing smell of bacon after a long shift, he would have smelled Lucy come into the diner before she even spoke. She always wore some kind of subtle, probably expensive scent that reminded him of cream-drenched strawberries.

He swiveled, ignoring Dermot's disapproving glower. She looked none the worse for wear after her adventures of the night before, fresh and bright and lovely.

She was wearing a leather jacket the color of deer hide, tailored and supple, with a scarlet scarf tied in some kind of intricate loose knot around her neck. She looked sophisticated and urbane and, as usual when he was around her, he felt like a dumb jock with more brawn than brains.

"If you saved your receipt," he drawled, fighting back against his own stupid sense of inadequacy, "I'm sure Mose Lewis at the hardware store will take it all back."

She made a face then plopped onto the stool next to him, leaned across the counter and gave Pop a big smacking kiss on the cheek.

"Dermot. You're as handsome as ever. I'm still waiting for you to get tired of this one-horse town and run away with me. You'd never have to pour a cup of coffee again."

The tips of his pop's ears turned red and he smiled, pouring her a cup of coffee.

When he spoke, the traces of Irish accent that still sprinkled his speech intensified. "I have to say, that's a verra appealing offer, m'darling, but I'm afraid I would miss my grandchildren too much."

"Ah, well. I guess I'll have to ease my broken heart with some of your luscious French toast. I've been dreaming about it since I left King County."

Pop beamed at this, as his greatest joy was feeding people—especially those who held a soft spot in his big, generous heart, which certainly qualified Lucy.

"Coming right up. You just sit there and enjoy much better coffee than you'll ever find in Seattle while you listen to my stubborn son apologize for his rudeness."

"I can't wait," she murmured.

Apparently, Brendan wasn't the only one who could wax sarcastic in the morning.

Since it *had* been rude and childish to call her names—and Pop likely wouldn't be quick to let him forget it—he took his medicine like a good boy.

"Sorry I called you an idiot," he muttered.

"Sorry you said it or sorry I happened to walk in just in time to overhear you?"

"Does it matter?"

To his surprise, she smiled a little, though she still had that unsettled, restless look in her eyes. "Not really, I suppose. Nicely done, Chief Caine."

Even big, dumb jocks could use good manners at times, especially when their Pop was standing close enough for a good whack on the knuckles with a wooden spoon.

"So. This is how the fire chief unwinds after an exciting night of serving and protecting the good people of Hope's Crossing."

"Sometimes. It's been a long shift and I'm starving. I didn't feel like cooking breakfast for myself or pouring a bowl of cereal. Since I already missed seeing the kids off to school this morning, I figured, why not?"

He wondered, not for the first time, why he always felt compelled to defend his actions around her.

"If I had a father like yours, I would come here every morning for breakfast."

He didn't miss the slightly wistful tone in her voice. Her home life hadn't been great, he knew, though only secondhand. Jess hadn't shared too many details but he knew Lucy's parents divorced when she was a girl, and she hadn't had a good relationship with her father's second wife.

"How is Iris House?" Lucy asked now. "Do you think it's safe for me to return?"

Though she spoke casually, he sensed an undercurrent of urgency that gave him pause. What was the big rush? She had spent the four months since Annabelle died basically ignoring her legacy. Why was she in a hurry now to stay there? First she showed up after midnight to a dark, cold, *locked* house when any logical person would have gone to a hotel, now she was trying to hurry along the investigation.

Some tiny part of him was tempted to drag the investigation out as long as possible in the hopes that any further complication would make her turn around and head back to Seattle, but that would have been petty and small.

"You should be fine. We've had our inspector go through it from top to bottom and everything appears in order. All the chimneys could use a thorough scrubbing before you use them. I can get you the name of a couple of chimney sweeps in town."

"That would be good. Thanks."

"I relit the pilot light, so you ought to have no trouble running the furnace at this point. You'll want to keep the windows open throughout the day to vent any lingering smoke. Should be a nice, sunny day for it."

"I'll do that."

"Most of the smoke damage seemed to be centered in that den area. You may want to have a cleaning company come in to do a professional job. Sometimes the smell can linger for a long time. I can get you a few of those numbers, too."

She wore an expression of vague surprise, as if she hadn't expected him to be helpful. "Again. Thank you."

"You're welcome."

They lapsed into an awkward sort of silence and he wondered once more why she had come back to town. This close, he could see a return of that fine-edged tension in the set of her mouth and the way she clasped a napkin tightly, as if to keep it from wriggling away.

"How long are you staying in Hope's Crossing?" he finally asked. "I've had a half-dozen people ask me that already, including Pop."

"Why would people automatically assume you know anything about my plans?"

"The very question I have asked myself numerous times, believe me."

Her mouth lifted a little at the corner and he almost thought she wanted to smile but she only picked up her coffee again.

"So?" he pressed.

"I...haven't decided."

He leaned back on the stool. "Now that doesn't sound like the Lucy Drake we all know. You're the woman with the plan, right? Always looking for the best angle, the next big thing."

Her fingers tightened around that recalcitrant napkin. "Not always," she muttered.

Yeah. Something was definitely up. He remembered that strange impression of the night before, that she was lost and even a little frightened.

He didn't like the sudden urge washing over him to wrap a comforting arm around her shoulder and tell her everything would be okay. That was more Dermot's venue, not his. He was just the dumb jock who was once married to her cousin.

And who had once shared a couple pretty heated kisses with Lucy, long before he ever started dating Jess.

He pushed that memory back into the deep recesses of his brain, right where it belonged. He had done his best for more than a decade to forget about that night.

"I thought NexGen couldn't get along without their hotshot marketing director. You don't have some kind of vitally important meeting to get back to in a day or two?"

She was now not so much fidgeting with her napkin as mangling it beyond recognition. "NexGen and I have…parted ways. I'm taking a small vacation to consider my options. A few weeks. A month. I haven't decided."

"Here?"

It was a stupid question, but he was so shocked that he couldn't think what else to say.

He figured when it came to jobs, people fell into four basic categories. Some hated them vehemently, others tolerated them, still others found great satisfaction in what they did. And then there was the fourth category, those passionate few who were basically defined by their vocation.

That was Lucy—and as a result, she had been amazingly successful for someone just barely on the north side of thirty.

Jessica used to always talk about what Lucy had achieved, her awards and honors and status. Sometimes his wife would glow with pride when she talked about Lucy. Other times she would be terse and moody after hearing about how far and how high Lucy had climbed in such a short time.

During those dark times, he wondered if she regretted her decision to marry him just a few years out of college and to give up her teaching career temporarily while the kids were young.

He hoped not. For the rest of their lives, his children would be without their mother. He would always be deeply grateful they had those first uninterrupted years with her.

"I needed a change of scenery," Lucy answered. "And since I've been putting off dealing with the house, I figured now was a good time."

He might not like Lucy much, given their complicated history, but he knew a little about loss. Leaving the job she had loved must be very difficult for her.

"Are you…doing okay?"

"You mean, am I going to be forced to live out of a grocery cart and a refrigerator box? I think I'm probably a few months out from that."

"I meant, are you doing okay, um, emotionally. Change is never easy, even if it was something you wanted. Especially after you lost Annabelle just a few months ago."

She looked surprised at the question and for a moment he saw a raw tangle of emotions in her expression before she donned a haughty sort of look.

"How refreshingly sensitive, Chief Caine. I never would have expected it of you."

He could feel his skin heat. "Forget I asked. Not my business."

Where was Pop with his breakfast, for crying out loud? All he wanted to do was eat his French toast and go home to sleep for a few hours before the kids got home. He wasn't in the mood to make nice to a prickly porcupine.

After a long, awkward moment, she finally spoke. "The truth is, I got fired."

Okay, he hadn't been expecting that one. Fired? Ms. Can-do-no-wrong Drake? What had she done to earn such a dramatic response? Last he heard, she was being groomed for a vice president spot, and now she had been canned? There had to be quite a story behind that one.

Judging by way she didn't meet his gaze after she dropped that little interesting bombshell, he had a feeling she hadn't meant to tell him. So why *had* she?

"That's tough. I'm sorry."

She gave him a wary look. "What? No sarcastic comments about how I probably had it coming?"

What had he ever done to make her think he was the kind of jerk who would kick a woman who had obviously hit a personal low point?

"Not my business. If you wanted to tell me, you would have."

"Our last product launch failed spectacularly," she said after a moment. "It was a PR nightmare. Our entire marketing campaign focused on how much more secure our newest software was than its closest competitor. Within minutes of the product launch, hackers set out to prove us wrong. Our clients have lost millions and the lawsuits have only just begun."

"How is that your fault?"

"Someone needed to take the hit, and after I got into a yelling match with the CEO and the product manager last week and called them both a few choice names, I was nominated."

"Ouch."

"As you can see, last night's stupidity trying to burn down Iris House was just the latest in a string of brilliant decisions on my part."

Before Brendan could come up with an answer to that, Pop came bustling out from the kitchen with two plates piled high with carbohydrates.

"Here you go. Two of the breakfast specials, French toast, just the way you both like it, with strawberries and almond butter."

"I can't believe you remembered that!" she exclaimed.

"You've only been coming in here for it since you were a wee girl."

Brendan thought he was the only one on the planet who ate his French toast like that. How strange, to find that Lucy shared that particular affinity with him.

"I remember because I always thought it funny that you and my boy here liked it the same way, given that you don't usually see eye to eye on many things."

Not much slipped past his pop.

"Isn't it?" she murmured.

She took a bite of her breakfast and closed her eyes in appreciation. "It's every bit as fantastic as I remember. You're a genius in the kitchen, my friend. Are you sure I can't talk you into running off with me?"

Dermot laughed, his usually weathered features once again turning pink with delight.

"I do hope you plan to stay in town longer than a few days. You look like you could use a few more mornings of my French toast."

She *was* too skinny, Brendan thought, as if she had been working too hard, though she did have a few nice curves he had no business noticing.

"You're in luck. At this point, I'm here indefinitely," she said with false cheerfulness.

Brendan's gut tightened. Indefinitely. That certainly sounded like she would stick around longer than a few weeks.

"Oh, that's lovely to hear," Dermot exclaimed. "What will you do?"

"I'm thinking about opening Iris House as a bed and breakfast."

"Are you, now?" Pop beamed at her.

"It seems like the right thing to do. Jess and Annabelle were always talking about it." She was careful not to look at Brendan while she spoke.

"They were, at that. That doesn't make it the right thing for *you*. I never would have figured you for an innkeeper."

"I know I don't have any experience at running a B&B. But I can certainly market the heck out of it."

Dermot laughed. "Indeed."

The door to the café suddenly opened and Pop looked up with a smile to greet the new customer.

"Oh. Katherine." His smile slid away, replaced by an even deeper blush. "Good mornin' to you."

"Hello." Katherine Thorne, a city council member and one of the town's leading citizens, walked into the café looking as smart and put-together as always.

Dermot suddenly fumbled the coffeepot and splashed some over the side of Brendan's cup. He glared at his son as if it were *his* fault, before reaching for a napkin to clean it up.

Pop had a long-term infatuation for Katherine Thorne. Brendan had no idea why his father had never done anything about it, especially when it was obvious to everyone in town that Katherine shared his infatuation and would certainly welcome something more than this awkward friendship.

Margaret Caine had been gone for more than a decade. His mother had died of cancer while he was still a running back for Colorado State, before his short-lived time in the NFL.

As for Katherine, she had been alone even longer, as her husband died years ago.

Brendan could see no reason why the two of them seemed locked in this dance where neither wanted to be the first to lead off. He only knew that watching them together was like chewing on last year's Halloween taffy, both sweet and painful.

"I'm meeting some friends for breakfast," Katherine said. "There should be about six of us at last count. If it's not too much of a bother, could we take one of the back tables, out of the way?"

"Of course. Of course. No problem at all. I'll just go make it ready for you and your friends."

Anything for his sweetheart, Brendan thought in amusement. Except actually *making* her his sweetheart.

Katherine watched after him for just a moment then turned back to greet Brendan. Her eyes widened when she spotted his companion at the counter.

"Lucy! Hello. How are you, my dear?"

Lucy gave Katherine a smile far more genuine than anything she ever bestowed on Brendan. "I'm fine. It's great to see you. You look wonderful. How's the bead business treating you these days?"

"Oh, I sold that ages ago. I loved it but the details of running a small business—taxes, inventory, personnel headaches—was sucking all the fun out of it for me. Now I'm just a beader. It's a much better fit."

"That's too bad. I planned to stop in while I was in town."

Brendan never would have pegged Lucy as a crafter. He might have thought she was only being polite if not for the sincere regret in her blue eyes.

Katherine smiled. "You still can, never fear. Make sure you do, in fact. You won't be disappointed. String Fever is as busy as ever. I sold it several years ago to Claire McKnight and she's done wonders with the place. You know Claire, of course."

"I don't think so. The name doesn't ring a bell."

"You might have known her by her maiden name. Claire Tatum."

"Oh, right. Ruth Tatum's daughter. I thought she married Jeff Bradford."

"She did. They were divorced shortly before I sold

her the store. A few years ago, she married Riley Mc-Knight. Do you know him?"

"Is that Alex McKnight's brother?"

"The very same, except she's now Alex Delgado. You *must* stop by her restaurant while you're here. Brazen. It's at the top of Main Street in the old fire station and is absolutely fantastic."

Lucy looked a little overwhelmed at the barrage of information. "Thank you for the recommendation. I'll try to do that. I guess Hope's Crossing has changed a bit since I lived here."

"Not that much. You'll find the same good friends and kind neighbors."

"Well, that's a relief," she murmured, though he hadn't missed the way her mouth tightened a little.

He had never had the impression that Lucy liked Hope's Crossing very much. Oh, she loved Annabelle and Jess and Iris House. She would visit on the occasional holiday and special occasion, like the children's christenings and Annabelle's past few birthdays.

He couldn't really blame her. From what Jessie had told him, Lucy had come to town an angry, rebellious teenager, forced to live with a great-aunt she barely knew. She had spent her last few years of high school at Iris House with Annabelle before heading off to college, but that didn't necessarily mean the town felt like home to her.

If she were looking for a place to lick her wounds, he wanted to tell her, she could do much, much worse than Hope's Crossing.

CHAPTER THREE

WHEN LUCY GREW up, she wanted to be just like Katherine Thorne.

The woman was the very epitome of class and elegance. Lucy had always thought so.

When Lucy had first been dumped on Aunt Annabelle, Katherine used to visit Iris House for the monthly library board meetings. Even when Lucy had been clad all in black with her piercings and her purple-dyed hair, Katherine had treated her with respect and kindness.

Few others had been able to see past all the attitude to the frightened, sad girl inside. Most treated her with suspicion and sometimes outright disdain, but Katherine had at least tried.

Lucy had never forgotten it. After she was able—in no small part thanks to Annabelle—to get her stuff together and move past that rebellious teen stage, she would sometimes stop into String Fever on trips back to Hope's Crossing during college breaks to visit Annabelle.

Invariably, Katherine would greet her with a warm smile of welcome and insist on catching up on her most recent semester and how her studies were progressing.

She remembered the woman as a bright spot of kindness in a dark time.

Now, as Lucy listened to Katherine talk to Brendan about a new fire engine the city had recently purchased, she was impressed all over again. First the library board with Annabelle years ago, now the city council. Apparently Katherine worked hard to serve the people of Hope's Crossing.

Dermot Caine approached them, his color a little more ruddy than usual, for reasons she didn't understand.

"Your table is ready," he said to Katherine. "Would you like to be seated or wait until the rest of your party arrives?"

The older woman made a face. "Oh. How rude of me. I've been monopolizing the conversation when you're here to have breakfast together."

"We're not together," Lucy said quickly, careful not to look at Brendan. "I mean, we're here together, obviously, but we didn't intend it. We both just kind of showed up at the same time. But not together, together."

She sounded like an idiot, a point that was reinforced when all three of them stared at her.

Brendan cleared his throat. "You know you're welcome to come over to the station and take a look at the new engine anytime. As hard as you worked to push the funding through, we ought to at least name it after you. Katherine. Has a nice ring to it, don't you think?"

"I've always thought so," Dermot said, then appeared flustered when the city councilwoman smiled warmly at him.

"Thank you, but I didn't do anything out of the ordinary. We all knew you needed it—it was just a matter of squeezing the funds out of our tightfisted mayor."

"Nobody squeezes William Beaumont better than you."

"His daughter seems to do a pretty good job of it. And speaking of which, she'll be one of my breakfast companions, along with Charlotte, Evie, Mary Ella and Janie Hamilton. Will you send them back to my table, Dermot? They should be arriving soon."

"Of course. Of course."

Katherine smiled, brushing her cheek against Lucy's. "My dear. It was lovely to see you again. I hope we get the chance to catch up before you leave town again."

"I'll make sure of it," she answered.

As soon as the woman left, Dermot seemed to find it necessary to retreat to the kitchen, leaving her and Brendan alone. Relatively alone, anyway, considering they were seated at a busy counter along with a half-dozen others, in a bustling diner filled with the pleasant sounds of clinking dishes and conversation.

She was still uncomfortably aware of him. Big surprise there, since she had the same reaction every time she was in the same room with him. His wife had been her best friend so, yes, that ridiculous awareness had led to some very awkward interactions over the years.

One stupid kiss more than a decade ago—a mere fifteen minutes out of her life—and sometimes, despite her very best efforts, she couldn't manage to think about anything else.

She let out a breath. She just had to try harder. If she was going to be staying in Hope's Crossing for a while, she would inevitably have to see Brendan. He lived down the street, and his children were two of her favorite humans on the planet.

She had to put that kiss a decade ago—and the subsequent weeks of confusion and heartache—completely out of her mind.

A moment later, he set his napkin down beside his plate and climbed off the round stool. "I guess I'll probably see you later. If I'm going to catch a few hours of sleep before Carter and Faith get home from school, I should probably take off."

"I can't wait to see them. I've got a few gifts for them, things I brought with me that I haven't gotten around to mailing. Could I drop them off sometime today?"

A muscle flexed in that strong jaw. "You know you don't have to shower them with gifts. They would love you, anyway, trinkets or not."

He made no secret that it annoyed him when she sent little toys or books to the children—or delivered them in person when she came to town. She was honest enough with herself to admit that might have been part of the reason she went to the trouble. She genuinely enjoyed picking out things for the children, but she considered needling Brendan a bonus side effect.

Yes, she was a horrible person.

If he had never flirted with her that long-ago night, never kissed her, never inspired such silly dreams— and never fallen hard for her best friend just a few weeks later and ended up marrying Jessie—their relationship might have been a much more comfortable one.

"I know I don't have to give them gifts, but I enjoy it. And who knows? Now that I'm unemployed, this might be the last time I can afford to bring them anything."

That was as close to a joke about the catastrophe her life had become as she had yet been able to manage. That had to be progress, right?

He studied her a moment, an unreadable expression on his features. He looked tired, his eyes a little red-rimmed and his hair slightly mussed, probably from taking off that helmet he'd worn at Iris House during the fire. He had crinkles at the corners of his eyes she didn't remember seeing before and a few little gray strands hidden in all that thick dark hair.

But he was still far too gorgeous for her peace of mind.

"The kids both have baseball practice this evening. We won't be home until later and then they'll have homework and their daily reading for school to do. Another day would be better."

She didn't need him to spell it out. He was clearly telling her that even though she was back in Hope's Crossing and living just up the street, he wasn't going to allow unfettered access to Faith and Carter.

The few bites of really delicious strawberry-and-almond sprinkled French toast she had managed to eat around her nerves seemed to congeal in her stomach. "Sure. I'll try to connect with you another day, then. I'm anxious to see them but I can certainly wait."

"I'll let you know."

He waved to his father, nodded to a couple other people in the diner then headed out without another word to her.

After he left, she spent a minute or two more picking at her breakfast, mainly because she didn't want to hurt Dermot's feelings by not savoring the meal he had prepared especially for her.

Why had she opened her big mouth and told Brendan about being fired? Of all the people in town, he was the one person whose reaction she had dreaded.

He had really been surprisingly decent about it. She had expected some kind of snide comment, but he actually had seemed sympathetic. Sometimes she didn't know what went on in his head. She only knew their encounters were usually so awkward and tense, she couldn't wait for them to be over.

How would she survive living in Hope's Crossing, where she was bound to run into him often?

The bells on the door suddenly chimed. She glanced up at the big mirror above the counter as a couple of women about her age walked in, laughing at something with their heads close together. Her heart gave a sharp, familiar ache at their friendship. Jessie had been her best friend most of her life, and Lucy missed her every single day.

She didn't have many other female friends, at least none that reached the level of closeness she had shared with Jess. Since she'd graduated from college and started working for NexGen, she had been so focused on her career, on climbing further and faster, she hadn't put nearly enough effort into building healthy relationships in other aspects of her life.

If she had a better support network, maybe she wouldn't have been left so shattered right now.

To her surprise, the women immediately walked over to her.

"Lucy! Katherine just texted us that you were here. How great to see you again!" A trim-looking woman with honey-gold hair and a sweet smile reached out and wrapped her in a hug.

It was a disorienting moment, as she had no clue who the woman was until she scrutinized her a little more closely. "Charlotte? Wow! You look fantastic!"

The last time she had seen Charlotte Caine, Brendan's sister, had been at Jessie's funeral, when the other woman had been about a hundred pounds heavier.

Charlotte smiled. "Thank you. It's been a fun journey. What a surprise to see you here at Pop's on a lovely Saturday morning! I didn't think you ever left Seattle."

Everyone in town would be wondering why she was back. How could she explain to them all that she had failed at the one thing she ever thought she was good at?

Maybe Brendan would tell everyone and then she wouldn't have to. No. Somehow, she knew he wouldn't. He might dislike her intensely, but she instinctively trusted him to keep this information to himself.

She had lost her job. The weight of her failure seemed to clutch at her chest. Who was she if she wasn't the go-getter marketing director at NexGen?

She made herself take a deep breath, forcing away those familiar snaking tendrils of panic.

"I decided it was finally time to figure out what I want to do with Iris House," she finally answered in a calm tone that left her inordinately proud of herself.

The woman with Charlotte—blonde and slim and stylishly, if casually, dressed—lit up at her words. "Oh, you're the one who owns that beautiful house?"

"Yes," she answered. It was still a tough admission. She didn't feel she had any rights to the place. Jessica should have inherited it, should have had the chance to turn it into the B&B of her dreams. She had adored every opulent inch of it.

Instead, Jess was gone, taken far too young during pregnancy by a heart condition no one suspected. Jess was gone, Annabelle was gone. Lucy was the only one of them left.

"I heard there was a fire there last night. Is it true?" Charlotte's friend said.

That's right. She had dozens of reasons to be embarrassed to show her face around town. "Yes. That was my fault. I arrived in the middle of the night and couldn't get the furnace to start. I tried to light a fire in one of the rooms and ended up with a chimney blaze."

"Is everything okay?" Charlotte exclaimed.

"Your brother seems to think so. He says I should be safe to return there this morning."

"That's a relief!" the other woman said. "I can't recall if we've met. I'm Genevieve Beaumont."

Ah. This was the mayor's daughter, who could wrap him around her finger. She thought she vaguely recalled seeing her at Annabelle's funeral, but she had been so grief-stricken, that time was a blur.

"Hello. I'm Lucy Drake. Annabelle Stanbridge was my great-aunt."

"She was quite a character. I've hated seeing her house empty these last few months. Iris House is one of those places meant to be filled with life," Genevieve said.

"I agree," she answered.

"What are your plans for it?" Charlotte asked. "Are you looking to sell? I can think of several people who might be interested."

"I haven't decided," she admitted. "I'm actually thinking about opening it up as a bed and breakfast, if the town isn't already glutted with them."

"Oh, that would be the perfect place!" Charlotte exclaimed. "People would love a chance to stay in one of the early silver mansions."

"I have no idea how much work awaits me. My plan after breakfast is to go through room by room and start making lists."

That panic began pressing in on her again. She felt completely out of her comfort zone with the whole idea—but maybe that was exactly what she needed. Maybe she had become too settled, too complacent with her life.

"If you need any help," Charlotte said, "Genevieve is just opening an interior design business. She does amazing work."

The mayor's daughter looked pleased and a little embarrassed at the endorsement. "I'm only just starting out. I'm sure Lucy has other plans in mind for what she wants to do with the place."

"Not really. I'd love for you to take a look at it and give me your thoughts."

Before Genevieve could respond, Dermot came out from the kitchen and spotted them.

"Why, look who's here! It's my lovely daughter and my lovely daughter-to-be."

Genevieve blushed at this, and both women greeted him with kisses on the cheek. Lucy studied the mayor's daughter more closely.

"You're engaged to one of the Caine boys? Really? You're a brave woman, Ms. Beaumont. No offense, Dermot."

He laughed cheerfully. "None taken. Believe me, I know exactly how brave she is to take on this particular son."

He hugged Genevieve again, who seemed to light

up with happiness. Lucy was aware of a sharp pang of envy that Genevieve apparently had been absorbed into the huge, boisterous, loving Caine family.

"Which brother?" she asked. "Let me guess. Aidan."

The tech genius had accrued a fortune in Silicon Valley and was worth millions, which would probably suit the elegant Genevieve. She had met him a few times over the years at various business functions.

Because of their shared connection to Hope's Crossing, he always found a few moments to speak with her, earning her jealous snake-eyes from some of her female associates, who tended to go a little out of their heads for Aidan's brilliant mind and his sexy-nerd good looks.

"Good heavens, no," Genevieve exclaimed. "I barely know Aidan. I think I've only met him two or three times. He terrifies me, if you want the truth."

"Jamie, then?" She never would have thought the sexy charmer of a helicopter pilot would settle down, even for someone as lovely as Genevieve.

"Wrong again," Charlotte said with a grin.

Lucy did a few quick calculations. She knew the older two of Charlotte's brothers were married. Surely not…Brendan. Impossible.

Why was it impossible? she asked herself. Jess had been gone more than two years. Did she really expect him to hold on to her memory forever? But still. Picturing Genevieve Beaumont as stepmother to Faith and Carter left a cold, tangled knot in her stomach.

"So you're marrying…"

"Dylan!" Genevieve said, with obvious relish, as if Lucy couldn't have made any other guess.

Just like that, the sickly feeling eased. "Dylan! Wow. That's…terrific."

And wholly unexpected. Last she heard, the youngest Caine brother had nearly died while fighting in Afghanistan and had been left with lifelong scars.

He seemed an odd pick for a woman who was obviously very aware of her appearance and who was starting an interior design business. But what did she know?

Nothing in Hope's Crossing was turning out as she expected.

She couldn't doubt the woman was deeply in love with Dylan, not when she saw the joy bloom on her lovely features.

"We're having a quiet sunrise ceremony this summer in a meadow near his house in Snowflake Canyon."

"Followed by a huge blowout bash that's going to take over the entire ski resort," Charlotte added dryly.

Genevieve beamed. "It has to be huge!" she protested. "What else do you expect from a double reception? Half of that is from your side."

"Who else is getting married?" Lucy asked, feeling a little lost.

Charlotte waved her hand, which Lucy now saw sported a tasteful princess-cut diamond.

"Oh, congratulations. I hadn't heard."

"Thank you."

"She's marrying Smokin' Hot Spence Gregory," Genevieve said.

"Spence? Really?"

"Yes. Spence." Charlotte's joy was softer than Genevieve's but every bit as genuine.

Though Lucy had lived in Seattle, she had been a

big fan of the Portland Pioneers and had even driven down a few times to watch Smoke Gregory's amazing fastball. His fall from grace as a Major League Baseball pitcher a few years before had been a personal blow—and the way he had clawed his way back from a dark place just as inspiring.

Maybe she should learn a few things from him.

"They're getting married at the church the night before Dylan and I are tying the knot. We've decided on separate ceremonies and a combined reception. Doesn't that sound fabulous?"

"It really does. Wow. A girl leaves town for a decade and everything changes. Congratulations, both of you."

"Thank you! We're meeting people for breakfast. You look as if you have nearly finished eating, but we would love to have you join us for coffee and conversation."

Lucy was sorely tempted, struck again by how very few female friends she had. She was suddenly greedy for friends—and not just any friends, *these* women.

At the same time, she wasn't sure she could pull off being warm and friendly when she felt so wrecked by everything that had happened the past few days. It wasn't every week a woman lost the job of her dreams or tried to burn down the only thing she had left.

"Another time, I would love that. Right now I need to head over to Iris House and take a look at the damages."

"Oh, good luck," Charlotte said. "We'll definitely catch up while you're in town."

"Genevieve, if you're serious about helping me with Iris House, I would greatly appreciate any input. Maybe we could make an appointment next week for you to walk through with me and at least give me some idea where to start."

The other woman looked thrilled. "That would be fantastic! I just had these really cute cards made up." She reached into the funky fabric bag she carried and pulled out a slim black case. She extracted a business card and handed it over to Lucy. "My cell, business line and email are on there. Call me and we can work something out. Do you have a card we can exchange?"

She had about a jillion and three of them, but they wouldn't do her any good anymore. "Not on me," she answered, which wasn't precisely a lie. "I'll call you, though."

"Great. I can't wait."

She waved goodbye to the women, left a bill on the counter to pay Dermot for her breakfast along with a healthy tip and then walked out into the town that would be her home for the foreseeable future, like it or not.

CHAPTER FOUR

"COME ON, HONEY. You can do it," Brendan urged his daughter.

"No! Don't let go, Daddy," Faith begged. "Please don't let go."

Brendan sighed as he held on to the back of her bike seat, wishing he could enjoy the sweetly warm April evening that smelled of life, new growth, somebody barbecuing down the street.

Another spring, another effort to get Faith to ride her bike without the training wheels.

Two years ago, she had begged him to take off the training wheels on her bike as soon as the snow melted. He had promised he would before the new baby came— but before he could follow through on his promise, Jess and the baby were both gone.

None of them had felt much like riding bikes that spring. When he pulled them out of the garage after the snow melted a year ago, Faith had insisted she wasn't ready to ride without the training wheels. He had pushed a little but not too hard. Jessie had only been gone a year and Faith seemed to need the comfort of the familiar.

But she would turn eight years old during the summer. The time had come for her to stop clinging so tightly to the familiar and venture into untried territory.

He worried about the tentativeness she had developed since Jess's death. She never wanted to try anything new—roller-skating, Girl Scouts, sushi.

She was an insanely smart girl, but she was beginning to let her fears rule her.

All of them had been in grief counseling for months after Jess and their unborn baby died. Maybe they weren't quite done in that department.

At some point, he had to fight back against the tyrannical hold Faith's fears had over her. He figured forcing her to lose the training wheels was as good a place to start as any and had removed them a week earlier, much to her dismay.

"Hey, Dad! Look! Here I go!"

Carter, still a month away from six, rolled past on his two-wheeler like Lance freaking Armstrong—but without the steroid abuse.

Carter seemed on the other side of the spectrum from Faith, totally without fear. He had begged Brendan to take off his training wheels the previous fall and he had done it with a great deal of trepidation, certain a five-year-old didn't have the balance or coordination yet. Training wheels existed for a reason, right?

At the same time, he had hoped maybe seeing Carter make the effort might spur Faith to try a little harder.

Instead, as she watched her brother master the bike in just an hour, Faith only seemed to cling tenaciously to her conviction that she wasn't ready.

"You're doing great, Car," he called. "Keep going."

"I loooove my bike," Carter sang out at the top of his lungs in one of his spur-of-the-moment song compositions as he rode past. "I love love love my bike."

He had to smile at the sheer exuberance Carter

brought to everything he did. What would he have done the past two years without both of his kids?

Probably wandered into the wilderness and became a hermit or something, growing a four-foot-long beard and living off beef jerky.

"Riding bikes is awesome and cool. I want to ride my bike to school," Carter sang.

Even Faith smiled at her little brother.

Brendan took that as an encouraging sign. "Okay, let's try one more time."

Her smile slid away. "I don't want to. Please don't make me, Daddy."

"You can do it, Faith. You just have to believe in yourself," he urged, feeling like the worst parent on earth for pushing her out of her comfort zone. On the other hand, wouldn't catering to her unreasonable fears be more harmful in the long run?

"I don't want to!" she protested.

"One more, that's all. I promise. And then we can put the bikes away and go for a walk."

"I want to ride a bike," she said, with traces of her mother's stubbornness—okay, and his, as well—in her voice. "I just want to ride a bike that still has training wheels. Why can't you put them back on?"

If the kid spent as much time trying to focus on her balance as she did arguing about why she couldn't, they would all be better off.

"One more time, Faith. Come on, kiddo. You've got this."

She glared at him but apparently accepted that he wasn't about to back down. With him holding on to the seat for balance, she started her wobbly way down the ride.

"Don't let go," she said. "Promise!"

He didn't answer. Instead, when she seemed to have sufficient speed and had reduced the wobble, he enacted one of those difficult parental betrayals and released his hold on her.

She rode about six feet before she realized he wasn't holding on anymore…and promptly fell over.

"Owwww," she wailed, not quite crying but close to it. "You let go! You promised you wouldn't let go!"

"I never promised I wouldn't let go."

"Yes, you did! You did!"

She wouldn't listen to him in this state, and he wasn't going to stand here arguing with her. Close to the end of his patience, he was about to tell her so when an unwelcome voice intruded.

"Wow, Faith! You're riding a two-wheeler? That's wonderful!"

Both of them turned around swiftly to find Lucy walking down the sidewalk toward them.

She looked lovely and bright and more casually dressed than he had seen her in a long time, in jeans and a plain green tailored cotton shirt that matched her eyes. With her hair pulled up into a loose hairstyle on top of her head, she looked pretty and sweet and far too young to have been the marketing director at a major software company until recently.

He was supposed to make arrangements with her to drop off a few things for Faith and Carter. He hadn't precisely forgotten; he had just done his best to put it out of his head so he didn't have to dwell on more thoughts of her that seemed to have intruded far too frequently since she returned to town.

"Aunt Lucy!" Faith exclaimed, her voice overflowing with joy.

Her father's minor treachery forgotten, she jumped up from the toppled bike and raced to Lucy, throwing her arms around her waist with an exuberant delight he rarely saw in his quiet, serious oldest child.

Lucy closed her eyes as she returned Faith's embrace with a soft expression on her features that brought a weird lump to his throat.

He and Lucy might not get along for a dozen different reasons, but he couldn't deny that she loved his children.

"What are you doing here?" Faith burst out. "I didn't even know you were coming! How long are you staying? Where are you staying? Will you be here for my baseball game next week?"

Lucy laughed at the barrage of questions hurled at her like a broken pitching machine spewing balls at the new batting cages in town.

"Whoa. Slow down. I'm sorry I didn't tell you myself. I made a really quick decision to come back to Hope's Crossing, and here I am. I'm sorry I didn't tell you. I didn't tell anybody. And I can't tell you how long I'm staying but I think it will be at least a month."

Faith's eyes widened. "*A month?* Really?" she whispered in a reverent sort of voice, as if someone had just handed her all her dreams on a shiny platter. Which Lucy apparently had just done.

"Yes. I'll be staying at Iris House. Just up the hill, right? I hope we have a chance to spend a lot of time together while I'm here."

"We can! Oh, we can," Faith said, at the same moment Carter came zooming past again on his bike.

Unlike his sister, Carter didn't seem at all fazed to see his usually absent honorary aunt. He acted like it was no big deal to encounter her walking down the street.

"Lucy! Hey, Lucy! Look at me!"

"Wow, Carter! You're doing great. Both of you riding without training wheels. That's so terrific. It's only a matter of time before you'll both be driving."

Faith giggled and grinned at Brendan, apparently forgetting for the moment that she was mad at him.

"I'm not really very good at riding a two-wheeler," Faith confessed after a moment.

"It takes a lot of practice. I bet you're terrific. Why don't you show me?"

Brendan worried she might start up her litany of excuses again. Instead, after a wary look at Lucy, she picked her bike off the pavement and climbed on with a determined expression.

He moved forward to hold on to the seat again, but before he could reach it, Faith pushed one pedal down and then the other. The effort was wobbly and unsteady and he thought for sure she would fall but after a few more feet, something clicked. She caught the rhythm or found her balance or *something*. By the time she made it to the next driveway, she was actually riding.

Faith gave a half excited, half terrified shriek.

"You're doing it, sweetheart," he called.

"That's fantastic! You're amazing," Lucy said. "See if you can make it to the corner and back."

"Come on, Faith. We can go together!" Carter exclaimed, obviously excited to see his sister riding after all the hassles of working to make it happen.

They rode off together, with Faith gaining more confidence with each rotation of the wheel.

"You're welcome," Lucy said, as the children pedaled out of earshot.

He gave her a long look. "Am I?"

"How long has she been trying not to learn how to ride a two-wheeler?"

He made a face. "About two years now. How did you know?"

She shrugged, keeping a careful eye on the children. He tried to do that, too, but found his gaze straying back to her despite his best efforts. "I've been watching from the house for the past fifteen minutes. Nobody but Carter seemed to be having a good time."

"Faith can be obstinate when she's in a mood."

"Poor thing," she said with a dry look. "She must have inherited that trait from Jessie."

The name seemed to shiver between them. Her best friend and his late wife.

"No doubt," he murmured and quickly changed the subject. "How's the house? Still smell like a campfire in there?"

She shook her head. "I found a couple of box fans in the cellar. I threw open all the windows on the ground floor and for the last two days I've been trying to blow all the air out. Now it smells like a Colorado April afternoon."

"That should help. You'll want to wash the curtains in that room, like I said, maybe have the upholstery on the furniture cleaned. Sometimes that smoke can cling for weeks, especially in textiles."

"I'll do that. Thank you."

They lapsed into silence, both watching the children

as they reached the corner. Brendan held his breath as Faith navigated the turn. She was a little shaky and he thought she would fall, but she set her leg down to help stabilize the bike and then picked up the rhythm again.

The kid was a natural. He had known she would be once she conquered her mental block and pushed past her apprehension. For that, at least, he owed Lucy.

"I'm sorry I didn't call you last night about coming over to bring the gifts you bought for the children," he said on impulse. "The evening got away from me, as they tend to do, with homework and laundry and dinner and everything."

"Don't worry about it," she said, her eyes filled with a sympathy he found as surprising as it was unwelcome. He didn't want her feeling sorry for him. Yeah, being a single father was tough, but he had plenty of help from his family and good neighbors.

"Whenever you want to come over should be fine. Tomorrow after school would work. I'm not on the schedule at the station for a few more days."

"Thanks. I would go get them now but I don't want to stop the forward momentum here."

The kids rode up to them just then. Faith even managed a credible job of staying balanced while she braked.

"Did you see that, Dad?" Faith's sweetly serious little face glowed. "I rode all the way to the corner and back!"

"I watched the whole time. You were terrific. I knew you could do it. It was just a matter of practice."

And a little bit of Lucy magic, he added to himself. It wasn't a completely comfortable thought.

"Can we go for a bike ride to the park?"

He chuckled. "Two minutes ago, you couldn't ride without your training wheels. Now you're ready to go across town to the park?"

"It's not across town. I meant the little park that's just on the other side of Tulip Street."

He had a hundred things to do that evening. Reports to file, bills to pay, dishes to wash. But he couldn't discourage her from practicing this new skill he had fought so hard for her to attain.

"Sure. We can go to the park. Stay on the sidewalk and don't cross the street until I get there."

"Okay, Daddy."

She beamed at him and rode off, still a little wobbly but really doing remarkably well, considering she had only actually been riding without the training wheels for about ten minutes.

He followed after her and had walked only a few steps when he realized Lucy was still standing where he had left her, in front of the Browns' driveway.

He turned around, struck by how lovely she looked there in the long shadows of afternoon with the fading sunlight haloing her hair and burnishing her skin.

He didn't want to notice that about Lucy or *any* woman. Not yet. He forced himself to push it out of his mind.

"You're not coming with us?" he asked gruffly, gesturing after the kids.

She blinked a little at his tacit invitation then smiled. "Oh. Yes. I could use a walk this evening."

He waited until she caught up with him, and they walked in silence for a few moments. The air was pleasantly cool. He always enjoyed this time of year, when the grass was beginning to green up again and the trees were bursting with buds.

"I had forgotten how pretty Hope's Crossing is in the evening," she said.

He had lived here most of his life, except the few years he was away on a scholarship playing college football and earning his degree and then the two short years he played pro football before a knee injury permanently sidelined him. To him, Hope's Crossing was just…home. But on a spring night in April, he could see the appeal of the well-kept, charming houses, the tree-lined streets, the mountains that encircled the town.

He waved to old Mr. Henderson, driving past in his beat-up old Chevrolet pickup truck. "It's a nice little town, especially for kids."

"I suppose that's true."

They walked a little farther and he raised a hand in greeting to two more people driving past.

"You must know everybody in town," she said.

"Not even close. We've got so many people moving in or building second homes in the area, it's hard to keep track. I just happen to know those two. And that one, my neighbor, Mrs. Peabody."

He waved at the longtime widow who used to teach him in Sunday school. He saw her shield her eyes with a hand as she tried to make out the identity of his companion and his stomach dropped.

He suddenly regretted asking Lucy to join him on this little excursion. Hope's Crossing was a small town. People were bound to take notice when their favorite object of pity, that poor widower Brendan Caine, started walking around town with a woman new to Hope's Crossing—or at least recently returned to town.

The last thing he needed were rumors starting up about him and Lucy. He didn't want anybody deciding to put more into this than exactly what it was, a casual walk to the park with his kids.

In reality, they were two people who disliked each other, linked only by the woman they had both loved and by the two children who rode ahead of them.

He needed to keep reminding himself of that and not allow himself to be seduced by a lovely evening, an even lovelier woman and the quiet enjoyment of a little adult companionship, for a change.

A WEEK AGO, if somebody had told her she would be spending a beautiful April evening sitting at a park in Hope's Crossing on a bench next to Brendan Caine, she would have laughed out loud at such a preposterous notion.

Life had the strangest way of throwing curveballs at a woman when she least expected it.

A week ago, she had been confident she had the world figured out—or at least her place in it. Now everything had changed, and she was left trying to find her way again.

Once again, she questioned her decision to return to Hope's Crossing. It had seemed so right at the time, coming back to this place where she had always found peace and comfort with Annabelle.

But Annabelle was gone and nothing would be the same.

Maybe she should have stayed in Seattle. She had a condo there she had paid cash for a few years earlier. She could have lived there basically rent free while she sent out feelers for other jobs. With her contacts in the industry, it probably wouldn't have taken her long to find something new. Being fired from her previous job didn't exactly look that great on her résumé but maybe her track record before the disastrous software launch would speak for itself.

Instead of following logic and sense, she had gone with her gut, for once, and had come back to the only place that had ever felt close to home.

Now, sitting next to Brendan Caine, she wondered again if it had been a huge mistake. He didn't want her here, that much was obvious—at the park or in Hope's Crossing. She hadn't missed his discomfort, just walking through town with her.

Too late to second-guess herself now. She was here now and just needed to make the best of things—and maybe that started with finding common ground with Brendan.

"I had a nice chat with your sister yesterday morning at the café," she said.

"Did you?"

"She looked fantastic. And she told me she's getting married to Spence Gregory. That must have been quite a shock for you and your brothers."

He shrugged. "They seem happy together. Spence was always a good guy. He just lost his way for a while."

Apparently, there was a lot of that going around.

"And I understand Dylan's tying the knot, too, with Genevieve Beaumont," she said. "Shock number two."

"Yeah. That one's a little harder to take in, but somehow they work together."

"How is her family taking it?"

"You mean their little princess hooking up with a disfigured war veteran?" he asked, his voice cold.

"Your words. Not mine," she answered in the same tone.

He studied her for a moment and some of the protective harshness seemed to ease in his handsome features. "Sorry. It's a touchy subject. The mayor and Mrs. Beaumont weren't very thrilled at first, especially since Dylan was unemployed for a while there. And of course, they didn't hesitate to let their objections be known far and wide throughout the land."

"I remember the Beaumonts. That doesn't surprise me."

"Gen stood up to them, which *was* a surprise. The way I hear it, she told them if they put her in a position to make her choose between her family or Dylan, she would choose him, every time."

Lucy decided she was liking Genevieve Beaumont more and more. "How romantic."

"Or something," he murmured.

"You don't think so?"

"It's easy to make grand sweeping statements like that. Not so easy to live with the consequences of them."

"But Genevieve must have stuck by her guns. They're getting married, right?"

"Dylan had a long, tough talk with Gen's parents. When he's not being all gruff and cranky, he can be quite a charmer, apparently. I think he must get it from Pop."

"Too bad that trait wasn't handed down universally to all the Caine brothers."

He snorted, a small, amused smile teasing the corner of his mouth. "Isn't it, though?"

She felt inordinately pleased that she had brought a smile to his face, even such a tiny one.

"He's also started a partnership with a fairly new contractor in town, Sam Delgado. From what I understand, they have more business than they know what to do with right now. And he's still a regular volunteer at A Warrior's Hope, the recreational therapy program Spence and Charlotte started for wounded veterans. A war hero, a volunteer, a thriving businessman. How could Laura and William possibly object to such a paragon for a son-in-law?"

"Not to mention he's the man their daughter loves."

"There is that."

He started to say something else but Carter called out from the swings in an imperious tone.

"Daddy! Push me."

Brendan sighed. "How did my children both get to be such bossy little things?"

She rose from the bench. "I've got this. Relax."

"No. It's fine."

"I'd like to. Would it kill you to let me help with the kids for five seconds?"

So much for any amicable accords. He was back to glowering at her—but at least he sat back down on the bench and made a gesture for her to go ahead.

She moved behind Carter and gave him a hard, swift push that had him giggling in delight.

"Higher!" the little daredevil exclaimed. This one was going to give his father all kinds of trouble during his reckless teenage years, she expected.

"Sure thing. Except I'm going to blame you if my arms fall off."

He giggled harder and swung his legs to help gain momentum.

"Faith says you're staying for a *month*. Is that true?"

"That's the plan, kiddo."

"Yay! Then you can come to my birthday party. It's next month. I'm going to be six."

"Do you know," she said, "I believe I heard a rumor somewhere that most five-year-old boys turn six on their next birthdays."

He giggled. "Will you come?"

"I'll have to see."

She didn't add that a lot could happen between now and next month. Given the tangled history between her and Brendan, she wasn't entirely sure she would be welcome at his son's birthday party in a month.

TWO EVENINGS LATER, Lucy juggled an umbrella in one hand, a bag from her favorite toy store in Seattle in the other and a box in both arms as she pressed Brendan's doorbell with her elbow.

She had always loved his house. It was comfortable and homey, built of a warm, rust-colored brick in the Craftsman style, with a wide front porch and two dormer windows. Situated on a higher plot in town, it had lovely views down the hill into downtown Hope's Crossing.

Jess's favorite rocking chair had a few old cobwebs underneath it, as if nobody used it much anymore.

She didn't have time to feel more than a sharp, familiar pang of loss over that before the door jerked open. Brendan stood on the other side, a cordless house phone cradled in the crook of his shoulder and neck and his fingers texting on a cell phone in his hand.

He appeared astonished to see her for all of two seconds before his features shifted into an expression of sheer gratitude. He grabbed the box out of her arms with one hand and practically yanked her inside with the other.

"I understand," he said into the phone in a clear tone of dismissal. "If you can't do it, you can't do it. Thanks, anyway. Talk to you soon."

He hung up and set the cordless receiver down on a cluttered table in the entryway at the same time he shoved the cell phone back in his pocket. "Lucy Drake, you are an answer to prayer."

She couldn't recall anyone ever saying *that* to her, especially not Brendan Caine. "I am?"

"Yes! Please tell me you're free for the next couple of hours."

She mentally perused her evening schedule and came up empty. As usual. "I should be free," she said, rather warily.

"Any chance you might be willing to stay with the kids for me? I'm supposed to be off tonight but I just got a call that three of our four full-time paramedics and four more of the volunteers are out with stomach trouble, probably food poisoning from some bad Chinese food they had for lunch, and we've had a string of accidents from the rain. I'm got to go in and cover until the overnight shift comes in. I know it's a lot to ask but the kids have already had their baths and are almost ready for bed."

She was stunned at the unexpected request but thrilled at the same time that he would even consider turning to her, a woman he so obviously disliked. "Of course. I'm happy to stay with them."

"None of my usual backup caregivers are available," he said, looking frazzled. "If you hadn't showed up, I was going to have to drag them in with me, pajamas and all, as a last resort. Thank you. I owe you."

"Not at all. I'll be delighted to spend a little time with them. You know I will."

"I'll try to get off as early as I can. Midnight would be the latest."

"No problem. I can get them to sleep."

"Thanks. I've got to run. Um, make yourself comfortable. Whatever you need. My cell number is on the fridge if you need me."

"We'll be fine."

"Thanks. Seriously. I owe you."

"You don't. I owe *you* for giving me the chance to spend time with them."

"Give me a second. I just have to change. The kids should be changing into pajamas. I imagine they'll be in any moment."

She waved him off and stood for a moment in the entryway of his house, left a little off-kilter by the unexpected turn of events.

This was good, though. She couldn't imagine anything she would rather do than spend the evening with her two favorite children.

She set the hefty box on the bottom step and put the toy store bag on top of it. She was shrugging out of her raincoat when Carter and Faith came barreling down the hall, their hair wet. Carter was wearing LEGO Star Wars pajamas, and Faith had on a nightgown sporting

Strawberry Shortcake. They looked startled to see her but rushed over with ready hugs.

"What are you *doing* here?" Faith asked.

"Well, my plan was to drop a few things off for you, but your dad just asked me to stay with you for a couple of hours while he runs into work."

"Yay!" Faith exclaimed just as Brendan emerged from down the hall wearing navy cargo pants and a white polo shirt with the logo of the Hope's Crossing Fire Department on the chest. He looked big and tough and dangerous.

Oh, and delicious. She couldn't deny that.

"Good news, kids," he said, grabbing a set of keys off a table in the entryway. "You get to stay in your own beds instead of sleeping at Grandpa's place or at Aunt Charlotte's. Your aunt Lucy has kindly agreed to keep an eye on you this evening until I can make it back."

Carter raced to her and gave her a complicated high-five. Somehow she managed to keep up. "Can we stay up until ten?" he asked.

"Eight-thirty," she countered. She figured that was appropriate when Brendan didn't protest the negotiation.

"Yay! That's half an hour later than usual," Carter exclaimed.

"Just this once," Brendan said. He scooped up his son and planted a kiss on his forehead. "Be good for Aunt Lucy."

"I'm always good," Carter insisted.

Faith rolled her eyes but didn't say anything. Brendan set the boy down and folded his daughter into a hug. "You, too. No staying up all night reading, got it?"

"Got it." She hugged him hard. "Good night, Dad. Be careful, okay?"

His mouth tightened a little, but Lucy watched him twist it into a smile that looked forced. "Will do, kiddo."

He straightened. "Thank you again," he said to Lucy. "Seriously. You saved the day."

"Right time, right place. I'm glad I could help."

He studied her for just a moment, and she wondered what he saw when he looked at her. She was no doubt bedraggled from the rainy walk to his house. She should have just driven, but it had seemed ridiculous when he lived less than a block away.

It didn't matter what she looked like, she reminded herself. Brendan didn't care. He had made that quite plain when he had kissed her senseless one moment and then fallen in love with her best friend the next.

"All right, my darlings," she said after he left. "Who wants to see what I've brought you?"

"Me! Me!" Carter exclaimed.

Faith chewed on her bottom lip. "Did Dad say it was okay?"

Brendan had known she had gifts for the kids. He had seen her carrying them in, and he hadn't *not* said it was okay.

She was going to take that as approval—though it annoyed her that he had apparently expressed enough displeasure about her gift-giving habits that perceptive little Faith picked up on it.

"It's fine," she answered.

"Okay," Faith decided. "Then I would like to see, too."

She tried not to overspend on the children, though

she had to check herself at times. She had been paid an exorbitant salary at NexGen, far exceeding her needs and her investments, and had few people to spend it on—a number that had dwindled in the past two years with Jessie's and Annabelle's deaths.

Her father, her stepmother, her half sister, Crystal, and the children. That was about the size of it.

She wanted to spoil Carter and Faith with trinkets and treasures but knew the things she gave them paled in comparison to actually making the effort to have contact with them through email, Skype and phone calls.

To that end, these gifts were small, but Carter adored the clever magnetic shapes that could be put together to form all kinds of structures, and Faith gave an adorable gasp of delight at the little elastic band bracelet loom and the supply of bands that came along with it.

"Oh! I've been wanting one of these to make bracelets for my friends," she exclaimed.

"Great. We can figure it out together. The woman at the toy store showed me how, and it looks simple enough."

"I'm so glad you're here," Faith said.

"I am, too, sweetheart," she answered—and to her surprise, it wasn't completely a lie, at least not when she was with the children.

She pulled out the heavy box she had carried down from Iris House. "The real treasure is in here, though."

"What is it?" Carter asked. "Can I open it?"

"You both can."

The children knelt on either side of the box and worked together to pull back the cardboard flaps.

"Books."

They both said the word at the same time, Carter with disgust and Faith in a reverent tone.

"Yes. Books. I found them up at Iris House. These were all your mom and my favorites when we werc children—*The BFG, Charlotte's Web,* Nancy Drew, Jack London, *The Hobbit.*"

"Hey, I saw that movie," Carter exclaimed.

"You need to read the book now."

"Only I can't read chapter books," he answered in a *duh* sort of tone.

"It's only a matter of time, kid. You'll be reading chapter books before you know it and then you'll want to read some of these books, I promise."

She pulled a boxed collection from the bottom of the box and held it out to Faith, who looked dazed with delight at the literary bounty. "And look at this. My very favorite. *Anne of Green Gables.* One summer when I came to stay with Annabelle for a few weeks, your mom and I made a pact to read the whole series by the time school started again. I think I was thirteen."

She actually *knew* she had been thirteen. It was the summer her father had left them, she remembered, when she had been lost and frightened, emotionally traumatized by a lifetime of being caught in the crosshairs on the battlefield of a horrible marriage.

When her mother—seeking attention, as always— made a halfhearted suicide attempt and was subsequently committed to the psychiatric treatment unit at the local hospital, Robert Drake had once more shrugged off responsibility for her.

How could he possibly be expected to take in a frightened girl? He had just moved in with his twenty-one-year-old girlfriend, and Pam wasn't at all prepared to handle that kind of responsibility. Besides, they just didn't have room. She would have so much more fun staying at Annabelle's, where her favorite cousin, Jessica, was living with her recently widowed mother.

For Robert, it had been the perfect solution. For Lucy, it was just another betrayal, made bearable only by Annabelle and Jessica and the magical escape she found that summer in books.

When her mother was released, she moved back to Denver with Betsy but she'd never forgotten those treasured hours reading on the shaded porch swing on hot July afternoons or under the big maple tree out back.

"You've read them, right?" she asked Faith now.

The girl shook her head. "Not yet. I've been wanting to but I never started."

She was not quite eight, much younger than Lucy had been when she'd read them. Maybe she wouldn't enjoy them as much.

Despite her worry, Faith looked delighted and picked the first book out of the collection and opened it up right there in the living room.

"What about me?" Carter asked, not to be outdone. "Which one should I read?"

She looked through the collection and pulled out *Charlotte's Web.*

"Have you read this? It's one of my favorites."

"Is that the one about the spider and the pig?" he asked.

"The very one."

"Daddy checked it out of the library for us once but we were reading something else and never had time for that one before we had to return it."

"Now you have your own copy and don't have to

take it back to the library. Why don't we start it tonight?"

"Okay!"

"Faith, do you want to stay out here and read your book or come into Carter's room and listen to *Charlotte's Web?*"

"I'll come with you."

Carter led the way back to his room, still decorated the way Jessie had left it, with a Western Americana theme: red, white and blue, with horseshoes holding up some shelves and a trail of stars stenciled around the ceiling.

It was a cute room for a boy, perfect for an active kid like Carter.

The sharpness of loss clutched at her chest again. Jessie had loved her family, being a mother, making a comfortable home for them. Of all the gross inequities in the world, Lucy considered it so unfair that this loving young mother with her life ahead of her would be taken from her family by a health condition nobody could have anticipated.

The room had two twin beds, maybe in anticipation for the day when Carter would have shared this room with his brother, who had been too gestationally immature to survive outside the womb after Jess went into cardiac arrest so suddenly.

Carter jumped onto one of the beds, and Lucy forced herself to push the sadness away.

"Daddy usually reads to me from the other one. You can do that, too."

She eased down onto the bed, and Faith curled up at her feet, pulling a throw over herself and listening raptly while Lucy began reading the story about a runt

piglet and the spider who was a very brave friend—
and a good writer, too.

By the time she finished the first chapter, Carter's
eyelids were drooping. Judging by his energy level
every time she saw him, she completely understood
why. An object in constant motion eventually had to
run out of steam. She didn't know if that was an actual physics principle, but it definitely applied to five-
year-old boys.

He closed his eyes at the same moment she marked
her page and closed the book. She slid off the bed and
pulled his blanket up over his shoulders, awash with
tenderness for this funny little man.

"You got through a whole chapter. That's great. My
dad usually falls asleep after about two pages while
he's reading to Carter," Faith confided in a whisper.

Like his son, Brendan put in a long, busy day, as
well.

"I guess it's lucky for both of us I made it this far.
Shall we go into your room and read about Anne coming to know Matthew and Marilla?"

"Yes!"

Together, they walked down the hall to Faith's room,
all pink and lavender and yellow, sweet as Faith herself.

"Oh. Look at that! That's the chair you told me about
on the phone a few months ago. I'd forgotten about it,
but it's just as lovely as you said."

It was a slim Queen Anne recliner with curvy lines
and a pretty material that seemed to bring together all
the colors of the room.

"Dad said somebody who liked to read as much as I
do needed a comfortable reading nook. He bought me

the light and everything. And it wasn't even my birthday. It was a just-because present. Those are the best."

"I agree." She smiled. "Do you want the chair or the bed for reading?"

"I'll take the bed." Faith settled in, hands clasped on her chest expectantly.

Lucy settled into the recliner—which was, indeed, comfortable—and proceeded to read a chapter from the book about an orphaned girl trying to make her way in her new home.

"I think that's enough," she finally said, though she would have read all night if she could, she was enjoying it so much.

"Anne is so *funny,*" Faith declared.

"She is," Lucy responded.

The girl was quiet as Lucy rose from the recliner, laid the book on her bedside table and tucked in her quilt a little more snugly around her.

"I wonder how her mom died," Faith finally asked, her voice low.

This poor little child, who had lost her own mother too young. Lucy wanted to cry suddenly that Jess would never have the chance to know the funny, sweet, courageous girl her daughter was becoming.

"If I recall from reading the series all those years ago, she was only a baby when both of her parents died of an illness."

"That would have been easier," Faith said, her voice solemn. "She probably didn't know them enough to miss them."

"Oh, honey."

She reached down to the bed and hugged Faith, wondering if the girl was open with her father about her grief or if she tried to protect him from it, as appeared to be her nature.

"It's normal to miss your mom," she said, choosing her words carefully. "You know that, right? Some part of you will always have a little hole. My mom died almost twenty years ago, and I still miss her."

Despite her emotional and psychological issues, Betsy had still been her mother. Lucy knew she probably missed what she *wished* she had in a mother more than the actual person, but the loss was no less acute.

"More than anything," she went on to Faith, "I wish that I could patch that hole for you and take away your sadness. But that would also mean taking away all your wonderful memories of your mom, and I would never, ever want to do that. You're sad because you miss her. I miss her, too. Your dad and Carter do, too."

"I know," Faith said, her voice small. "I miss her so much sometimes. Carter doesn't remember her much. He was only three. I do, though."

"He'll remember her most through the memories you and your dad share with him about her."

"Sometimes I'm mad at her, too," Faith said in a rush, as if the confession had been churning inside her for some time, just waiting for a chance to slip out.

Lucy was almost positive Faith hadn't shared *this* with her father. She sat on the edge of the bed and pulled the girl's hand into hers. "That's normal, too, honey."

"Why did she even need another baby? She had me and Carter. She would still be here if she hadn't decided to have another baby."

Just how much did Faith know about the circumstances around Jessie's death? Lucy chose her words carefully. "Your mom used to tell me when we were girls that she wanted a half-dozen kids, just like the Brady Bunch. Three boys and three girls. She loved your dad's big family and wanted one, too. It's not that you weren't enough for her, honey. She just had so much love in her heart and knew another baby would make that love grow even more."

"It didn't, though."

Lucy sighed. "She didn't know she had a problem with her heart. None of the doctors even knew. She spent all her life with it and had you and Carter and it never gave her any trouble. She had no reason to think having the new baby would be any different from having you or your brother."

She hugged Faith, feeling the slenderness of her bones beneath her nightgown. "You know she would never have chosen to leave you, right?"

Faith sniffled a little but didn't cry. "I guess."

"You were her sunshine. Always. I know it hurts not having her here, but the best thing you can do is think about all the good you still have. Your dad, Carter, your grandpa Caine and all your aunts and uncles and cousins."

"You."

The tears she had been fighting ever since Faith first asked her about Anne Shirley's mother welled up, and she had to swallow hard against the emotion in her throat. "Me. Yes. Always."

"I know. I know I have all that. Sometimes I just get a little sad."

"Nothing wrong with that. The sad times in our lives help us appreciate those moments of beauty and joy." She rose. "You need to try to sleep now. You've got school tomorrow, and your dad won't be very happy with me if he finds us still up gabbing when he gets back. If you want, I can read here in your comfortable chair while you fall asleep."

"No. I'll be okay." She smiled sleepily. "I'm really glad you're here, Aunt Lucy."

She kissed the top of the girl's wispy blond hair. "I am, too, darling."

CHAPTER FIVE

THE HOUSE SEEMED almost eerily quiet without the children running around, filling the space with their laughter, their questions, their disparate personalities.

She walked down the hall toward the kitchen, accompanied only by the sound of the rain still pattering against the windows and the creak of an occasional floorboard in the old house.

Odd, that she lived in the huge, echoing mansion by herself but didn't feel nearly as alone as she did right now, walking through Brendan's place—probably because all the clicks and whooshes at Iris House were as familiar to her as her own heartbeat.

She felt a little like an intruder, creeping around where she shouldn't. How ridiculous was that, when he needed her here to help him with his children?

This was a comfortable house, she had to admit, warm and airy. But something still seemed missing.

The kitchen was a mess, with dirty dishes piled in the sink and a glass casserole with the sticky remains of what had likely been their dinner on the stovetop.

Since she had nothing else to keep her busy—and maybe she wanted to prove to him that she could be useful for more than just bringing unwanted gifts to his children—she unloaded the dishwasher. She had to do some opening and closing of cupboards and drawers to figure out where things belonged, the worst part about working in someone else's kitchen, but she figured it out.

After that was done and the remaining dishes loaded again, her stomach rumbled. She hadn't eaten since lunchtime. Her plan had been to take the gifts down to the children and then head back to Iris House to make a sandwich.

She thought about ignoring the rumbling but the residue left on the casserole had looked like chicken enchiladas and had smelled delicious. She was sort of a rabid chicken enchilada fan.

She opened his refrigerator and found a container with the leftovers, along with an unfinished meal on a plate covered in plastic wrap that she guessed had been Brendan's.

Assuming he wouldn't mind, given the last-minute favor she was doing him, she left his plate alone but spooned a rolled tortilla from the leftover container onto a plate of her own, added some of the sauce and warmed it in the microwave.

The food was fantastic, easy on the heat index but every bit as good as something she would find in her favorite Mexican restaurant in Seattle. After she just about licked the plate clean, she loaded it and her fork into the dishwasher, gave the countertops one last swipe with a cloth and then wandered into the family room.

She had probably been here before when she had visited Jess, but she didn't remember spending any time in this room. The space was dominated by a big-screen TV and two big plump leather reclining sofas.

Right now, it was also cluttered with toys. She

should have made the children come in before bedtime to clean up their mess. Since she hadn't thought of it—and since she didn't like the idea of Brendan having to do it himself when he came home after a long day—she spent a few moments clearing the floor before she collapsed onto the sofa, exhausted from her day.

She flipped through the television shows and finally settled on a news program.

The stress of the past few days must have been more exhausting than she realized. The last thing she remembered was some apple-cheeked reporter with an unnaturally chipper voice trying to ask a hard-hitting question of a politician.

She must have fallen asleep. When she awoke, she had the strange, crawly sensation of being watched.

She blinked her eyes open, wondering if Carter or Faith had awakened her. Instead, she saw a big, wide-shouldered figure standing in the doorway, and she gasped, visions of psycho killers flashing through her mind.

"Whoa. Easy. I'm sorry I startled you. It's me. Brendan."

The voice pushed through the panic, and she drew in an unsteady breath. Brendan. Of course. How could she possibly have mistaken him for anybody else?

She drew in a shaky breath. "Well. There go several years off my life I won't get back."

He turned the dimmer lights up in the room. "See? Only me."

As if that made her feel any more comfortable. "I'm sorry. I was sleeping and woke up to find you standing there. It would creep anyone out. Even you."

"Probably." He smiled a little, but she thought suddenly that he looked weary. Beyond weary, actually, bordering on deep fatigue.

"What time is it?" she asked.

"Almost one. I'm sorry to be so late. Things were a little busier than I expected, and this is the earliest I could get away."

"Don't worry about it. If they need you back at the station, I'm fine staying all night. As long as you don't jump out and scare me when you come back."

Through his exhaustion, she saw glimmers of surprise in his expression that left her melancholy. Why did he seem so shocked that she could be compassionate and helpful when the situation called for it? This was only further evidence of his poor opinion of her.

The feeling of trying so very hard to please someone impossible seemed entirely too familiar. She didn't have to look very far to see why—a girl growing up with a difficult, demanding, overbearing father knew that feeling like she knew her own imperfect face in the mirror.

Brendan always viewed her as nothing more than Jessie's pain-in-the-neck ambitious, driven cousin, who showed up at inconvenient moments.

Okay, not *always*. One magical night, he had flirted with her and kissed her and had led her to start spinning ridiculous dreams about something that would never be. That night seemed like a distant scene in someone else's life, something she almost thought she might have made up in her head, especially after he started dating Jessie just a few weeks after making her think he might actually be interested in her.

She wasn't going to say he broke her naive twenty-one-year-old heart, that getting over his rejection of her had been one of the hardest things she'd ever had to do. That would be giving him entirely too much power, and she wasn't willing to go that far.

"I'm done for the night," he answered, and she pushed stupid thoughts of the past away. "The shift is covered now, and the guys with food poisoning are already feeling better. Thanks for saving the day."

"No problem." She rose from the sofa. "Let me grab my things from the kitchen and then I'll get out of your way."

He followed her as she retrieved her raincoat and umbrella.

"Did you ever catch dinner?" she asked him.

"No. I'll grab a bowl of cereal or something before I crash."

"Don't forget, you've still got a plate of enchiladas in the refrigerator you can warm up."

"I might do that. The phone call from my assistant chief came just as we were sitting down to dinner."

"I thought as much."

How many plates had he left uneaten over the years?

"I had a few bites of your chicken enchiladas," she told him. "I hope you don't mind, but I hadn't eaten dinner yet when I came over here."

"Not at all. I hope you had more than a bite. There was plenty. You stepped up and saved my bacon. The least I can do is feed you."

"They were very tasty. You're not a bad cook."

He made a face but seemed pleased with the compliment. "With Pop around, learning to cook at our house was mandatory, not optional. All of us were required to learn at home and then to work at the café at some point in our lives. Pop had me flipping pancakes before I could talk."

She tried to picture him as a dark-haired little boy surrounded by his brothers, both older and younger, trying to learn how to cook. It was difficult to make the image stick when she was confronted by the big, hard reality of the adult Brendan Caine.

"I love your dad."

"You and half the women in town. Young and old, he charms them all. Too bad for you, but his heart belongs to Katherine Thorne...though he'll never admit it."

"Katherine? Really? I had no idea they were a thing."

"I'm not sure what *kind* of thing they are. They've never even dated, if you want the truth, but you should see the way Pop blushes whenever she comes into the café."

She smiled, charmed by the idea of two people in that season of their life being flustered by each other. Brendan hadn't specifically mentioned that Katherine returned Dermot's feelings, but she must. Lucy had always liked Katherine Thorne and considered her to be a woman of good sense. What other choice would she have but to care for someone as wonderful as Dermot?

"Oh, they're perfect together! Don't you agree?"

She realized she was still smiling when Brendan didn't answer, only continued staring at her mouth with an odd expression that made her feel suddenly hot and restless.

"You don't like the idea?"

He blinked a few times, and she remembered the poor man was exhausted and probably didn't like much of anything right now. Especially *her*.

"What idea?"

"Your pop and Katherine. But it doesn't matter right now. I should go. I hope you'll be able to rest for a few hours. Good night, Brendan. Thanks for giving me the chance to be with Carter and Faith tonight. We had a marvelous time."

She picked up her umbrella and headed for the front door. He followed along just a few feet behind, and at the door, he opened a closet to grab his jacket.

The crazy man intended to walk her up to Iris House. She stopped there with her hand on the doorknob. "It's half a block. You don't have to come with me."

"Yeah. I do."

"What about the kids?"

"They'll be okay for five minutes."

"This from the fire chief?"

"I'll be in sight the whole time and can be back in sixty seconds from anywhere on the block. If it makes you feel better, I've got a baby monitor I use when I'm working out in the yard after they're in bed. I just need to plug it in. The signal reaches at least as far as Iris House so we can hear if either of them wakes up."

She wanted to insist he march right into his bedroom and catch some of that sleep he so obviously needed. But then, she'd never exactly been the Mother Hen type, and this seemed an odd time to start. Besides, she was just too tired to get into it with him.

She waited a moment while he found the monitor and set it up in the hallway so he could hear the children if they called out, then he stuck the handset in his pocket and they walked out into a quiet night, cool and lovely with gleaming streets and the breeze heavy with the scent of rain-drenched pine.

At just past 1:00 a.m., most of Hope's Crossing slept. She could see a light on below here and there, but most houses were dark. Once, she knew who lived in most of the houses on this street, but it had changed since that brief time she lived here with Annabelle so long ago.

Change was inevitable. Nothing stayed the same in life. Why hadn't she kept that in mind these past few years at NexGen and prepared a little better for it?

She breathed in deeply of the sweet air that made her want to go on a long walk in the mountains, something she had learned to love during her time here in high school.

She certainly hadn't done enough of enjoying the outdoors in Seattle. She had lived in a beautiful place but working sixteen-hour days didn't allow much free time to enjoy it.

That wasn't a problem now. She had nothing *but* time.

They were almost to Iris House when she finally asked the question that had been plaguing her since he dragged her into his house and told her she was an answer to prayer.

"How do you manage everything now? The kids, your job. It can't be easy. Do you ever think about working somewhere with a more regular schedule?"

"It's a juggling act sometimes, but I have a lot of help. Pop. Charlotte. Erin—that's Andrew's wife. I try to work around the kids' schedule, and I also have a good babysitter and quasi housekeeper who comes in and spends the night when I'm on the overnight shift. Linda Madison. She actually lives right there."

He pointed to a house that was two doors down from Iris House, now dark and shuttered.

"The name seems familiar but I can't picture her."

"She taught at the elementary school for years. Second grade. She was good friends with my mom. And Annabelle, too."

"Oh, I think I remember her now. Red hair and those big, swoopy kind of glasses."

"That's her. Her hair is still red but her glasses are smaller now, you'll be happy to know."

"Whew. That's a relief."

He lifted his mouth a little but didn't give in to a full-on smile.

"She doesn't have any grandchildren so she's kind of adopted mine, which works out great for everyone. The only problem is, she's gone on a once-in-a-lifetime cruise through the Panama Canal for the next few weeks so I'm on my own," he said, just as they reached the iron fence encircling Iris House. "We're managing, though. Most of the time."

He reached to open the gate for her. "So you're really going to turn this old place into a bed and breakfast?"

"That's the plan for now. Who knows? I may change my mind and decide it's too much work. It's probably smarter to just sell it and let someone else assume all the risk and the effort."

"You're not usually the sort to back down from a challenge."

"Not usually. But I've also learned over the years to pick my battles. Sometimes the fight just isn't worth it."

"True enough."

"You'd better get back to the children."

"Yes. Good night. Thanks again."

"You're welcome."

He turned to walk home but on impulse she followed him through the gate. "You know I love being with Faith and Carter, right?" she said. "Right now I've got nothing else pressing on my time. I would be happy to help you with them whenever you need, at least until Mrs. Madison returns."

His gaze narrowed in the slice of moonlight between two clouds. "I don't need your help. I've got it covered," he answered, his voice clipped.

Just what she needed tonight. Another stupid rejection. "Of course you do," she returned in what she hoped was a calm voice instead of the angry words she wanted to snap back.

"Sorry I presumed."

She reached for the gate behind her and struggled with the latch in the darkness. After a moment, he sighed and reached out to help her open it. His hand covered hers, the strength and size and *heat* a vivid contrast to the cold, wet metal.

"Lucy. I'm sorry. I'm a bear tonight."

"Tonight?" she asked caustically.

"Yeah. Most of the time, probably. Tonight is… worse than usual. A couple of hours ago, we were called out to a double fatality. A couple of tourists. A young couple from Nebraska. The guy was speeding in the rain up the canyon and flipped their rental."

In that wedge of moonlight, she thought the lines looked a little deeper beside his mouth. "Oh, no."

"Fatalities always hit my guys hard, even when we don't know the people. It's a reminder that we're all a heartbeat away from losing everything we care about."

He would know that more than most. Her heart

squeezed in her chest, and she couldn't help reaching out to touch his arm.

Again, his heat seemed to draw her like a warm fire on a cold winter's night. Without the chimney fire, of course.

"I'm sorry," she said softly.

He gazed down at her for a long moment and something seemed to shiver awake between them, like a great slumbering creature that had just shaken off a long subterranean hibernation and finally wandered into the sunshine.

"A little more grumpiness than usual is completely understandable," she added.

Though she didn't want to give up the heat and comfort of touching him, she forced herself to withdraw her hand. "I meant what I said about the kids. I really do love their company. They can help me at Iris House as I go through each room and start cleaning out."

"I appreciate the offer. If I can't make things work the way we usually do things, I know where to find you. Good night."

He waited by the gate until she had let herself into the house. Once she closed the door behind her, she looked out through the wavy original oval glass pane on the front door and watched him walk back through the rain-slick streets, remembering another rainy night so long ago.

It was late May, she remembered. Memorial Day weekend. She had been twenty-one and had just finished her undergraduate degree in computer science and marketing in a fast-paced three years. She had taken an internship at NexGen but wasn't due to start for a few weeks so she had decided to come spend some time with Annabelle and Jessie, who had graduated from college the year before and was teaching first grade at Hope's Crossing Elementary School.

Unfortunately, she planned the trip without talking to Jess, and it turned out her cousin had already made plans for the weekend to fly to San Diego with some friends so they could hit the beach after a long Hope's Crossing winter.

She had invited Lucy along, but Lucy was going to be spending the summer being extremely underpaid in an expensive city and had decided she couldn't justify the cost of the trip.

Jess offered to stay home, too, so they could enjoy a visit together, but Lucy knew her cousin didn't have an unlimited budget, either, and would lose the money she had already paid for her share of the trip, so she encouraged her to go.

Friday night, she had been at loose ends at Iris House and one of her friends from high school, Sara Benevidez, had called her, wanting to go listen to a live band at The Speckled Lizard—a rather disreputable bar in town where some of the cute tourists tended to hang out.

She had agreed, though cute tourists were definitely not on her radar. She had decided not to date until she had met a few of her career goals.

She could picture that beautiful spring night at The Liz vividly. The honky-tonk band that hadn't been half-bad, a little dancing, a few margaritas, a little light-hearted conversation. In Boulder, she was so focused on her schoolwork that the renowned party scene there had sort of slipped by her. That night, it had felt great to let her hair down and remember she was a twenty-something about to embark on the rest of her life.

And then Brendan walked in with one of his brothers. Jamie, the helicopter pilot.

She recognized them as Caines right away. Big, built, great-looking.

She'd never met Brendan, but she knew who he was. He was five years older and something of a legend around Hope's Crossing. He had been a star running back on the high school football team and had gone on to play college ball and had a few pretty good years for the Broncos before suffering a career-ending injury.

She figured she had nothing at all in common with a former professional athlete. Still, he rated off the charts on her own personal yum scale. The dark hair, those blue eyes, the chiseled features and wide shoulders.

After Jamie Caine came over to talk to Sara—who had apparently gone out with him a time or two, as had half the women in town—somehow they ended up sharing a table with the brothers. Sara and Jamie had been flirting heavily and not paying attention to either of them, which left her matched up with Brendan by default.

He had just moved back to town after years away to take a job with the fire department, and she had found it incredibly sweet that he was moving back to help protect and serve his hometown.

Something about the beautiful spring night and the giddiness of having a man like Brendan look at her with interest—and maybe the simmering anticipation coursing through her veins at being about to embark on a new life—brought out a side of her she'd never expected. Where she was usually focused, serious, intense, that night she was actually vivacious and fun and flirty, all the things that seemed to come so easily to her friends.

They danced, they laughed, they talked…and she lost a little of the heart she usually protected so carefully.

When he walked her back to Iris House, he told her he wanted to see her again, but he was leaving for a couple of days on a quick hiking and fishing trip with Jamie while his brother was home on leave.

She explained she was leaving the day before he got back for Seattle and her internship.

His disappointment had been incredibly gratifying. She did scribble her email and phone number on a piece of paper she found in her handbag and he promised he would be in touch as soon as he returned.

Then at the front gate that she could see gleaming black in the moonlight, he had kissed her.

She let the curtain flutter close now, remembering. It had been intense and passionate, probably the most incredible kiss of her entire life. A kiss filled with promise and possibilities, with the budding of something wild and sweet and wonderful.

She had gone to sleep that night—and for the next week—replaying that kiss in her mind, dreaming about him, wondering about him.

He had never called her, of course.

When he came back to town from his trip, he met Jess in all her tall blonde gorgeousness, and the fickle man forgot all about the strange, intense tech geek he had only known for a night.

Why shouldn't he? Jessie had been everything he was looking for. Sweet, warm, kind. And *there*. She loved Hope's Crossing and wanted to stay in town and start a family, just like Brendan.

She loved football and his family and him.

They were perfect for each other—which hadn't made Lucy feel any better about the situation when Jessie called her all giddy about the great guy she was dating and about how he might be The One.

She sighed now and moved away from the door and into the huge, quiet house.

She had tried to be happy for Jessie when, after a year of dating, Brendan proposed. After all, he was everything Jessie had ever dreamed about, and *Lucy* certainly wasn't in the market for a big, gorgeous ex-football player turned firefighter, right?

After her internship, she had taken a permanent job at NexGen and moved quickly up the ladder. As Jessie and Brendan settled down and bought the house she had just left, as Jess became pregnant quickly, as sweet Faith came along, Lucy threw all her energy, her effort, her loneliness into her career.

As a result, she became the youngest director in the history of the company and had been on track to a vice presidency within the next two or three years, everything she told herself she wanted.

That chance meeting on a long-ago night had meant nothing for either of them.

So why couldn't she seem to get it out of her head?

Lucy freaking Drake.

Brendan stomped down the street without looking back at Iris House. He was angry with the world right now—at the food poisoning that had dragged him back to work on a night he wanted to be with his kids; at the stupid, pathetic tourist who didn't understand the concept of driving safely for conditions and had paid for it with his life and the life of his new bride; at Lucy for showing up at his doorstep right when he needed her…and then for making him feel things he didn't want to, ever again.

For two years, since Jessie and the baby died, everything inside him had been on ice. A frozen block of nothing. He had been going through the motions, focused mostly on two things—doing his job and being the best damn father he could manage to Faith and Carter.

He had achieved a place where, while he wouldn't exactly call it peace, at least he wasn't the crazed, grief-stricken, hot mess he had been in those first months after that life-changing-in-a-heartbeat moment when the doctors had come out of the E.R. treatment room to tell him his wife and child were gone.

Gone.

An otherwise healthy mother of two had been taken by a shocking, extremely rare complication of pregnancy, coronary artery dissection, a tear in an artery that allowed blood flow in places it shouldn't be in the heart.

She had gone into cardiac arrest in the grocery store and his own paramedics had been called to take her to the hospital. He'd been home with the kids when he got the phone call and by the time he frantically dropped Faith and Carter off with Mrs. Madison and flew to the hospital, she and the baby were already gone.

It had been more than two years and he had eased into a routine of sorts as a widower. Everything had been going along fine. He had learned how to juggle a dozen plates at once and was doing his best to keep things rolling at a decent pace.

Now Lucy Drake, with her dark curls and her big green eyes, had to blow back into his life and change *everything.*

He didn't want to be attracted to anybody. He wasn't ready for the surge of his blood or the pound of his heart—and he sure as hell wasn't prepared to be attracted to Lucy.

She had never liked him and made no secret of it. She was abrasive and rude and went out of her way to try hitting all his hot buttons.

At first, he figured he deserved it. She was the first and only woman he had been a complete ass to.

They had kissed once—a pretty amazing kiss, yeah—and he had been really attracted to her, despite their differences.

A week hiking around the mountains around Hope's Crossing on that fishing trip with Jamie had left him plenty of time to think, though, and the bald truth was, while Lucy had been great-looking and fun and exciting, she wasn't what he wanted in life.

He loved his hometown and now that he was back, he couldn't imagine living anyplace else, while she had been brimming over about the excitement of city life and how she couldn't wait to move to Seattle and start her fast-paced career.

He'd known he wanted to build a family and a home here, so what was the point in starting a relationship with a woman who had made no secret she wanted none of those things?

End of story, he'd figured.

He hadn't called or emailed her as he promised,

figuring the heat between them would fizzle and die without an oxygen source. Though he felt like a jerk about it, he didn't quite know how to explain to someone as smart and savvy as Lucy that he was entering the dating game with an eye on the long play.

He figured, it had only been a kiss. Her heart wouldn't exactly have been broken. Besides, she was busy with a new job, a new city, and had probably forgotten all about him.

Then he met Jess one afternoon at her summer job waiting tables at one of the restaurants at the resort and fell hard for her, not even knowing at first that Lucy was her cousin and best friend until their third date, when she had finally given him her address and he realized she lived at Iris House with Annabelle Stanbridge.

He had awkwardly asked Jess about Lucy, and she had gushed about how much she loved her cousin and was so proud of her. He had almost stopped dating her right then, figuring things had become too messy, but Jess had been sweet and warm and he had needed that in his life at the time.

Still, Lucy had always been the fly in the ointment of their peaceful marriage. He always left their interactions feeling vaguely guilty, like he was some big, heartless player—not to mention that she had done her best to talk Jessie out of marrying him, which still rankled.

By the time he reached his house and let himself in, some of his anger had ebbed. So he had been attracted to her for a few minutes there tonight and had wanted to kiss her.

What did he expect? A beautiful woman, a lovely, rain-soaked night scented with lilacs and springtime, and a man who had been alone for more than two years. There was a recipe for disaster if he'd ever heard one.

It was only a normal physiological reaction. He wouldn't let it happen again, so what was the sense in thinking about it?

CHAPTER SIX

"THANK YOU SO much for stopping by. I have to admit, I have absolutely no idea where to start."

Genevieve Beaumont walked into the foyer of Iris House and set down a large leather tote on the carved table by the front door so she could untwist a scarf from around her neck.

"That's why I'm here. Believe me, I have more than enough ideas for both of us, and I told you, I have been *dying* to have a look inside Iris House. I should be thanking you for giving me the chance. This will be *so* much fun."

Lucy had to admit, Genevieve's enthusiasm was infectious. She hadn't really considered any of the work that needed to be done on Iris House in the *fun* category but perhaps this walk-through could help shift perspective a little.

"Where should we start?" she asked

Genevieve pulled a bound notebook out of her satchel. "Let's first sit down and talk about any ideas you have for using the space and then we'll do the tour. Does that work?"

"Sounds good."

Lucy led the way into the parlor, with its elegant period furnishings and thick moldings.

"Oh, I love the custom woodwork in here. They

just don't put the same time and effort into houses these days."

Genevieve perched on one of the camelback horse-hide sofas. "This is so exciting! Okay, tell me what you want!"

If she knew that, she wouldn't need Genevieve, would she? She made a face. "I want a finished product that isn't too ostentatious or flashy but is romantic and elegant. I want people who stay here to remember it forever. A decade from now, I'd like them to say, 'George, remember that charming little inn where we stayed in Hope's Crossing? We had the *best* time there. We should go back. Today!'"

Genevieve chuckled. "Okay. Specifics are good. Anything else?"

"The house has ten bedrooms. Eight of those have en suite bathrooms. The other two don't but they're small rooms, anyway. I'm thinking we could combine them with two of the other rooms to make them large suites with sitting rooms."

"Oh, I like that idea. It will cost you, though."

"Everything's going to cost me," she muttered. Fortunately, she had money in savings, and Annabelle had left a comfortable inheritance that would help tide her over through the transition.

"What about the owners' quarters? Have you thought about which rooms will be yours? We can't leave that out of the equation. You'll want a private space where you can retreat at the end of the day when you're tired of dealing with guests."

"I'll be here at start-up but my intention is to hire someone to run the B&B for me for the long-term."

"So you won't be staying here?"

"No. Only here for a few months."

She really needed to start putting her résumé out there. She'd had a few of her networking contacts already ask what her plans might be. So far, she had remained mum, preferring to focus on Iris House for now.

That couldn't continue indefinitely, of course. The nest egg was comfortable but not coast-the-rest-of-your-life comfortable—especially with the renovations she needed to make to the house.

Besides, sitting around doing nothing but living off her previous gains wasn't in her nature, anyway.

She and Genevieve talked a little more about a possible color palette and the multiple-use potential for the main floor public rooms, like weddings and large parties. Finally Genevieve stood. "I can't wait another moment. Let's see what we have here."

They started on the top floor and worked their way down. Genevieve exclaimed with delight at something in each room—a wide, deep window seat in one, a built-in oak bookshelf in another, an oversize clawfoot tub in another.

By the time they made it to the main floor, it was obvious Genevieve saw far more potential in the house than Lucy, which was the first encouraging sign she'd had since coming up with this harebrained idea.

"My Dylan and Sam Delgado would love to get their hands on this house."

"I don't think I've met Sam."

"He's pretty new in town, but you might know his wife. Alex McKnight. She runs a great restaurant in town, Brazen. You have to go there while you're in town! Did you know Alex?"

"I did. She was a few years older than me but I think we had a few mutual friends."

"Well, Sam, her husband, did a lot of work at A Warrior's Hope. He's fast and he does a great job—even better now that Dylan works with him."

The pride shone through her voice like a lighthouse beacon and Lucy smiled.

"What's A Warrior's Hope? You're not the first person in town who's mentioned it to me."

"Oh, it's a fantastic program that was started up last year to provide recreational therapy to help injured veterans. We run summer and winter sessions and provide help to about six or seven veterans in a session, all through donations of time and resources. The whole town has really rallied around it."

"And you and Dylan are involved?"

"Charlotte and Spence actually started the program. Dylan and I were dragged into their volunteer workforce kicking and screaming, you might say, but now we both really enjoy it. Okay, I probably enjoy it more than he does, but he still comes to help when he can."

"That's terrific."

"You should help," Genevieve exclaimed. "You were a marketing director. I bet you could give Spence some fantastic ideas about how to get the word out about what they're doing!"

"I don't know—" she began, but the rest of what she would have said was cut off by the chiming doorbells.

She couldn't say she was sorry for the diversion. She did believe volunteer work was a necessary and important part of life and had donated time as a mentor at a woman's shelter in Seattle.

Right now, though, she was barely keeping herself

together—and the past hour had only reinforced just
how much work she had to do at Iris House before it
would be ready for guests. She was too overwhelmed
to even think about taking on a volunteer commitment
right now. Maybe if she were staying in Hope's Crossing for the long-term…

"Will you excuse me?"

"No problem." Genevieve held up her tape measure. "I'll just write down the dimensions of some of
the rooms and make some notes while you answer the
door."

Even as she couldn't wait to find out Genevieve's
vision for the house, she had a feeling those notes were
going to cost her plenty before they were done here.

She was focused on the possibilities as she headed
for the front door, her mind picturing Iris House filled
with guests and laughter and life again.

Just before she reached the door, the bell rang again
with an edge of impatience she didn't miss. She pulled
it open then could only stare for at least ten seconds,
not at all prepared for the man standing on the other
side.

"Dad!" she finally exclaimed when she could force
her brain to start clicking again. "What are you doing
here?"

Robert Drake raised one distinguished gray eyebrow
as he let himself into the house without an invitation.
He looked around the foyer and Lucy was suddenly intensely aware of the jeans and practical russet cotton
work shirt she had chosen for the tour with Genevieve.

Robert was wearing a tailored blue dress shirt and
Savile Row tie, of course. She had very few memories
of him in casual clothes.

He reached in to brush his cheek against hers. "Why do you sound so surprised? Is it so unusual I would want to see my oldest daughter when she moves into the state whcrc I reside?"

Unusual was an understatement. Her interactions with her father rarely moved beyond the infrequent phone call or hastily dashed email. She was a part of Robert's past he preferred not to dwell upon.

That he would actually drive the hour and a half from Denver to see her was beyond remarkable.

"How did you even know I was in Hope's Crossing?" she asked.

"Crystal mentioned it a few days ago."

"Did she?" For a moment, she couldn't remember even telling her half sister she was coming back to Colorado, then she remembered a few quick texts they'd exchanged the day she set out from Seattle. So much had happened, that seemed another lifetime ago.

"Yes," Robert answered. "She said you were planning to stay a few months and work on Iris House. What's the story? What happened to NexGen?"

She had absolutely no desire to tell him anything about it, but her father would push and push until she caved and gave him the information he sought. Robert was something of a legend at extracting information. He wasn't one of the foremost criminal defense attorneys in the state because of his knitting skills.

He was a complicated man—brilliant, intense, focused and completely impossible to please.

And now she had to tell him she had failed rather spectacularly.

"NexGen and I have parted ways. Creative differences."

"What did you do?" he asked in a resigned voice.

What else did she expect? Of course he would never step up and say that if they were crazy enough to fire his baby girl, the company must be run by a bunch of butt-scratching baboons.

"I did my job and I did it extraordinarily well. We had a poor product launch and I took the hit for it, despite my otherwise successful track record."

"You can't rest on your laurels. You should know that. Do you think I sit around looking at newspaper clippings of all the cases I've won? No. Not one of them matters where it counts. The only important case is the client I'm defending right now."

"I'm choosing to look on the positive side," she answered, which was only a little lie. "I haven't taken a vacation day in eight years. I needed a break and Iris House needed some attention before it crumbles into a wreck that will have to be condemned. I decided to take a few months off to recharge my batteries and take care of things here before I shift focus back to my career."

"What are you going to do with it? I hope you've decided to sell it, as I've been advising you since Annabelle died."

She wasn't sure her father could ever be placed in the category of advisor. She remembered one conversation about the house, at Annabelle's funeral, when Robert had told her she would be crazy to hang on to a money pit like Iris House, especially with real estate prices finally on the upswing in resort communities.

"I'm still mulling my options. I'm considering turning it into a bed and breakfast. That's what Jessie and Annabelle wanted."

"Those things never make money," he said dismissively. "You're better off dumping it while you can, trust me."

As usual, her father's clear disdain for one of her ideas only made her more determined than ever to do it.

Because, yeah. She was mature that way.

She suddenly remembered Genevieve and her tape measure. "You know, Dad, I've actually got an interior decorator here. We were just having a tour. If you can give me a few minutes to finish up with her, perhaps you and I can run somewhere and grab lunch. Someone just recommended a new place in town, Brazen."

"I'm actually on a fairly tight schedule." He shifted his weight and for the first time, she thought her father looked uneasy about something. "I actually also came to—"

Whatever he intended to say was cut short when Genevieve herself actually came down the sweeping staircase with her clipboard in hand.

She paused about halfway down when she caught sight of them in the foyer below. "Oh. I'm sorry. I didn't mean to interrupt."

"No. It's fine," Lucy answered, and the other woman continued down the staircase.

"Genevieve, this is my father, Robert Drake. Dad, this is Genevieve Beaumont, my interior designer."

She saw at once that Gen recognized her father. No surprise there, he and her stepmother were very well-known in Denver social circles. From all accounts, Genevieve used to move in those same circles.

"I believe we've met," she answered. "It was a few years ago at a charity event for the Denver children's hospital."

"Oh, yes." Robert smiled vaguely, and Lucy could

tell he didn't remember at all. She wanted to tell Genevieve not to feel too badly about it. Her father barely remembered *Lucy* most of the time.

"I believe I'm finished taking pictures and measurements. I'll upload everything and rough out some ideas. Meanwhile, you figure out your final budget and we'll come up with a game plan. Why don't we meet again next week? We can grab some lunch and talk over the fabulous possibilities of this house. I'm so excited about this project."

She wanted to hug Gen right that moment for backing her up, but she didn't want her father to think they were more girlfriends than client and decorator.

"That would be great. Thank you again, Genevieve."

"You're welcome. Seriously, Iris House is just as amazing as I always imagined it would be. I'll be in touch."

She let herself out of the house and in her wake, Lucy was aware again of the distance between her and her father. So many old pains seemed to bubble and seethe beneath the surface like a geothermal pocket under the earth.

"She seems a trifle young to be an interior decorator, wouldn't you agree?" Robert said after Genevieve left.

No, she didn't agree. And what did age have to do with anything? "She comes highly recommended by people I trust," she said.

She led the way into the parlor. "Can I get you a drink after your drive? Coffee? Mineral water?"

"No, thank you. I'll find something on the drive back."

This was turning stranger and stranger. He obvi-

ously had an agenda for the visit. She only wished he
would bother to share it with her.

"Can you at least sit down?"

He did, perching on the edge of the camelback sofa.

"Okay, Dad," she said after another awkward pause.
"We both know you didn't come out here to talk about
my renovation project or the road bump I've hit on my
career path. Why are you really here?"

Robert stretched an arm across the top of the sofa,
a relaxed pose she could see was just that—a pose.

"I need to ask you a small favor."

"A favor."

She blinked, not quite sure how to respond. In all
her thirty-one years, she had no recollection of her father asking her for anything.

"It's about Crystal."

Okay, that was unexpected. She loved her sister, but
the girl was a *teenager*. They texted and occasionally
talked on Skype, but that was about the extent of their
relationship.

"Yes. The situation between your sister and Pam
is…difficult. Your stepmother's health is not good. You
know that."

"No. I didn't know. I'm sorry. Last I heard, her mul-
tiple sclerosis was in remission."

"She's relapsed," he said, with a slight note of cen-
sure in his voice, as if his second wife could control her
medical condition by sheer will. "The last few months
have been difficult on all of us. She's struggling right
now and doesn't have the strength and energy she had
even in February. Our stress and worry over Crystal
isn't helping the situation."

She knew Crystal had been in a few scrapes here

and there. For some incomprehensible reason, her half sister seemed to delight in flaunting her misdeeds to Lucy, as if she thought they would earn her points with her.

Whenever she confided something to her, Lucy had done her best to steer Crystal toward a different direction, one that wouldn't leave her drunk or stoned or stuck with a teen pregnancy like something on an MTV reality show.

"Pam needs peace and quiet right now to recover her strength, and Crystal just can't seem to understand that, no matter how many times we both explain it to her."

Crystal probably understood exactly what her parents wanted of her. And like Lucy, she was probably just as determined to do the opposite.

"I'm sorry," she murmured. "This must be a difficult situation for all of you."

"Two days ago, she was expelled from school for having marijuana on the school grounds."

For a defense attorney who made a very good living off the dregs of society, Robert took a very dim view toward such things, as she remembered all too acutely.

"Well, that was stupid of her, wasn't it? Everybody knows you keep your stash under your mattress."

He frowned at her. "She claims she was only holding it for someone else. A boy she won't name."

"Ah. The old *I swear it's not mine* defense."

"Something like that. Criminal charges are pending, as well, though the school trustees and the juvenile court authorities are taking their time, considering, well, my standing in the legal community."

Given his shark reputation, she could imagine they

weren't keen to charge Robert Drake's daughter with a crime unless they had an ironclad case against Crystal.

"My point is, this is just the latest in a string of poor decisions on your sister's part. Sneaking out to go drinking, cutting classes, hanging out with a disreputable crowd."

Like the sorts of people who paid her private school tuition through their attorney fees? she wondered.

"She's on a difficult path, and something needs to be done quickly to steer her back onto the straight and narrow."

"So let me guess. You want me to talk to her. Give her the benefit of my thirty-something years on the planet and explain to her that she's trying to get attention in all the wrong ways. That I've walked in her shoes and know the dangers of that particular path. That keeping her grades up and her nose clean is really the only way she'll be able to get into a good college, and a good college is the only way she'll make something of her life. I'll talk to her but I can't guarantee it will have any results."

"I appreciate the offer," Robert said, with another surreptitious glance at his watch. "Actually, I had something else in mind."

"Oh?"

He looked around the spacious room. "This is quite a large house. How many bedrooms?"

"Ten," she answered, suddenly wary.

"Plenty of room, then, for one fifteen-year-old girl."

She stared at him. "What?"

"It's really the perfect solution, don't you agree?"

"Perfect? Perfect for whom?"

She could feel the beginnings of a panic attack fluttering in the wings, trying to get her attention. No. Please no. She couldn't show that weakness to her father, too, and have him tell her she was as crazy as her mother.

"This would be perfect for everyone. Crystal adores you. You know she does. She's always talking about that weekend she flew up to Seattle and stayed at your condo with you and about the awards you've won and the exciting trips you take. She wants to be just like you someday, you know."

Her father was *very* good at what he did, weaving suggestion and flattery into an inescapable silken web.

"I care for Crystal, too," she began.

She had wanted to hate Crystal, once upon a time, for having everything Lucy didn't. The doting mother, the father who hadn't walked out on her. A steady home.

Her existence had changed Lucy's life, and she should have despised her for it, but from the very beginning, Crystal's dimpled smile and sweet auburn curls had worked their way into her heart.

"That doesn't mean she should come stay in Hope's Crossing with me," she said.

"What do you want me to do, Lucy? She can't stay in our home. It's too much for us right now. Pam needs to focus on regaining her health, and she certainly can't do that when she's stressing every moment over another wild mistake your sister makes. This is a critical time in your sister's life. Surely you, of all people, understand that."

Her face burned and she felt as if her father were throwing every one of her past mistakes in her face. Yes, she had been a troubled teenager. Who could blame her, for heaven's sake? Betsy had been a mess, unstable even before Robert walked out on them to find his true love with his second wife, and completely out of control afterward. Robert seemed to have no problem leaving his child with a mentally unstable alcoholic so he could build a new life. How could she *not* resent that?

She had engaged in all sorts of risky behavior in a pointless effort to get her father to notice her.

After her mother's death, Lucy had gone overboard on the rebellion. Drinking hard, partying with the wrong people. She had even run away a time or two. She had made life horribly difficult for Pam, so resentful of this young woman her father had chosen and their efforts to start a new family when he couldn't be bothered with the one he had.

Remembering her past sins, that wild-child past, mostly left her feeling embarrassed—and deeply grateful that somehow sheer luck had kept her from ending up dead or in jail.

"Crystal has been expelled because of the pending charges," Robert said. "With only another month left in the school year, we decided it wouldn't make sense to start her in a new private school. We're giving her through the summer to try to shape up on her own. If she doesn't, military school may be the only option left to us."

She tried to imagine her creative, artistic, dramatic sister in military school and couldn't make the picture fit. It would crush her. Why couldn't Robert see that?

She supposed she shouldn't be surprised. Apparently he couldn't be bothered to truly look at either of his daughters.

"And you think *I* can be some kind of substitute for military school?"

He shrugged. "Why not? You can put her to work here. She can help you with this place. By the looks of it, you have plenty to do around here. A little elbow grease will be good for her. You'll see. You two will have a great time together."

And once more, Robert could wash his hands of a particular problem and feel as if he had done his duty. Just as he had done when he left Lucy with Annabelle, he wanted to drop Crystal off to become someone else's problem.

Instead of a kindly old aunt, he was dropping Crystal off with her not-nearly-as-kindly older sister.

That panic attack fluttered a little harder. "Dad—"

"I know it's a great deal to ask of you."

No kidding. Apparently she had managed to achieve some tiny measure of maturity over the years because she somehow managed to refrain, barely, from rolling her eyes.

"I will, of course, be happy to cover the cost of her food and lodging while she's staying with you," Robert went on.

"I haven't agreed to let her stay with me," she said, still somehow offended that Robert didn't think she had the wherewithal to cover her sister's care. Okay, she might have just been fired but for the past three years, her salary, including her stock options, had probably exceeded his.

"How could you possibly refuse?" he said. "This is really the best outcome for everyone involved."

She could see how it was certainly the ideal solution for her father—which was always his first and last priority.

As for Lucy, she did *not* need another complication in an already-tangled life. She was scraping bottom, at a personal low point. What could she possibly have to offer a troubled fifteen-year-old girl right now?

She gazed around the parlor with its ornate moldings and the Tiffany chandelier that had been imported from Paris, so familiar and beloved to her now—in contrast to the first few weeks after she had been sent here to live with Annabelle.

She had hated it here, had felt as if she were being exiled to the deepest, darkest wilderness.

Iris House had been a convenient dumping ground then, too. One of her mother's frequent halfhearted suicide attempts had actually worked a few months earlier—probably by accident, Lucy always suspected. She expected no one was more surprised than Betsy that that particular pill combination had worked so effectively. Robert was busy with Pam and their efforts to conceive and didn't have time or energy for her petty rebellions.

Annabelle had opened her home and her heart to Lucy. With astonishing patience and endless compassion, she had taken a wounded, angry teenager and turned her into a fairly tolerable young woman.

If not for her aunt, she didn't know where she would have ended up. Probably on the streets somewhere. She probably wouldn't have gone on to graduate with top marks from Hope's Crossing High School and summa cum laude from college.

Lucy knew her strengths. She wasn't Annabelle,

not by a long stretch. She had none of her aunt's patience or quiet faith.

In Lucy's favor, she *did* love her sister. If she could help Crystal straighten her path a little and perhaps avoid some of her own painful mistakes, didn't she owe it to the girl to try?

"Did you talk to her?" she asked, wavering. "Does she want to come to Hope's Crossing?"

"This isn't about what she wants anymore," Robert said in that same unbending voice she remembered loathing so much as a teenager. "For the last year she has made choice after choice that has led her to this point. Now she will have to understand this is her *last* choice. It's you or military school."

She sighed. She couldn't consign her sister to that, not if she had any chance of helping her. "Two weeks. She can stay for two weeks. At the end of that time, we can reassess the situation. Maybe a few weeks without the stress will be enough to give Pam the rest she needs to rediscover her coping skills."

"Excellent."

Robert didn't try to argue with her. Maybe a two-week reprieve had been his goal all along. "You won't be sorry."

She was *already* sorry. With each passing second, she wanted to tell her father she had changed her mind, but fickleness was another sign of weakness she wouldn't reveal to him.

"I can have her here tomorrow." He rose from the sofa. "I have meetings all day but I'll arrange for someone to bring her out—unless you're going into Denver for some reason and can save me the trouble."

He couldn't even be bothered to dump off his own

child? She supposed she should be grateful he made the effort to drive out to speak with her about it today, instead of asking this huge favor via his Bluetooth.

She rose, as well, not willing to let him own that position of power. "I'm sure you can clear your schedule for a few hours so you can bring her out yourself."

A muscle tightened in his jaw at her unstated rebuke. He looked as if he wanted to argue, and she made a little mental wager with herself at what excuse he would use. *I'm a busy man. My time is valuable. I'm doing the best I can.*

Instead, he managed to surprise her. "Perhaps I can rearrange some things."

"Good. I'm sure that would mean a great deal to Crystal."

"I doubt that. I'm not exactly on her list of favorite people right now."

He seemed completely baffled by the admission, as if he didn't understand how either of his daughters could be so difficult and contrary as to actually mind years of his distance and disapproval.

"It's a ninety-minute drive from Denver. Perhaps you can find a little common ground on the way," she said, though she doubted it. Robert would probably spend the whole time on his phone.

She walked him out and said goodbye with a dutiful kiss on the cheek.

"Don't waste too much time away from your career here," he warned when they reached his Mercedes. "You start to lose credibility if you spend too long out of the game."

"Thank you for the advice," she said.

"Oh, and put Crystal to work mowing the lawn. It needs a trim."

He waved and backed out of the driveway. She watched until his taillights disappeared around the corner, wondering what in the world she had just done.

CHAPTER SEVEN

STUPID, LOUSY LAWN MOWER.

With a vow to work out her triceps a little more diligently in the future, Lucy pulled the ignition cord on Annabelle's mower. The dumb thing chugged a couple of times, but that was it.

"Come on," she growled, trying again with the same results.

Next order of business, she was definitely going to hire a lawn service.

She had started out with such high expectations, too. That was the greatest frustration.

Forty minutes ago when she had pulled the mower out of the garage, it had started on the first try. She had been filled with a ridiculous sense of accomplishment—which had quickly faded when the mower coughed and sputtered and eventually died after only two passes along the front yard.

For the past half hour, she had been wrestling with the thing, trying to start it up again with no success.

She was apparently going to have to hire a lawn service sooner, rather than later. Worse, she would have to leave the lawn half-mowed and looking horrible when her father and sister arrived the next day.

It was her own fault for letting Robert's gibes pinch at her. Yes, the lawn needed a trim but it could have waited. Now, because of one offhand comment he made, she was stuck with this mess of her own creation.

And yes, thank you. She fully understood the symbolism in regards to the rest of her life.

One more time. She would try the stupid mower one last time before throwing in the towel and hunting through the phone book to find someone to take care of it for her, which was probably what she should have done in the first place.

The one pull turned into two then five then ten, all with the same results. The only things she got out of it were aching muscles and a new appreciation for lawn mowers that had push-button starters.

She slumped in the grass, disheartened and tired, trying to figure out what to do next. Maybe she could borrow a mower from the neighbors to mow the front yard or hire a small engine repair technician to make an evening house call.

She was mulling her options when an SUV pulled into the driveway.

Brendan.

As if her father's visit and unexpected request wasn't enough, her wonderful day just needed this, another interaction with the surly and difficult fire chief of Hope's Crossing.

"Having trouble?"

No. She and her lawn mower were simply sitting out on the grass together, enjoying the lovely evening.

"I can't get the stupid thing to start."

"Yeah, that's sort of what I figured when I saw you sitting here." He sauntered over with the typical male confidence that he could rev up anything with an engine. "You check the gas?"

She frowned. "Yes, I checked the gas. It might be a few years since I've mowed a lawn but I do know enough to check the gas level. It was low but I filled it out of a can clearly marked *lawn mower gas*. I figured that was a safe bet."

He nodded and crouched down beside the mower, fiddling with a couple of things she didn't even know *could* be fiddled with as one of the back doors of his SUV opened. A moment later, Faith slid out and skipped over to them.

"Hey, Aunt Lucy! Guess what? I finished *Anne of Green Gables* today. I loved it *so much*. I'm going to read *Anne of Avonlea* next."

"It's a good one."

"Thank you for bringing over all the books," she said. "I didn't even know my mom had all those books. Dad and Carter are starting one of the Hardy Boys books. Dad said he read that one when he was a kid! Didn't you?"

"I did," he answered, not looking up from monkeying with the lawn mower.

He got up with that inherent grace so surprising in a man of his size.

"Let's try it now," he said.

He grabbed the pull crank, gave it a good hard yank and the mower growled to life.

Seriously? She had just spent thirty minutes trying to start the dumb thing, and he had it purring to life inside of five?

She wanted to growl, too.

"How did you do that?"

"I know this mower well," he called over the engine. "I've been taking care of Annabelle's lawn for years. It's a little temperamental and sometimes needs a little persuading, especially in springtime at the start of a new mowing season. You should be good now."

"Thank you."

She wasn't sure how she felt to learn he had been helping Annabelle with her yard care all this time. If she had given it any thought at all, she would have just assumed her aunt would hire somebody to take care of it for her, but as a child of the Depression, Annabelle could be funny about some things.

She had artwork in the house worth tens of thousands of dollars at the same time she clipped every single coupon out of the newspaper and drove a twenty-five-year-old sedan.

It made sense that Brendan would have stepped up to take care of his wife's elderly aunt. Jessica and Annabelle had been very close, since Jessie and her mother had lived at Iris House for three years longer than Lucy had.

In Hope's Crossing, people reached out to help each other. Since she had been back, she was beginning to remember that about the town—and when it came to family, that help was only magnified.

She and Faith watched Brendan make one trip to the end of the grass, then turn around and head back in their direction. She waited for him to give her the mower, but he turned around again for another pass, looking as if he had absolutely nothing better to do but mow her lawn on a lovely spring evening.

After a moment, she walked across the new-cut grass and stood beside him, hands on hips.

"Okay," she yelled over the mower's noise. "You can stop now. I've got this."

"So do I."

"Caine. I mean it. Stop." In another minute, she was going to be stomping her foot like Carter in the middle of a tantrum.

"This will take me fifteen minutes, tops," he called.

She wanted to argue with him but (a) he was bigger than she was, and (b) she hadn't wanted to mow the lawn, anyway, and (c) it was a little tough to make a clear point in an argument over a growling lawn mower engine.

Not knowing what else to do, she finally threw her hands up—both literally and figuratively—and headed back to Faith.

"Are you late for something?"

She shook her head. "We were just going to grab some dinner at Grandpop's place. We can wait."

"I need to pull some weeds. Want to come talk to me while I do it?"

"Sure," she answered, looking thrilled. "What about Carter? He's still in the car."

"We'll take care of that." She headed to Brendan's SUV and opened the rear passenger door. If he could help himself to her lawn mower, she could help herself to his son.

"Hey, kid." She grinned at Carter in his booster seat.

"Let me out," he demanded.

She grinned as she unhooked the complicated straps. "Want to help me dig in the dirt?"

"Yeah!" he exclaimed.

They headed to the flower garden that circled the house and the porch.

"Since you're going to dinner later, you better not

get dirty or your dad will be mad at all of us. Just a second. Wait here."

She hurried into the house and found a couple of old work shirts of Annabelle's. In a drawer in the mudroom/washroom cabinet, she retrieved several pairs of gardening gloves she had seen there earlier.

When she returned to the children, Carter was bent with his nose almost to the sidewalk, watching a bug inch its way across the pavement.

"Look. It's a roly-poly," he said. "If you pick it up, it rolls into a ball. Watch."

He picked up the bug with a careful concentration she found adorable and laid it out in the palm of his other hand. The bug lived up to its billing and rolled up, tail to head.

"Isn't that cool?" he exclaimed.

"Very." She smiled as she helped him set the bug back in the grass then pulled his arms through the sleeves of Annabelle's denim work shirt and rolled up the cuffs. The shirt was cavernous on him but did a pretty good job of covering up his clothes from neck to knee.

"Now gloves," she said, and helped him get his fingers in the right spots.

When she finished helping Carter, she turned to do the same with Faith but found the independent miss had already covered her clothes with one of the work shirts and found some gloves on her own.

"Which are the flowers and which are the weeds?" Faith asked, studying the garden with a frown of concentration.

"That, my dear, is an excellent question." She pointed to a prevalent plant. "I know for sure that's a weed, at least when you find it in your flower garden. It's an elm seedling that sprouts from seeds that blow off the trees."

"You mean if we left the little thing alone, it would grow into a big tree like that one?" Faith asked.

"Eventually. Let's start with pulling all the elm seedlings you can see. It's kind of like a treasure hunt."

The children both jumped into the spirit of the thing and for the next fifteen minutes she and Faith worked together to the accompaniment of Carter yelling, "There's one! There's another one. Hey, I found another one!"

In between, they talked about Carter's kindergarten teacher—super pretty; about a problem Faith was having with a schoolmate—aka, mean girl in training; and about which park in town had the fastest slide, which Lucy vowed to test at the earliest opportunity.

This was exactly what she needed, she thought. Listening to the children chatter seemed to miraculously lift her worries about the next day and her sister's arrival. She felt far more centered than she would have from mowing the lawn.

They had made it around the front of the house when she heard the mower shut off. A few moments later— long enough, apparently, for Brendan to return it to the shed behind the garage—he walked around the side of the house, looking big and masculine in the early-evening light.

He caught sight of them kneeling in the dirt together and paused, an odd expression on his features that made her insides do a long, slow shiver.

After a moment, he moved closer, and she rose and pulled off her gardening gloves.

"Lawn's all done."

"You didn't need to do that," she said.

"It took me all of fifteen minutes. I told you it would. No big deal. It's not a very big lawn, in case you didn't notice."

She suddenly realized she must sound surly and unappreciative, not her intention. "Thank you. It's been a…rough day. This was an unexpected kindness."

"You're welcome. And I'm sorry about your rough day."

She shrugged. "They happen."

"Yeah. I've had a few of those myself." He didn't quite smile but it was a close thing. For a moment, she was overwhelmed by how gorgeous he looked there in the warm golden evening light and she couldn't help remembering the last time she had seen him, a few nights earlier when he had walked her home and they had talked in the rain-soaked moonlight.

"I'm starving," Carter said with grand dramatic fervor, as if he were going to expire any moment now from malnutrition.

"I know, I know," Brendan said, tousling his son's head. "But what are a few hunger pangs compared to helping our neighbor? Now we can enjoy our dinner even more knowing we've done something nice for someone else."

Maybe it was the general turmoil of the day or her emotions that were already on edge, but the sweetness of the life lesson between father and son there in Annabelle's spring-wild garden touched a deep chord inside her.

"Hey, Dad. Can Lucy come have dinner with us?" Faith asked suddenly.

"Oh. I don't..." Lucy started, but Carter cut her off.

"Yay! I want to sit by Lucy!" he exclaimed. "Grandpop is gonna make me my own pizza. I bet you can have one, too. He puts a smiley face on it with the pepperonis!"

She smiled, crazy about this boy who found joy in roly-poly bugs and pepperoni smiley faces.

"That sounds delish. Dinner would be great, but I'm pretty messy here."

"We can wait for you to wash up," Faith said eagerly. "Can't we, Dad?"

He gazed down at his daughter with a helpless sort of expression, the look of a man who didn't know how to undo a situation his children had just created.

The awkwardness of the situation might have made her laugh a little if his reluctance to spend any time with her didn't sting so badly.

The polite thing would be to make up some excuse to the children for why she couldn't eat with them. She was busy. She had an entire garden to weed. She was in the middle of a load of laundry.

She certainly didn't want to go where she was plainly not wanted.

At the same time, she didn't *want* to say those things. She loved being with Carter and Faith, and the idea of a solitary dinner was depressing, especially in light of her difficult afternoon.

"We'll be happy to wait," Brendan finally said. He even managed to make the lie sound believable to her. "Carter won't mind a few more minutes, will you, bud?"

Carter looked like he minded very much, but he finally shrugged. "I guess not."

All three of them looked at her with varying degrees of expectation. Again, she thought of all the excuses she could make. Brendan would prefer if she did, she knew, but she suddenly didn't want to give him that convenient way out.

She had gone along with the program when it came to her father and what he wanted from her. She wasn't at all in the mood to give Brendan his way on this, too.

"I can hurry," she said. "You won't starve in five minutes, will you?"

Carter did his best to put on a brave face. "I guess not. I hope Grandpop still has pepperonis when we get there."

"He will," Brendan assured his son.

"You're welcome to come in and wash up, as well," she said. "I did my best to keep them clean."

"We'll do that. Thanks," he answered, as Lucy flew up the stairs and rushed into the house.

A little defiance could be good for the soul sometimes, but she couldn't help wondering just what she had accomplished by pushing Brendan outside his comfort zone. He was like one of Carter's bugs. She had a feeling he was only going to curl in tighter to protect himself.

Dinner. With Lucy and all this uncomfortable subtext shimmering around them.

Once more, his life felt like a Hail Mary pass spiraling toward him way out of reach, completely beyond his ability to control.

How in the hell had that happened?

He had no idea how to tell Lucy he would rather she didn't come with them to dinner. He suspected she knew yet had agreed to come, anyway, for reasons that baffled him. As usual. Most of the things Lucy did baffled him.

It was too late now, so he would just have to make the best of the situation.

"Come on, kids. Let's wash up."

He shepherded the kids to the bathroom off the kitchen and supervised while they scrubbed fingers and the few smudges of dirt on their faces.

When they returned to the graceful living room—Annabelle always called it her parlor—Faith immediately opened her book while Carter headed for the bottom drawer of an old carved-leg chest where Annabelle always kept die-cast cars and trains and dolls for visiting children.

They were very good at entertaining themselves—one of the greatest blessings of parenting these particular two little creatures, he had always thought. Their preoccupation left him free to look around the room. He spotted a thick notebook and what looked like a stack of fabric samples and color palettes on the coffee table.

He picked up one of the books and was leafing through it when Lucy returned looking fresh-scrubbed and pretty. His gut twisted, but he told himself it was just hunger.

He and Carter both needed to be fed at regular intervals.

He held up the sample book. "You're serious about the bed and breakfast, then."

"Why does everyone keep asking me that?"

"I don't know. Maybe because I never thought you wanted any more ties to Hope's Crossing. You seemed in a big hurry to leave, back in the day, first to college and then Seattle."

"I was never running away from Hope's Crossing. Just running *to* something else. There's a big difference."

"And now you're back."

"For now," she said, and he told himself that little stomach twist *this time* was relief.

"We're all different people, aren't we?"

"For what it's worth, I'm definitely serious about the bed and breakfast. If all goes according to plan, I'm hoping to have guests here by the Fourth of July."

"I hope it works out for you," he answered.

"Are we ready *now?*" Carter asked, apparently at the end of his tether.

"I'm ready," Lucy said.

"Let's go, then."

The children chattered with Lucy all the way out to the car and after they took off. He didn't think Carter even stopped to take a breath in the ten minutes it took to drive downtown and find a parking space near the Center of Hope Café—while he just tried not to think about how strange it was to have someone sitting beside him in the passenger seat again.

The moment they walked together into his pop's restaurant, he knew he had made a huge mistake.

Dermot stood behind the counter speaking to a customer. When he spotted his son and grandchildren, his eyes lit up with the usual warm delight—and then he spotted Lucy walking with them and his expression shifted almost comically. Shock, delight and something that looked suspiciously like hope gleamed in Dermot's eyes.

Crap. The last thing he needed was for Pop to get the wrong idea about him and Lucy and start spinning any little matchmaker schemes. He was having a tough enough time reminding himself that he wasn't ready for this yet. He didn't need added pressure from his father.

"Hi, Grandpop!" Faith beamed at Dermot. "Can we sit in our usual spot?"

Dermot walked around the counter and knelt down to kiss his granddaughter on the cheek and solemnly shake hands with Carter, as he always did. "You certainly may, my darlin'. I've been saving that table just for you."

"Did you know we were coming?" Carter asked, eyes wide.

"Well, no, now that you mention it. Maybe I was hoping, though."

The children giggled at his Irish malarky, which he had in abundance.

"And Lucy, my dear. How lovely to see you again. How are you getting along in that big old house by yourself?"

"So far, so good," she answered, kissing him on the cheek and earning a delighted blush in return.

Brendan hadn't been joking when he told her half the women in town adored his father. The truly humbling thing about Dermot was that he didn't even have to try. He showed genuine interest and concern for everybody, and people responded instantly.

Dermot led them to their favorite spot, a booth in front of the window, where they could watch any excitement on Main Street while they waited for their food.

"Tonight's special is the macaroni and cheese. A

particularly good batch, if I do say so myself. I experimented with a little Gruyère cheese tonight, on Alex McKnight's recommendation."

"Oh, that sounds delicious. I think I'll have that," Faith exclaimed, as if she even knew what Gruyère cheese was. Hell, Brendan barely knew what it was.

"Not me!" Carter sang out. "You know what I want, Grandpop."

"Hmmm. Liver and onions again? Or my special fried worm stew?"

"Ewwww. No! Pizza. Pizza. Pizza. With pepperonis and a smiley face."

"I think I can manage that. Son. You?"

"I'm in the mood for a Reuben tonight, in a fog."

Dermot beamed, as he always did when his children—or other customers—used diner slang.

"In a fog?" Lucy asked with a baffled look.

"It means with a side of mashed potatoes," Brendan explained.

"Ah. Well, is there a way to say I'll have a grilled chicken wrap with a side salad?"

"You just did, my dear." Dermot grinned. "Coming right up. And to drink?"

Brendan was tempted to ask for a good, stiff whiskey, but Dermot didn't carry a liquor license at the café. The kids had chocolate milk and he and Lucy both requested water with lemon.

"Excellent," Dermot said. "Now, which of my darling grandchildren would like to come in the back with me and help me put the pepperonis on a certain pizza?"

"Me!" Carter exclaimed, jumping up.

"Oh, may I come, too, Grandpop?" Faith asked.

"Of course! The more the merrier! Come along, then."

The children slid out again, and Brendan was tempted to go along with them as soon as he realized their absence left him alone with Lucy. They were seated on opposite sides of the booth, and without the children's buffering presence, it felt entirely too much like a date.

As soon as the laughing trio headed for the kitchen, an awkward silence descended. Brendan blurted out the first thing that came to his head. "I thought I saw your father today, driving down our street."

He knew at once by the way her mouth tightened and her hands clasped in front of her that the subject wasn't a comfortable one.

"That's certainly possible," she answered, avoiding his gaze. "He stopped in this afternoon for an unexpected visit."

"You don't sound pleased."

She appeared fascinated by the weave of her place mat. "Not particularly."

He should change the subject, but he couldn't come up with an alternative on the fly. Give him a break, he hadn't been on a date in about a decade. Not that this was a date or anything.

She had thanked him earlier for mowing the lawn and said she had a rough day and needed a little kindness. Did that have to do with her father?

"He must be happy you're back in Colorado."

"Why would you think that?" she asked, her tone stiff.

"Well, he drove all the way from Denver to say hello, didn't he?"

She made a noise that wasn't quite a snort. "Something like that," she answered.

She was quiet for a long time, and he started racking his brain to come up with another topic of conversation, until she finally spoke. "He came to ask me to let my half sister stay with me. She's fifteen years old and...troubled."

"And he wants you to take her?"

"My father is very good at finding someone else to deal with the messes in his life. Annabelle took me, didn't she?"

"You consider yourself one of the messes in your father's life?"

"He certainly did. I hit those rebellious teen years just as he was marrying for the second time and settling down. I was what you might call a difficult child, especially after my mom's death."

Her mother had committed suicide. He knew that from Jess and felt an unexpected wave of sympathy for the confused and grieving teenage girl she must have been.

"I was moody and angry all the time, had a pathologically difficult time following rules and didn't get along at all with my father's second wife."

"Understandable, after everything you went through."

"Not according to the great Robert Drake. So he somehow talked Annabelle into taking me in."

He could imagine that had felt very much like another abandonment to her. First her mother escaped her obligations and left behind a world of pain by taking her own life, then her father chose his new wife over his own daughter.

He couldn't even imagine it. His children were his life.

"It worked out okay for me, I guess," she said. "Once I was away from that environment, I did better and remembered I actually liked school, when I wasn't trying to hand my dad a screw-you along with every report card. I made it through high school and went on to college."

"You worked hard and were successful because of it."

She looked surprised at his words. "I guess he's hoping maybe history will repeat itself with Crystal."

"Did you agree to take her?"

She fiddled with her silverware. "Conditionally. I'm giving her two weeks to see how she likes Hope's Crossing and living with me."

"And then what?"

"We'll have to see how things go." She was quiet for a minute. "It's going to be a disaster, isn't it?"

After more than a decade as a firefighter and emergency medical technician, he had dealt with enough accident victims to recognize the thready note of panic in her voice.

"Don't worry. You're going to be great," he answered, in the slow, measured, calm tone that usually helped in these situations.

"How do you know?" she demanded. "What do I know about being responsible for a teenage girl? I've never even had a pet!"

"I know, because I've seen you with my kids," he answered. "You love them and they adore you. I've let you stay with them and I would completely trust you to do it again. That's about as ringing an endorsement as a guy like me can make. Relax. You're going to be great with your sister, Lucy. You obviously care about her or you wouldn't have agreed to do what your father asked. As far as I'm concerned, that's half the battle when it comes to kids."

She drew in a breath and he could see some of the panic begin to fade. "Thanks. I appreciate you talking me down. I might need another pep talk before these two weeks are up."

"Anytime," he murmured as the kids returned with Dermot—and he was shocked as hell to realize he meant the words.

CHAPTER EIGHT

As THEY WAITED for their food, Lucy talked and laughed with the children and tried to do her best to figure out why she felt as if in those brief moments of conversation, something significant had shifted between them.

His words seemed to settle inside her, warming and calming her.

I've seen you with my kids. You love them and they adore you. I've let you stay with them and I would completely trust you to do it again. That's about as ringing an endorsement as a guy like me can make. Relax. You're going to be great with your sister.

Since he'd started dating Jessie so long ago, Brendan and Lucy's relationship had been adversarial. She had been hurt and rejected that he had picked Jess over her, and those dark feelings had brewed inside her like a lurking infection, just waiting for a moment of weakness to growl to life.

She hadn't treated him well.

She burned to think of some of the sly comments she had made to Jess about him when they were dating. It had been petty and small of her. At the time she'd justified it to herself—really, how could he possibly be any kind of decent guy if he would lock lips with Lucy one minute and start dating Jess seriously just a couple weeks later?

She had figured he was a dog, just another athlete who liked to play around on and off the field, and at first she had been honestly concerned he would break Jess's sweet, fragile heart.

Even after Brendan and Jess had been dating for a year and he proposed, Lucy had continued her subtle campaign to undermine the relationship.

After the wedding, she had forced herself to stop, realizing Jess had made her decision. They appeared to love each other, and Lucy knew she was hurting her cousin by so actively disliking her choice in a man.

That didn't stop her from being cool to Brendan on the phone or on her rare visits to Hope's Crossing.

Now, looking back, she was ashamed of herself. Okay, she had some hefty baggage that made it particularly difficult for her to cope with rejection. That was no excuse for letting her hurt get in the way of being a good friend to Jess and maybe becoming a friend to him, too.

The more time she spent with him, the more she was coming to see beyond her old resentments.

By all indications, he had been a good husband, a loving son, a devoted father. Just now, he and the children were playing I Spy, a game they had probably played a hundred times before at the café.

She would like to be friends with him. Was that even possible, given their history?

"I spy, with my little eye, something green. No wait. It's yellow. No wait. Now it's red," Carter said.

"It's the stoplight, isn't it?" Brendan guessed.

Carter giggled. "Yes. How did you know?"

"No fair!" Faith protested. "You can't do things outside. We've told you that like a hundred times!"

"Sorry. I keep forgetting."

The door to the café opened, and a family—handsome father, well-dressed mother and two teenagers—walked in.

Her dinner companions had very different reactions to the new customers. She was almost certain she heard Brendan swear under his breath, but Carter gave a shout and Faith laughed softly.

"I spy, with my little eye. Uncle Andrew and Aunt Erin and Ava and Josh."

His just-older brother, she realized.

While she could see similarities between the two men, Andrew was much leaner than Brendan, with the slightly pale look of someone who spent most of his time behind a desk.

The other Caines looked pleased to see Brendan and his children. Andrew's wife—Erin, the children had called her—gave Lucy a surprised look before she quickly concealed it.

She wanted to tell the woman they *weren't* on a date, that this was a dinner invitation extended only out of polite expedience, but that would have been far too awkward. Better to keep her mouth shut and let his family members draw their own conclusions.

"If I'd known you were coming to Pop's tonight," Andrew said, "I would have called you. We could have hogged one of the big tables in the back and eaten together. Better yet, we could have called Charlotte and Dylan and made a party of it."

"Like we don't see enough of each other as it is," Brendan muttered. "I can't spray a fire hose in this town without hitting a blasted Caine."

"We're everywhere, aren't we?" Andrew said with a grin.

He smiled expectantly at Lucy, and after a slight uncomfortable pause, Brendan nodded to her. "You remember Lucy Drake, Jessie's cousin?"

"Oh, yes! Sure. Good to see you again."

"Lucy, my brother Andrew, his lovely wife, Erin, and their kids, Ava and Josh."

"Hello.

"How nice that you still stay in touch with Brendan and the children." Erin gave her a warm, friendly smile, and she couldn't help smiling back.

"He doesn't make it very easy, but I try."

Dermot came out of the kitchen and beamed with delight at more of his progeny. "What a happy day this is for me! More of my favorite people in one place."

They all hugged and kissed as if it were Thanksgiving dinner and they hadn't seen each other since last year. She knew that wasn't the case. The children had told her they gathered with the Caines every Sunday for dinner at Dermot's house.

What would it be like to be part of such a warm, boisterous family? Probably wonderful for the long-term but right now she was left feeling a little overwhelmed, not sure exactly how she fit in.

She ended up retreating into herself a little, becoming an observer rather than a participant as she listened to their conversation about the teenage son's baseball season prospects.

"Get the Caines talking sports and we'll never be able to eat," Erin said after a moment. "Come on, guys. I'm sorry for the interruption."

"No problem," Brendan said. "See you all later."

Dermot walked away with them, and the absence left a silence behind that was filled by a couple a few tables away, speaking louder than normal.

"I'm fine, Judy," the man said, which was an odd conversational gambit, she thought. "Stop fretting over me."

"You're not fine," Judy snapped back. "Why do you have to be so stubborn? I can tell you don't feel well."

Lucy shifted her attention and saw the man *didn't* look well. He appeared to be in his late fifties, balding, with an odd gray cast to his features. He was sweating, great droplets gathering on his forehead, despite the comfortable temperature in the café.

"That was fun, seeing Aunt Erin and Uncle Andrew," Faith said. "Don't you think so, Dad?"

"Sure. Great fun," Brendan replied.

"Hey, we should take a bike ride to their house sometime. It's not very far, is it? Maybe only two miles."

"Less than that. Only about a mile. That would be great," Brendan replied, just as the woman across the way grabbed her companion's arm.

"Come on, Martin. You're scaring me. Let's go back to the hotel where you can lie down."

"Stop nagging," he repeated, so loudly this time it drew even Brendan's attention. The man stood up, staggered a little and fell over with a kind of gurgle, knocking his silverware to the floor with a loud clatter.

"Martin!" the woman shrieked. Before she could even slide her chair out, Brendan was out of their booth and on the ground with the man.

"What's happening?" Carter asked.

"I'm not sure, honey," Lucy said as Brendan began trying to rouse the man.

"Is that man dead?" he asked.

"Be quiet, Car," Faith said, looking stricken.

"Come on, kids. Let's go find your aunt and uncle."

She grabbed their hands and ushered them away from the dramatic scene, where Brendan was now undoing the man's shirt and feeling for a pulse.

They headed into the other part of the dining room, out of view of the action.

"What's going on?" Erin asked when she saw Lucy and the children.

"I'm not sure. A man is having some kind of health issue. Brendan is helping him. Can Faith and Carter stay with you for a minute while I see if he needs help?"

"Of course. Kids, slide over and make room."

Andrew rose and headed to the other area of the café, presumably to help, as well, while their teenagers did as their mother asked.

"We were just about to play twenty questions!" Erin said. "Who wants to go first?"

Lucy waited until she was sure they were settled then rushed back to Brendan's side. She had been away for no more than sixty seconds but Brendan had started chest compressions, with competent, practiced motions.

"I don't know what happened," the woman said. "He was just talking to me and then he fell over. What's wrong with him?"

"Does your husband have any history of heart disease?" Brendan asked between compressions.

"His cholesterol is high and his blood pressure is a little bad. He's been working on it. That's all."

"What can I do?" Lucy asked.

"Call 9-1-1," he said without breaking rhythm.

"On it," Andrew said from nearby with his mobile to his ear.

"Pop, you've still got that portable defibrillator, right? Where is it?"

"Oh, my goodness. You're right! I've had it ever since—well, for the last two years. I should have thought. It's in the office. I'll get it right away."

He raced from the room much faster than a man in his sixties should move and returned a moment later with what looked like a suitcase.

Brendan turned to Lucy. "Any chance you know CPR?" he asked her.

"Yes," she answered. "I recertify every year."

She didn't have to tell him why. Probably the same reason Dermot kept an AED—automated external defibrillator—in his restaurant. Because someone they all loved had died of a cardiac arrest.

"I need you to handle the compressions while I set up the AED. Can you do that?"

"I think so."

"Keep that beat, just like I'm doing. You know the drill, right? Think of the Bee Gees, 'Stayin' Alive.'"

She had never done this on anything but a dummy, but she moved into position and took over from him, aware of the adrenaline pulsing through her. It was far different on a human, and she suddenly was reluctant to push hard enough to compress his rib cage. A man's life was at stake, however, so she forced herself to get over her squeamishness.

He stood watching for a second to make sure she had the correct rhythm then he opened the suitcase and turned on the machine.

"Ma'am, does your husband have any implanted medical devices?" Brendan asked.

"No. No, of course not."

"We need to get that necklace off him. Anything metal will conduct electricity."

He pulled off the small gold chain with the St. Christopher's medal the man had been wearing.

"Now, Lucy, I'm going to attach these paddles here, but I don't want you to stop what you're doing. You're doing great. I'll just work around your hands."

He spoke with such calm in the midst of the chaos that she took a deep breath and felt even more tension leave her shoulders.

He grabbed a couple napkins and wiped at the man's chest then attached two adhesive pads. The whole process took maybe thirty seconds in all.

"Okay, now, on my signal, I want you to step away while the machine checks his heart rhythm."

She complied, hands in the air. He pushed a button on the AED and the machine gave a computerized voice prompt. *Analyzing heart rhythm. Do not touch the patient. Analyzing. Stand clear.*

What felt like an eternity later but was probably only a few seconds, the machine said, *Shock advised. Charging. Stay clear of patient.*

"Everybody, back up," Brendan said.

The machine gave a voice prompt again. *Deliver shock now. Press the orange button now.*

Brendan complied and the machine again spoke. *Shocking! Stand Clear!*

The man convulsed but then went still again.

"Come on, Martin. Come on," Brendan urged.

Shock delivered. It is safe to touch the patient. Begin CPR.

"Do I start compressions again?" Lucy asked.

"Yes, for two minutes then we'll try to shock him again."

She started up again and after about six or seven compressions, Martin gasped, just like in the movies.

"Brendan."

"Stop for a second." He checked the man's airway, but Lucy knew the defibrillator had done its job. The man's color had greatly improved, and she felt his chest rise and fall.

"He's breathing!" she exclaimed. The man's wife cried out just as the door to the café burst open and two paramedics rushed in.

"What do you got, Chief?" the older one asked.

"Male Caucasian, approximately sixty-five years old, nonresponsive, not breathing. We just shocked him with the AED and restarted cardiac activity."

"Nice work. You've always had a way with a defibrillator."

"What can I say? It's a gift."

Brendan stood up. On the surface, he looked as calm as ever, but she could sense the tension seething through him.

"Judy?" Martin said, his voice raspy and weak.

"I'm here, darling!" Judy knelt on the floor of the diner and looked up at both of them with a look of deep gratitude. "You saved his life! That was amazing!"

"He's not out of the woods yet," Brendan said gruffly as the paramedics swarmed the scene, lifting the man onto a gurney and attaching him to oxygen and all kinds of sensors. "My guys here are going to transport him to the Hope's Crossing hospital, where we're lucky enough to have an excellent cardiac team. They may end up sending him to a larger hospital in Denver for treatment, depending on what caused the event."

"I don't care. He's alive."

The woman reached out and hugged Lucy. "Thank you. Thank you so much. He's everything to me."

"I didn't do much, only followed orders. It was Chief Caine here who did all the heavy lifting. He's the expert."

"Chief Caine? Are you the fire chief?"

"Yes, ma'am," he answered.

She gave a ragged-sounding laugh. "Can you believe that, Martin? You're the only one I know lucky enough to have a heart attack at the same time the Hope's Crossing fire chief and his wife are having dinner across the aisle."

Lucy wanted to correct the woman, but it didn't seem worth the trouble, not under the circumstances.

"Thank you again," the woman said. "I don't even want to imagine what might have happened if you hadn't been here."

"I like this outcome much better than the alternative," Brendan said with a forced smile.

Lucy again sensed his tension. How did he do it? Go out on cardiac emergencies when his own otherwise young and healthy wife had died of a heart attack? It must eat him alive, wondering why he could save men like Martin yet hadn't been able to save Jessie or their baby.

No one could have saved them. She wanted to tell him that. She had done a great deal of research on the rare condition that had killed Jessie. Lucy knew the mortality rate was high and even if he had been right next to Jessie with an AED, she still likely wouldn't have survived.

"Well," she finally said. "That was a little more excitement than I expected in Hope's Crossing."

He let out a long breath. "Don't make the mistake of thinking because a place is small, nothing of significance happens there. The smallest moments in a person's life can be life-changing."

The other paramedics loaded the other man up on the stretcher and started to roll him out to the waiting ambulance when one of their radios crackled with static.

"Auto-pedestrian accident, Main Street and Silver Sage Road."

"That's just a block from here," Brendan said. "Who's the other team on duty?"

"Chen and Myers," one of the EMTs answered. "They got called a half hour ago to a fall at the senior center. They might be done by now."

"But probably not."

"Yeah. Probably not."

"Do you need to go help?" Lucy asked. "I can take care of Faith and Carter. I'll get them tucked in just like last time."

He looked torn. "Are you sure?"

"Yes. No problem. I'm happy to do it. You told me you trust me, remember?"

"You certainly proved yourself tonight."

She knew she shouldn't find such a glow of satisfaction from his words but she couldn't seem to help it. Yes, she had been the marketing director for a Forbes 500 company and had moved up the ranks extraordinarily quickly, overseeing an international staff of five hundred people. She had traveled around the country on the corporate jet, had spoken in front of many industry leaders, all the tech movers and shakers.

But she had never helped saved a man's life before tonight. All her other accomplishments in life seemed ridiculously paltry in comparison to this one thing.

"Thanks, Lucy. I owe you, again."

She shook her head. "You don't. I'm happy to help. It's what friends do for each other, right?"

He studied for a long moment, as if struck by her words then smiled that slow, rare smile of his.

"I guess they do," he answered. He hurried to the other side of the restaurant to hug his children and explain the situation to them, then tossed her the keys to his SUV on his way out the door.

CHAPTER NINE

"I wish you could stay in Hope's Crossing forever and ever."

Carter gave her a sleepy smile, and Lucy's heart turned over in her chest as warmth soaked through her.

"Oh, darling. What a nice thing to say."

"It's true," he insisted. "We could ride our bikes together in the summer and go skiing in the winter, and you could come to my birthday party. It's in three weeks."

"I think you've mentioned it a time or two," she said with a smile as she tucked in his blanket.

"Because it's going to be *so fun*."

"I'm sure it will. I'll be here for that, I promise."

As for the rest—the forever and ever part—she didn't know how to answer him. Stay in Hope's Crossing? It was impossible, wasn't it?

She loved the restaurants, the art scene, the excitement of city life. And she *had* loved her career: the creative challenges, the problem-solving, the heady rush of success. She wasn't at all ready to give that up.

She knew the chances of being able to stay in Seattle were probably not the greatest, when she was ready to start putting out feelers. She certainly wasn't going to find another comparable job in Hope's Crossing.

"I can't wait to do those things with you while I'm

here," she said. "But not tonight. It's late and you've had a big day, mister. Time for you to get some sleep."

"Okay," he answered, already half-there.

She kissed his cheek, smelling soap and laundry detergent and a few lingering scent molecules of little-boy sweat.

"Good night, sweetheart."

"Night, Aunt Lucy. I love you."

With a lump in her throat, she turned off his light and closed the door then crossed the hall to Faith's room, where the girl was sitting up in bed with *Anne of Avonlea* open across her lap.

She didn't seem to be reading, though, mostly gazing into space. When she sensed Lucy's presence, she looked up.

"Oh. Hi. Are you done with Carter?"

"Yeah. He was pretty pooped, I think." She walked into the room. "How are you doing?"

Faith shrugged. "Okay, I guess."

This serious little girl needed more wacky fun in her life. A good water-balloon fight or a dance-a-thon or a pie-eating contest.

She perched on the edge of the bed. "What's up? You seem upset."

Faith sighed. "I'm okay. Just thinking about that man at the café tonight. He almost died, didn't he? Of a heart attack."

Like her mother. Poor little lamb. "But he didn't. Your dad saved his life. Wasn't that amazing?"

"I guess." Faith looked down at the stitching of her quilt.

"You don't think so?"

"He's always doing that. Pulling people out of

wrecked cars and going into burning buildings and climbing up big mountains to get hikers who fell and stuff."

Lucy thought that was just about the *definition* of amazing. "How many kids do you know who can say their dad spends his days helping people?"

Faith fidgeted with her blanket. When she met Lucy's gaze, her eyes were troubled. "Sometimes I just wish he had a regular job, you know? Something where he couldn't get hurt. If he dies, too, me and Carter won't have a mom *or* a dad."

The simple observation rocketed straight to her heart. This was obviously not the first time Faith had fretted about such a possibility. As a frequent worrier herself, Lucy could completely relate to the way those dark thoughts could creep over any brightness and hope.

She felt completely out of her depth having this conversation and prayed for the wisdom to say the right thing.

"What you say is true. But I know your dad, and I know he's a careful guy. Every single moment he's working, I'm sure he's thinking about you and Carter and doing whatever is necessary to stay safe. The day I had the fire at Iris House, he was very concerned with safety, for me and his other firefighters and for himself."

"He could still be hurt, no matter how careful. I heard Aunt Charlotte say that to him one time when she didn't think I was listening."

Lucy ran a hand over Faith's hair. "Your dad loves you more than anything. You know that, right?"

Faith nodded.

"It would be really horrible if something happened to your dad, but that's not going to happen."

"Can you promise?"

She sighed. She wanted to, more than anything, but she also refused to lie to the girl. Faith was too smart to believe in hollow words, anyway.

"No. I'm sorry, I can't. But no matter what, you would still have your grandpop, your aunt Charlotte, everyone else who cares about you. And me. Especially me."

She wasn't sure whether her words helped the situation at all, but Faith seemed to relax a little.

"It was pretty cool that my dad saved that guy."

"Darn right," she answered. "Now shall we read about Anne a little more?"

Faith held out the book for her. Lucy read until she saw the girl's eyelids droop and even close a time or two.

"I'd say that's enough for now." She pitched her voice low.

"I'm not sleepy," Faith mumbled.

Lucy smiled. "Of course you're not. You can read a little more if you want."

By that point, Faith's eyes were completely closed. Lucy kissed her cheek, adjusted her quilt and turned off the bedside lamp before walking from the room and closing the door.

She stood in the hallway between the bedrooms, second-guessing everything she had said to Faith before they had finally started reading.

The whole conversation about Brendan's risk potential was a minefield. She had navigated it as best she could, but now she wasn't confident she had said or done the right things.

Should she have assured Faith that Brendan wasn't going anywhere so she could clear that worry off her mental plate? Or was it better not to give the girl platitudes but to be frank and honest in hopes of better preparing her for every eventuality?

She had no idea.

She did remember that same sort of worry tormenting her when she was young and her parents were fighting again—that something would happen to one or the other and she would find herself all alone in the world.

Unlike Faith, she hadn't been able to claim a large, loving extended family. Only Annabelle and Jess—an elderly aunt and a distant cousin. Now they were both gone, leaving her only with her father, a stepmother she wanted to think had become a polite friend of sorts over the years and the half sister who needed her.

Oh, Lord. Her sister was coming in less than twelve hours.

She wasn't at all ready.

Instead of going out to dinner with Brendan and his children and then offering to babysit while he went off saving the good people of Hope's Crossing from themselves, she should have been back at Iris House, taking care of the thousands of things she needed to do before undertaking the challenge of a difficult teenager.

She could at least make a list. Organization was one of her biggest strengths. She hurried into the kitchen and grabbed a magnetic notepad off the refrigerator and a pen from the little nearby painted tin can pencil holder that one of the children had probably made in art class.

She sat down at the table and started writing down thoughts as they came to her. The easy ones: change the bedding in the room she thought would work best for Crystal. Find out what she liked to eat. Stock the refrigerator with teen-friendly foods. Get a lock for Annabelle's small wine collection.

Each thought spurred about a dozen others and the more she wrote, the more thin tendrils of panic began to tangle and snarl around her.

She didn't know a damn thing about teenage girls. She was going to screw everything up, and Crystal would end up hating her, hating Robert, hating Hope's Crossing.

She would probably run away and end up on the streets somewhere, a teenage junkie forced to sleep on steam vents in some rat-infested alley, with all her belongings in a backpack she stashed under a Dumpster.

The panic attack she had been fighting since the moment she opened the door of Iris House to find her father standing on the porch reached out and grabbed her by the throat.

No. Not now. She drew in a sharp breath then another. Why was the air suddenly so thin in here? She inhaled again, feeling light-headed with fear and the sick realization that she wasn't going to be able to fight off this one.

Some tiny, functioning corner of her brain knew it was a reaction to seeing that man literally die in front of her and then be brought back to life, an aftershock to the whole mixed-up emotional morass of Jessie's death under similar conditions and missing her so much and spending so much time with the children she had left behind.

Add to that her angst about the impending stress of having Crystal at Iris House, and this panic attack was a greasy black inevitability.

The rest of her didn't give a damn for the reasons; she only wanted it to stop.

She couldn't breathe, and the room seemed to spin and spin and spin.

She was hot, sweating, dying.

Her stomach churned, and she was certain she was going to throw up, right there in Brendan's kitchen. She gripped her chest with one hand and the edge of the table with the other, trying to breathe, to will down the trembling and her rapid-fire heartbeat.

She wasn't going to die. She wasn't going to die. This was only in her mind.

The mantra wasn't working this time, no matter how loudly she tried to scream it inside her head.

She was so turned inward with the battle, she only vaguely heard a door open somewhere in the house.

She heard Brendan's voice as if he spoke from the wrong end of a telephone handset. "Sorry I'm late. That took a little longer than I'd planned, which is kind of the story of my life. I ought to get that phrase printed out on a three-by-five so I can just hand it out to all the people I leave waiting for me."

She couldn't have responded for anything, though the graying of her vision was starting to recede with each word he spoke. Brendan was here. He was washing his hands at the sink, his back to her. She forced herself to focus on his solid strength, to pause, to think, to breathe.

"I swung by the hospital," he said. "You'll be happy to know, our friend was doing great by the time I left.

Laughing and joking with the nurses on the cardiac floor and already driving his wife crazy."

Oh, dear heavens. She couldn't let him see her like this. She drew in a sharp breath and then another. "That's...good."

Too late. He turned from the sink, his gaze intent at her thready tone.

"Are you okay? You don't look well."

"I'm f-fine. I need to go. I'll...see you later."

She lurched for the door, grabbing it with hands that still trembled like she had just been tossed headfirst into a frigid reservoir.

"Wait. Stop. Sit down," he ordered. "You're clammy and have no color whatsoever. What is it? What's wrong?"

"I'm fine," she repeated. *Please. Just let me go.*

He moved to block her path with surprising speed for such a large man. Apparently, he hadn't been an NFL running back only because he filled out a jersey so well.

"You're nowhere near fine, Lucy. Come on. Sit down and I'll get you a drink of water."

"I don't need your help."

She wanted to snap and snarl the words, but they came out more like a pitiful whimper.

Though the panic attack was already fading and her heartbeat had begun to slow, she was weak, battered, wrung out—as if she had just floated serious rapids without a life raft.

"Sit down, damn it, before you fall over." He shifted quickly into paramedic mode. "Your breathing is shallow and coarse and your skin is pale. Do you have asthma? Are you having any chest pain? When was the last time you had a physical?"

He asked the questions with careful calm, but she could hear the grave concern twisting through his voice. She knew exactly what he must be thinking.

It's not a heart attack, she wanted to say, but the words wouldn't come.

"Have you had an episode like this before?"

More of the black fear faded. She swallowed hard and felt tears burn in her throat. She always burst into tears after the bad ones.

She had to tell him. He would only push her and push her until she did. She was going to have to tell him, even though the humiliation was far worse than anything else.

"Panic attack," she managed. "It's already starting to fade. See? My hands aren't shaking as much. In about…five minutes, I'll be perfectly f-fine."

She waited for his expression to change to one of disgust or unease. Instead, he simply gave her a startled look and then went to the sink to pour her a glass of water.

"Here. This might help."

She grabbed the glass from him and swallowed, as parched suddenly as if she'd been racing to Wild Iris Ridge in a windstorm.

Simply swallowing—some physical, tangible action—seemed to help calm her. She sipped again; at the same time she also focused on modulating her breathing.

"Better?" he asked after a moment.

She wanted to hide her face in her arms and pretend he wasn't there watching her out of those concerned blue eyes. Instead, she forced herself to face him as those snaking tendrils of fear continued to recede.

"Yes," she answered when she was moderately certain she could speak without her voice trembling. "I'm…sorry you had to see me fall apart. Bad timing on your part. If you had come home just a few minutes later, you would have completely missed out on all the fun."

He sat down in the chair next to her at the table, his expression still tight with concern.

"How long have you been having panic attacks?"

She sighed, seeing no point in obfuscation or denial. He had just seen her greatest weakness. He couldn't think any worse of her.

"I had the first one the week of Annabelle's funeral. It scared me to death. I thought I was having a…" Her voice trailed off and she couldn't bring herself to say the word.

"Heart attack," he answered, his voice heavy as he sat there in the kitchen chair his late wife had probably picked out.

"Yes," she answered, feeling small and stupid. "It went away after only a few minutes and I thought it must have been stress or…or grief or something like that. After the second one, I went in for a battery of tests. I knew when they called for a psych consult, I was in trouble."

Again, she waited for him to look at her with disgust, but he seemed amazingly calm about the whole thing, now that she was no longer completely freaking out in the middle of his kitchen.

"I understand there are several available medications for panic attacks. Have you tried anything?"

"A few. I just started a new one. It helps but isn't a hundred percent effective." She curled her hands together in her lap. "I'm sorry you had to find out."

He made a dismissive sort of gesture. "You have a medical condition. I can see no reason to be embarrassed about it, any more than you should be about diabetes or high blood pressure."

She didn't want him to be decent about this. It only made her feel more guilty about the way she had treated him over the years.

"It's not quite the same, but I appreciate your efforts to make me feel better," she said.

"I don't see a difference. Panic attacks are the result of a biochemical reaction in your brain. You're not crazy and it's not some kind of weakness on your part. Is that what you've been thinking?"

"I tell myself that, but it doesn't make me feel any better—not when I feel like there's this evil little demon walking around with me every moment for the last four months, just waiting under the surface to burst out and say hello and completely take over my psyche."

"Did the panic attacks have an effect on your job?"

"You mean, was I fired because I freaked out in the middle of a staff meeting? Not directly, but I missed a couple of meetings for doctors' appointments and then had to play catch-up. You played football. You know how disastrous it can be on a team when one player's head isn't in the game. Eventually, the team has to cut the guy who's keeping them from the championship."

"Did you bother explaining to anybody what was going on? Or did you just try to soldier on by yourself?"

He probably knew her well enough to guess the answer to that.

"It doesn't matter. It's done. They fired me, with complete justification."

"The panic attacks are the real reason you're back in Hope's Crossing right now instead of out there trying to find a new position, aren't they? You've come home to the one place in your world where you felt safe."

She wanted to cry all over again. How was it possible that Brendan Caine, of all people, had figured that out before she did?

He was absolutely right.

The two years she'd lived with Annabelle had been the most calm, stable, comfortable time in a childhood ruled by chaos and insecurity, first through the constant arguments of her parents and then by her father's negligence and her mother's drinking and instability.

"Now you dispense mental health counseling, too?"

"Whatever it takes," he answered with a slow smile.

"You're very good at it," she admitted. "I suppose you're right. Annabelle and Iris House have always been an island of calm for me, a place where I knew I was loved, no matter what."

To her further humiliation, he picked up the list she had been composing before the panic attack hit. "This is what set you off, isn't it? Your sister coming tomorrow."

"What if I fail? What if I can't help her, can't provide that quiet calm that Annabelle gave to me?"

"You said it yourself. Annabelle provided a place where you always felt loved. Forget your lists. Just give your sister that."

She drew in a shaky breath, far more calmed by his

words than she knew she should be. "Thank you. I appreciate the comfort and the insight."

"Anytime."

"And now that you have seen far deeper into my brain than I feel completely comfortable with, I'm going to go home so we can both get some sleep."

"Are you sure you're okay?"

"Yes. I'm usually a little shaky for a while after a bad one, but I should be fine."

She stood up and headed for the door. He was there to open it before she could reach it, surprising her again with his speed.

"Let me grab the monitor and I'll walk you up to your place."

She wanted to argue with him, but the truth was, right now she needed to borrow a little more of his strength and that calm center of his that drew her like a warm fire in the middle of a howling blizzard.

WHO EVER WOULD have believed brash, confident Lucy Drake suffered from panic attacks?

As they walked up to Iris House, Brendan mulled the fascinating dichotomy of her. Everything he knew about her would have given him the impression she charged through the world, conquering challenges right and left.

Finding out she struggled in this way lent a vulnerability to her that was as startling as it was…appealing.

He was actually glad she wasn't perfect. It made her far more down-to-earth and approachable, though he didn't think she would appreciate the perspective.

He was intensely aware of her walking beside him, soft and warm in the moonlight. Her head only reached the top of his shoulder, and he could smell her shampoo—or whatever kind of goopy girl hair product she might use. She always smelled like strawberries. Ripe, juicy, summer-night perfection.

"Thank you again for helping me with Faith and Carter," he said as they approached the house. "Did everything go okay with them?"

"You mean, before I had the meltdown?"

He nudged her a little with his elbow. "You said that. I didn't."

"If I didn't say it before," she said after a moment, "thanks for being understanding about everything."

"There was nothing to be understanding about. But you're welcome."

"To answer your question about the children, everything went fine. You have to be the luckiest dad in the world. They're lovely, both of them."

He smiled, deeply grateful for his children. "We might have a different story to tell when they start hitting their teenage years, but for now, yeah. They're pretty awesome."

"I should tell you," she said, just as they reached the iron gate at Iris House, "I had quite a serious discussion with Faith this evening."

He wasn't surprised. His daughter had a huge heart, with a giant capacity for love and pain. "Oh, no. Who is she worrying about this time?"

"You. She's afraid you might go out on a call one night and not come home."

He muttered an expletive. "Not the first time I've heard that from her. I don't know how to ease that particular fear, other than to quit my job. I'm not ready to do that."

"I don't think she expects that of you."

He wasn't so sure of that. Jess had wanted him to quit. It had been one of the few things they'd argued about. She couldn't understand how he could possibly love a job that occasionally put him in harm's way. Since he had always loved the paramedic side of things, even before he became the fire chief, she had wanted him to go on to medical school, something that wouldn't have fit his personality in the slightest.

"I've tried to explain to Faith that even if I had the safest job she could think of, there are no guarantees in life. Something could still happen to me."

"That's basically what I told her. Maybe a little less blunt. For the record, I think you're doing a great job. It can't be easy on your own, but your children are healthy, well-adjusted little creatures."

More of that soft warmth soaked through him. "Thanks," he answered. "That means a lot."

They walked up the steps to the porch, and she unlocked the door and turned on the light inside. He needed to get back to the kids—monitor or not—but he was hesitant to leave until he was certain she was okay.

"How are you doing now? Better?"

"Much." She managed a small smile that only looked a little tremulous. "Thank you. I'm only sorry you had to see it."

"Sorry *anyone* caught you in a weak moment or that the eyewitness was me in particular?"

He wouldn't have dared ask the question if not for this new intimacy that seemed to swirl around them. He might have credited it to the shared experiences of the evening—when you save a man's life together, you do tend to have a new sort of bond, not to mention that he had seen her in a moment of rare vulnerability during the last vestiges of her panic attack.

Somehow, it seemed as if they had turned yet another corner in their relationship.

She was quiet for a long moment and he wasn't sure she was going to answer him.

"Ah. That is a good question, isn't it?" she finally said.

"You can be honest, Lucy. You don't like me much. That's not some big dark secret. You never thought I was good enough for Jess."

As soon as he said the words, he regretted them. Why couldn't he just enjoy this new peace between them?

"Maybe you're not as smart as you think you are," she answered softly, her eyes large in her slender features.

He snorted. "I never claimed any kind of brains. I think it's fair to say, Aidan got more than his share of smarts among the Caine males."

"That's not true."

He stepped forward. He knew it was a mistake under the circumstances but she was too lovely there with those big green eyes and he couldn't seem to help himself.

"Yeah. It is. For instance, a smart man would never think about doing this," he said just before he kissed her.

CHAPTER TEN

Okay, this couldn't be real.

She couldn't really be standing in her foyer wrapped around Brendan Caine, being kissed by him as if he couldn't get enough. For one brief, wild moment, she wondered if she had passed out in his kitchen during the panic attack and thumped her head on the edge of the kitchen table or something.

That would be a far more reasonable explanation than the reality of being here in his arms, his mouth intent on hers, his hands pulling her closer and closer.

Kissing him might seem surreal and unexpected. That didn't mean she wanted him to stop anytime soon.

She wrapped her arms around his neck, desperate for more. He had talked earlier about how she came back to Hope's Crossing in search of her personal happy place, a place to feel safe and secure.

This. This was safety and peace, unlike anything she ever expected. She wanted to burrow into his big, broad chest and stay there forever.

She didn't know how long they kissed, but eventually they came up for air. Brendan was breathing hard, his pulse racing beneath her fingers. He stared at her for a long moment, looking stunned and a little wary.

"Wow," he finally said. "That was…"

Delicious. Toe-tingling? Wildly, lusciously wonderful?

"Completely unexpected," she finished for him.

He cleared his throat and she had the feeling he had intended to say something else. "Yeah. That, too. I'm sorry, Lucy. I didn't intend for that to happen."

Even as her heart cracked a little along a familiar fault line, she tried for insouciance. What else could she do? "Do your lips often act of their own accord, then?"

He made a face. "Apparently."

"As do mine. Apparently."

He drew in a ragged breath. "Well. This is a complication I didn't anticipate."

That made two of them. She was exhausted suddenly and wasn't at all sure her emotions could endure many more complications.

The day had been long and strange, the most bizarre she could remember.

First her father's unexpected and unwelcome visit, then helping to save a man's life. Throw in a nasty panic attack, followed by a kiss from the man she had tried to shove out of her head for more than a decade and she was suddenly exhausted.

"It doesn't have to be a complication," she finally said.

"Oh?"

"We can just both pretend nothing happened. It was a fluke. An aberrant moment of shared insanity."

"True enough."

He smelled delicious, like sage and leather. And he had tasted even better....

She caught herself. Oh, for heaven's sake. She really needed to stop noticing things like that. Better to focus on the scents of spring that still wafted through the open doorway. The new leaves on the trees; moist, overturned soil; fresh-cut grass.

Only a few hours ago, he had been mowing that grass for her. How had everything changed so quickly?

"We can blame my panic attack. I mean, isn't it obvious? I'm not in my right mind tonight. Otherwise, I never would have let you kiss me."

"Or kissed me back."

That had probably been a little hard for him to ignore when her tongue had been tangling with his. She flushed. "Or kissed you back."

"I started it. It was wrong of me to take advantage when you were already upset about the panic attack. For what it's worth, I'm sorry."

"Look, let's both just let it go and do our best to forget about the whole thing."

She hadn't had much luck trying to forget the last kiss they shared on another spring night, but there was always a first time, right?

"Sounds like a plan," he answered.

She gripped the open door and tried to ignore the wobble in her knees. It was only fatigue, she told herself.

To her vast relief, he headed for the doorway.

"Good night," she said.

"Night, Lucy." He paused with that lopsided smile she was beginning to crave like strawberry cheesecake.

"For the record," he murmured, just a few feet away from her, "it might have been crazy but that was one hell of a kiss."

He trotted down the steps and headed down her sidewalk.

She watched him move through the darkness for only a moment before she wrenched her gaze away and forced herself to go into the house.

She did *not* understand the man. Why would he possibly want to kiss her? Twenty minutes ago, she was a trembling, emotional wreck.

She had spent all these years telling herself the connection that she'd felt so long ago with him had just been her imagination. A few too many margaritas; a little too much dancing; a warm, lovely spring night perfect for flirtation.

After he started dating Jessie, she had tried to cover up her hurt by pretending she didn't like him, anyway.

He only had to kiss her before she recognized the lie for what it was.

Lucy sat in her parlor with her father and sister, wondering just what she had done.

"Are you sure you wouldn't like something to drink?" she asked Crystal. "I bought regular Coke, Diet Coke, regular Pepsi and Diet Pepsi because I wasn't sure which you would prefer."

"What about Diet Mountain Dew? Do you have that?"

Naturally, her sister *would* have to pick the one beverage she hadn't stocked up on. All that angsting in the grocery store over which one to buy had been for nothing.

"No. I missed that one. Sorry. We can go to the store later and pick some up. If you have anything else you particularly like, make a list."

"How about margarita mix? Can we get that?"

"Crystal." Robert looked up from the message he

was sending into his phone long enough to snap out his daughter's name.

"Oh, right. I forgot. You're tossing me into a black hole where fun isn't allowed."

"We can have fun," Lucy protested. "We'll have all kinds of fun. Iris House isn't exactly a women's prison."

"Close enough." Crystal slumped onto the couch and Lucy's heart sank even further.

Her half sister obviously did *not* want to be here. From the moment she and their father walked inside, she had just about seethed with snarky attitude, lots of eye rolling and sarcastic comments.

Lucy wanted to call the whole thing off. She supposed it had been idealistic of her to think Crystal would be happy to see her. Her relationship with her sister had always been a good one. She had assumed that would be enough to carry them through a couple weeks of togetherness.

Now she wasn't so sure.

"You want a women's prison?" her father asked, his voice hard. "You're in enough trouble right now, young lady. It wouldn't be that much of a stretch for us to arrange the genuine article. I've been doing my best to keep you out of the juvenile corrections system, but maybe I need to just back off and let you deal with the consequences of your actions."

Crystal opened her mouth to make some sharp retort but apparently thought better of it, under the circumstances. Instead, she crossed her arms over her chest and slumped lower into the sofa.

Ah, the old silent treatment. Lucy had used that one with regularity when she was Crystal's age.

"I'm really excited to have you stay with me." She crossed her fingers at her side and hoped her sister didn't notice. "We're going to have a great time. You'll see. Hope's Crossing is a great town."

"Why can't I just stay home?"

"You know why," Robert said in that same absent tone as he continued his email. "Your mother isn't well right now. She's exhausted and weak from her MS flare-up."

Crystal's lips tightened. "And that's my fault?"

"You haven't exactly helped the situation. All this stress is taking a toll on your mother. She needs peace and quiet for a few weeks."

"Sure. Get rid of the annoying brat. Why not?"

As Lucy might have predicted, all that teenage attitude rolled off their father like raindrops on Gore-Tex.

"Oh, give it a rest," he said wearily. "I don't have time for more of your histrionics. I've already taken more time than I should have, driving all the way out here. I have meetings this afternoon and need to head back to the city."

"Sorry I dared waste a few minutes of your precious time," Crystal muttered.

Robert sighed, raising his glasses up a little to squeeze the bridge of his nose. For the first time she could remember, her father actually appeared less than impenetrably composed. He looked tired.

He wasn't as young as he'd been when Lucy was the belligerent fifteen-year-old throwing barbs at him. If she wasn't careful, she might actually feel a little sorry for him.

"Again, the attitude isn't helping matters," he said. "I can't see what's so heinous about this situation. You have the chance to enjoy a two-week vacation with the older sister you love. You're always saying you want to spend more time with Lucy. This is the perfect chance, so tell me again why you're throwing a tantrum about it like a three-year-old."

"Lucy doesn't want me here any more than you and Mom want me around at home!" she snapped out.

"Not true," Lucy protested. "I'm excited to spend a little time with you."

She justified the lie because she figured it wouldn't help the situation if Crystal knew Lucy probably wanted her at Iris House *less* than Pam and Robert wanted her at home.

"Why?" Crystal demanded.

Lucy faltered for about three seconds to come up with a reason her sister might believe but that tiny pause was disastrous.

"Yeah. That's what I figured," Crystal snapped. "Why can't I go home?"

"Your sister invited you to stay with her in Hope's Crossing for two weeks, and that's what you're going to do in order to give your mother a chance to rest and regain her strength."

"Do you want me to stay in my room and write ten thousand times, *From now on I'll be a good little girl and drink the Kool-Aid my Fascist dad forces down my throat?*"

"An excellent place to start," he retorted.

Had she been this awful? Lucy wondered. Worse, probably. How had Annabelle endured it?

"I'll be in touch," he said. Lucy waited for him to hug the daughter he wasn't going to see for two weeks, but he only rose and walked toward the front door.

She followed him, ever the good hostess. Of course, he didn't hug her, either, or even thank her for the sacrifice she was making for his younger child. She didn't expect him to.

"Don't worry. I'm sure by tonight she will get over her pique so she can be more excited about spending a little time with you."

"And if she doesn't?"

"We'll put an end to this," he said, his voice matter-of-fact and without any trace of softness. "She might think spending time with you at Iris House is akin to being consigned to a women's prison, but she will think very differently after she spends a few weeks at Rock Crest."

The military school had always been her father's favorite threat with her. Maybe one of his daughters ought to call his bluff one day.

"I'll be in touch," Robert said again.

"Goodbye, Dad."

He paused at the door, and to her surprise, he kissed her on the cheek. "Thank you for this. I know it will be an imposition on you. I want you to know, Pam and I both appreciate it. You returning to Hope's Crossing right now came at an ideal time for us."

"Glad I could help," she said dryly.

Really? Could he be so oblivious to her own personal life trauma? The death of all her hopes and dreams? She had been abruptly terminated from the job she loved, and he couldn't see beyond his own needs.

He waved and headed to his waiting Mercedes, and she returned inside to the angry shadow of her own teenage turmoil.

When she returned to the parlor, Crystal was texting something on her cell phone—something amusing, apparently, judging by her smirk.

For just an instant as she realized she was now responsible for this person who exuded teen angst, Lucy's heart seemed to squeeze in her chest.

No. She could handle this, she told herself. She was tough and smart, and she had walked this particular road from the other side.

"Let's take these bags up to your room and get you settled in," she said.

Crystal looked as if she wanted to make some kind of snide comment, but she apparently thought better of it and shrugged instead. "Whatever."

She stuck her phone in the pocket of her very tight shorts and grabbed the smaller suitcase, leaving Lucy to take the larger one.

She thought about saying something but had a feeling she was going to have to pick her battles carefully over the next weeks.

CHAPTER ELEVEN

FORTY-EIGHT HOURS after Crystal came to Iris House, Lucy had just about decided her entire *world* was now a battlefield.

Her sister argued about every single rule she had set up for the house. She left her things all over the place. She refused to help with the dishes—or the laundry or the gardening or cleaning out any of the rooms. She was disrespectful and pissy from the moment she woke up until she went to bed.

By the evening of the second day, Lucy wanted to tear her hair out, clump by frustrated clump. She tried to remember Brendan's advice to provide a steady source of love to her troubled sister, but she didn't know how in the world she was supposed to do that when Crystal had more impenetrable defenses than the offspring of a hedgehog mated with an armadillo.

She and her sister were locked in a battle of wills and the only solution was something drastic.

She was in the room she had designated as an office, going over the notes and sketches Genevieve had left her that morning when Crystal poked her head in. As usual, her makeup was about an inch thick, heavy on the eyeliner with her brows plucked to within a millimeter of their lives.

"Something's wrong with your Wi-Fi," she snapped.

"Is it?" Lucy asked blandly, pausing to glance at a mock-up Gen had done of the third-floor turret bedroom designed as an exquisite romantic honeymoon suite, complete with elaborately painted ceiling and four-poster bed.

"I've been trying for like fifteen minutes and it won't let me on."

"Maybe you're not using the right password," Lucy suggested blandly.

"It's the same one I've been using for like two days. It's not my problem, it's yours."

Lucy opened her laptop and clicked on her web browser, which immediately went to the news index she used as her home screen.

"Hmm. Strange. Mine's working fine."

"Check it. Seriously, I've been trying for fifteen minutes."

"Oh, that's right. I changed the password. I guess you need that one."

Crystal gave her a disgusted look. "Hello? Why didn't you tell me that when I said it wasn't working? What's the new password?"

Lucy casually flipped a page in the sketchbook. "I'm sorry but I'm not prepared to divulge that to you at this time."

"What? Why not?"

"My house, my Wi-Fi, my rules. Using the internet around here is a privilege that you earn by being civil, something that has been in short supply the last two days."

"You're saying I can't get online?"

"The city library has Wi-Fi, I understand. You'll have to apply for a library card in order to use it, which takes an adult signature. I might consider signing it, but, again, we have that little civility issue."

"I'm supposed to Skype with my friend Devin in like twenty minutes! What am I supposed to do?"

"I'm sure you'll figure out something. You're a smart girl. Oh, I should mention, Dad's already called your mobile company and put strict limits on your cellular data usage. No cell phone workaround."

"OMG. You're worse than my parents! I hate it here *so much!*"

After two days, any semblance of patience Lucy might have possessed before this whole thing started was long gone. "Call Dad yourself, then. He can be here by bedtime. I'm sure your place at Rock Crest is already reserved, especially after the conversation I had with him this afternoon."

Crystal looked like she wanted to throw something. Instead, she sat down. "What do I have to do to get the password for the day?" she asked with exaggerated patience.

"Spend an hour with me running errands in town without all the attitude."

The sister who used to beg Lucy to come visit her looked as if this was the harshest torture anyone had ever been forced to endure. Worse than the rack or waterboarding or bamboo shoots under her fingernails.

"What's the alternative?"

"No alternative. Take it or leave it."

"One hour and I get the new Wi-Fi password?"

"You'll have the password for twenty-four hours. Tomorrow I change it again and your behavior that day will determine whether I share it with you."

Crystal's frustration was palpable, but Lucy could also see her sister realized she had no alternative.

"Fine. One hour running errands. I'll have to call Devin and tell her. When are we going?"

Lucy closed the sketchbook. She hadn't expected Crystal to capitulate so quickly—but then her sister's entire life seemed to be devoted to her social media activities.

"Right now is fine with me. Let me just run a brush through my hair and grab some lipstick."

Five minutes later, they headed for her BMW.

"Can I drive?" Crystal asked, with more enthusiasm than she had yet shown for anything else.

"Nice try. You don't have a license yet."

"I have a learner's permit."

"Which your father is keeping in his possession until the charges against you are dropped."

Crystal glowered and climbed into the passenger seat.

"I'll make a deal with you," Lucy said. "If you help me clean out the top turret bedroom tomorrow, in the afternoon we can drive out to this quiet road I know outside of town and practice a little."

That seemed to mollify her sister a little. At least she appeared to stop sulking as they drove to downtown Hope's Crossing.

Lucy found a parking place not far from her destination, Dog-Eared Books & Brew.

"I won't be here long," she said.

"I've got an hour to kill," Crystal muttered, wandering over to the magazine racks.

Lucy headed for the small business section and

picked up several books on opening and operating a successful bed and breakfast.

When she returned to the magazine racks, she offered to buy Crystal the copy of *Teen Vogue* she was leafing through, but her sister declined and said she had it already.

"Was there something else you wanted?" she asked, praying this temporary détente would continue.

"No," she answered tersely then appeared to try to relax her tone. "I think I'm good."

"I need to pick up a special order and pay for them then I'll have these rung up."

Lucy wandered to the checkout, where the woman running the register looked vaguely familiar. That was the problem with living in a small town—she kept bumping into people she was almost certain she knew but couldn't quite remember.

"Hi," she said. "I placed a special order for a few books and got a call this morning that they had arrived. The name is Lucy Drake."

"Oh, right," the woman said with a cheerful smile. "Just a moment."

She looked under the counter and pulled out three books on Victorian architecture and design.

"These are beautiful. I was hoping you wouldn't pick them up for a few days so I could have more time to look through them."

Lucy smiled, drawn to the woman's open friendliness. "You can borrow them when I'm done."

"Deal." She cocked her head. "Lucy Drake. You're the one living in Iris House now, aren't you?"

"Yes."

"I live just a few blocks from you. I'm Maura Lange. I was Maura McKnight back in the day."

This was Alex McKnight's older sister, she remembered. Like everyone else in town, Maura had been friends with Annabelle. As Lucy remembered, she'd been a single mother raising a toddler on her own when Lucy had been in high school.

"You've got a great shop here. I'm sure I'll be back. Books and coffee are two of my favorite things."

"We are kindred spirits, then. It's great being able to incorporate all the things I love into one store."

"You've done a good job."

"Thank you. Listen, we have a book club that meets about once a month. I don't know what your reading tastes are like—aside from the obvious renovation guides—but we generally read a really eclectic variety. This month we're reading a young adult fantasy we've all really enjoyed. We're meeting Friday if you'd like to join us. We're always trying to draw in new members to shake things up."

"That's very kind of you," Lucy exclaimed. A moderately civil sister, an armload of new books and a potential new friend. This was turning out to be most definitely a red-letter day.

Maura slid a business card across the table, then flipped another one over and grabbed a pen from the caddy by the computer monitor. "If you give me your email, I can send you all the details."

She scribbled it down.

"Welcome back to Hope's Crossing. It's so great to see someone in Iris House again. I've always loved that place."

Everywhere she went in town, people told her how

much they loved her house. It was both disconcerting and heartwarming.

After the bookstore, she had to fill up her car with gas and then they headed for the grocery store.

On the way, she tried to pick Crystal's brain about the things she loved to eat but didn't learn much, other than her sister hated fish and refused to eat veal or lamb.

"I can just stay in the car," Crystal said as Lucy pulled into a parking space at the distant edge of the grocery store. "I don't mind."

"And do what? You have a limited number of texts now and you've probably already exceeded those. Come in with me. You can pick out a few things you might like to eat."

Crystal's jaw worked for a moment, but she finally forced a pleasant expression. "Sure."

Lucy slid out of her car, just as a familiar SUV pulled into the space next to them. Her heart started to pound and her hands suddenly felt clammy.

She hadn't seen Brendan since the night they had kissed, a memory that seemed to be seared into her mind.

She wanted to quickly rush into the store and pretend she didn't see him but already Carter was waving excitedly at her out the back window.

"Wait a moment, Crystal," she told her sister, who had already started for the store.

"Why?"

"These are some friends of mine," she answered. "I should say hello."

During the past difficult two days, she had done her best to put that stunning kiss out of her mind in order to focus on her problematic sister. It hadn't worked all that well, she acknowledged. Now, as she watched him climb out of his SUV in all his big, tough gorgeousness, she couldn't seem to focus on anything else.

The children opened their respective doors and rushed to her, Carter slightly in the lead since his side was closest to her. Faith must have helped him out of the booster seat straps.

"Look at that! Two of my favorite kiddos."

"Hi, Aunt Lucy," Carter exclaimed, throwing his arms around her waist.

Over his head, she saw Crystal's heavily mascaraed eyes widen. "Aunt Lucy?" she asked. "What's that about? Do we have some long-lost relatives I've never met?"

"It's a long story," she answered her sister. "Their mom was my cousin on my mom's side and also my dear friend."

"Where did you go the other day?" Carter demanded. "I thought you were going to be there for breakfast but Daddy said you went home."

Not before he kissed me senseless.

She finally dared a glance at Brendan and found him watching her intently.

She could feel her cheeks soak with color. "I never planned to stay for breakfast, Carter. Only until your dad got back."

She hugged Faith, remembering their last intense conversation. "How are you, my dear?"

"Okay," Faith said. "I'm almost done with *Anne of Avonlea.* I might have to wait to read the next one because I have to do a book report on *Matilda.*"

"Hey, I read that book when I was a kid," Crystal

said. Faith turned with interest, taking in the double pierced ears and the tight clothes.

"Hello. I'm Faith Caine," she said.

Lucy winced. A seven-year-old had better manners than she did. "Sorry. This is my sister, Crystal. Crystal, this is our neighbor Brendan Caine the fire chief in Hope's Crossing, and these are his children and my honorary niece and nephew, Faith and Carter Caine."

She held her breath a little, wondering if her sister would make some snide comment. Instead, she nodded with something almost resembling politeness.

"Hello," she answered, and while her tone wasn't exactly warm, it wasn't belligerent, either.

"Where do you live?" Carter asked.

The girl looked a little taken aback by the question. "With my mom and dad in Denver."

"Crystal will be staying with me for a few weeks," Lucy explained.

"You're lucky," Faith declared. "I *love* Iris House. I wish I could stay there all the time. It's like a castle."

"It's because of the cool turret. That's where my room is. I can see the whole town from the windows," Crystal said.

If Lucy had false teeth, she would have spit them out at the enthusiasm in her sister's voice. For forty-eight hours, Crystal had despised the very idea of Iris House, and now she was expounding on the architectural details.

"That's so cool!" Faith exclaimed.

"Are you buying groceries, too?" Carter asked. "We're all out of eggs, milk and bread."

"Good job remembering the list, kid." Brendan said, the first words he had spoken since pulling into the

parking lot. "We should probably get on it so Lucy and
her sister can do the same."

At his prompting, they headed as a group toward
the grocery store. Just a few yards past their parking
spaces, Faith suddenly jerked to a stop.

"Did you hear that?" she said, suddenly alert.

"What, bug?" Brendan asked, stopping beside her.

"Something's in that big garbage bin. I just heard
it. I think it might be a baby crying!"

Brendan eyed the Dumpster in question. "A baby?
Honey, I think you're imagining things."

"I think I heard it, too," Crystal said with a frown.
"Listen."

They all went quiet, even Carter—something of a
miracle. The world seemed to cooperate for a moment
as no cars drove past.

As she strained her ears, Lucy heard the faintest of
sounds, more a squeak than a cry.

"Did you hear it that time? I think it's coming from
the Dumpster!" Crystal said.

Brendan eyed the bin with reluctance. "It's probably a rat."

"Ew!" Faith wrinkled her face while her brother
looked thrilled at the possibility.

The sound came again, faint but distinct.

"What if it *is* a baby?" Faith pressed. "What if somebody accidentally threw it away? We can't just leave
it there!"

"It's not a baby."

"How do you know if you don't look?" she said with
uncharacteristic mulishness.

"I bet it's an alien, like E.T.," Carter said. "I bet he

fell in, but he doesn't have hands, only tentacles, so he can't open the lid and now he's stuck."

"We have shopping to do," Brendan said.

"Just take a look, Dad. Please? I don't want to leave a baby in there."

"It's not a baby," he repeated, but with a sigh, he headed to the garbage bin and held open the metal cover. He peered inside. To Lucy's surprise, Crystal walked up next to him to look in, as well.

"Oh. Oh, my gosh. Do you see that?" her sister exclaimed.

"I see it," he said grimly, flipping the lid of the container all the way open.

"What is it?" Lucy asked. She couldn't resist joining them just as Brendan lifted out a box that looked as if it had once contained oranges.

"Is it a rat?" Faith asked. Though she was the one who started the whole thing, now she looked too apprehensive to even peer into the box.

"No," Crystal answered. "Puppies."

Brendan reached into the box and pulled out two little handfuls. They were black with brown markings, perhaps the size of a grapefruit with big dark eyes and shaggy faces. The only difference she could see was that one had more brown on the face, while the other was predominantly black with bigger brown markings on the body.

"Somebody threw away two puppies?" Faith exclaimed, looking as if her belief in all humanity had just been destroyed.

"It looks as if there were three. One, uh, didn't make it."

"Oh," Faith whispered sadly. She reached for one of

the puppies before Brendan could stop her—or before Lucy could warn her about fleas or any other manner of stray animal-borne ickies.

Crystal reached for the other one in Brendan's hand. "Oh, the poor little things. I can't believe somebody threw these cute guys away. How sad! Why didn't they take them to a shelter or something?"

This soft, gooey creature was her sister, who had flipped her nothing but sarcasm and attitude for the past forty-eight hours?

"Who knows?" Brendan answered. "People can be jackasses. Maybe they figured since the one died, the others weren't far behind."

"They're not brand-new, are they?"

"No. They look a few weeks old. Their eyes are open, anyway."

Lucy knew less about dogs than she did about fifteen-year-old girls. At least she had once been one of the latter. The closest she came to a dog was the adorably ugly but much-beloved French bulldog Annabelle had had, François. The dog hadn't done much, just trotted along on his short, stubby little legs as he followed Annabelle everywhere.

François had been fifteen, ancient in dog years, when he died just a few months before Annabelle. That had seemed a blessing to her, that they went close together.

"Does Hope's Crossing have an animal shelter?" Lucy asked.

Brendan nodded. "It was built a few years ago. Lee Peterson runs it. I'll give him a call, see if he can take a couple of young puppies or if he knows anybody who would foster them until they're old enough to be adopted."

"Why couldn't we foster them?" Crystal exclaimed.

Oh, no. Just what she needed, another element of stress in her life.

"Crystal," she began, but her sister held up the puppy that just filled both of her hands.

"They're so gorgeous. Look at this face! They're just babies. They need love and attention, not a shelter somewhere where they're crammed in with a bunch of other dogs."

Again, she couldn't quite believe this was the same surly teenager she had endured for two days.

"You're only going to be here a few weeks, remember?"

"We could take care of them for those few weeks, just until the shelter can find a more permanent place. It won't be hard. We can keep them in the utility room off the kitchen. I'll feed them and everything. Please, Luce. I've always wanted a dog, but Dad would never let us get one."

That, more than anything, made her waver. How many times had she begged her parents for a dog or a cat or even a gerbil? Robert insisted their lives were too busy for the mess and the responsibility—which, now that she thought of it, was basically a metaphor for her father's entire approach to parenting.

Lucy had always liked animals. She had a few friends with dogs in Seattle and would even sometimes borrow one for a few hours, just to take a walk with it or throw a ball into the Sound for it to retrieve.

She had never taken the step into ownership because

of her sixteen-hour workdays. Right now, however, she had nothing but time.

"I suppose we could give one of them a home for a few weeks. I think two would be more than we can handle."

"We could take the other one!" Faith looked as if this idea was the answer to her prayers.

Brendan, on the other hand, didn't look nearly as thrilled. "Oh, honey," he began, but Carter cut him off.

"A dog! A dog! We're getting a dog!" He started wiggling his hips back and forth like a celebratory end zone dance.

"Hey!" he called to a woman pushing a shopping cart past them. "Hey, guess what? We're getting a dog."

The woman turned with a smile, and Lucy realized it was Mary Ella McKnight, her favorite English teacher, whom Genevieve told her had recently married the town's wealthiest resident, Harry Lange.

"Are you?" Mary Ella said, pausing.

"We just found these dogs in the trash," Faith said. "Somebody threw them away. Isn't that the saddest thing you ever heard?"

"Tragic," she agreed, smoothing a hand over Faith's blond hair. The sweet girl just brought out the urge to nurture in people, Lucy thought. "So you're taking one home?"

"Temporarily," Brendan said quickly. "I guess. Just until we can find a permanent home for him."

Mary Ella looked at the little puppy in Faith's arms, where Carter was now leaning over and tickling him under the chin.

"Good luck with that," she said with a commiserating sort of look.

"Just look at him! He is such a cutie," Crystal said, cuddling the dog under her chin.

"Ours is cute, too," Carter said.

Faith cradled the puppy in her arms. "They're both adorable. The cutest puppies *ever.*"

"First order of business will be the vet to have them checked out and to pick up a couple flea collars," Lucy said. "Any chance there's an animal clinic open this late?"

Brendan, she saw, had the expression of someone trapped in a situation spiraling out of his control. "No idea," he answered. "Let me text Dylan and Drew. Both of them have dogs and would have a better handle on the vet situation in town than I do."

He pulled out his phone and sent a quick message, which was answered about twenty seconds later. As he read the screen, his mouth twisted into a smile that left her a little achy and, okay, jealous.

She wanted a big, boisterous, helpful family that could make her smile under otherwise stressful circumstances—not to mention that she was suddenly discovering she wanted to be the one who could make Brendan find a little enjoyment in life again.

"What's funny?" she asked.

He looked up from his phone. "Nothing, really. It's just that Dylan answered right away. He sent me the vet's phone number and everything. Since he was injured in Afghanistan, he hates texting—it's the one-hand thing—but he dearly loves his dog. He must have Tucker's vet on speed dial."

Brendan phoned the number and she listened in on his half of the conversation as the children cooed over the puppies. When he hung up, he confirmed everything she had surmised by her eavesdropping.

"That was the Monte Vista Veterinary Clinic. It's off the highway down by Silver Sage Meadow. They're only officially open for another half hour, but the receptionist said they could stay a little late to take a look at the puppies, since it's an emergency."

He gazed at his children and the puppy Faith held, clear reluctance in his expression.

"Do you want me to take both puppies?" Lucy asked, her voice low. "Despite what I said earlier, we can probably handle it. Crystal would love having both to take care of. Who knew a puppy would be the breakthrough I've been looking for with her, right? And it would get you off the hook. One puppy can't make much more mess than two and they might be better off together."

"It's tempting. Believe me. Our lives are hectic enough without throwing in the complication of a puppy."

The puppy licked Carter's face, and the boy giggled, his face turned toward father with an expression of sheer joy.

Brendan sighed. "But how can I break my kids' hearts now?"

Emotions welled up in her chest—not only because of the sheer adorableness of a cute little boy getting the love from a puppy saved in the nick of time from a grim fate, but because of Brendan. He clearly didn't want a dog, and she could totally sympathize. But he was a wonderful father, willing to take on a challenge that would only bring more chaos into his world in order to provide a little bit of happiness to his children.

How was she supposed to guard her heart against a man like that?

She would *not* let herself fall for him, Lucy told herself sternly. The last time she had let her emotions rule the day over logic and reason—when she started weaving ridiculous dreams about *him* after only one kiss—she had been left raw and heartbroken for months.

"We'll meet you there, then," she answered. "I guess our groceries will have to wait."

CHAPTER TWELVE

BRENDAN PULLED INTO the parking lot of the veterinary clinic to the sounds of a squeaking puppy and two squealing children.

When, exactly, was his life ever going to return to some semblance of normal? he wondered as he parked his SUV and helped the children out of the backseat.

Since the moment Lucy Drake came back to Hope's Crossing, nothing seemed the same.

Lucy parked beside him as he was unhooking Carter's straps. Her younger sister climbed out holding the puppy.

"Guess what?" Carter told her with delight. "Our puppy peed in the backseat!"

Lucy winced. "Sorry," she muttered to him.

"Makes me glad for leather seats. We got most of it with paper towels and I should be able to scrub down the rest."

They walked into the clinic, and only after he was inside and spotted the woman standing behind the counter did he realize how awkward this could be. He should have asked Dylan or the receptionist he spoke with on the phone the name of the veterinarian.

Dr. Elizabeth Lynde was a very nice woman in her early thirties who had recently moved to Hope's Crossing to start a veterinary practice.

Their paths had crossed the summer before at a barbecue one of his firefighter buddies had dragged him to and she had later called him up to ask him out on a date to go to the movies with her.

After his initial shock and, yes, panic, he had quietly thanked her for the invitation but told her he wasn't quite ready to date yet. When he was, she would be the first one he called.

In retrospect, he should have just gone out with her. She was a nice woman and he enjoyed her company, but the whole dating thing still seemed so strange.

Of course, that didn't seem to stop him from kissing Lucy until he couldn't think straight.

He tried to push that mistake of a kiss out of his mind, which wasn't exactly easy when she stood next to him smelling of vanilla and strawberries and looking lovely in jeans and a white tailored blouse that now had dog hair on it.

He never did get the chance to ask Elizabeth out. Last he heard, she was dating an accountant at the ski resort.

"Hey, Brendan. My assistant told me you called. How are you?" She leaned in and air kissed his cheek.

"Great. Thank you."

He suddenly wished again he had been able to generate a little more interest toward her. The Hope's Crossing dating pool wasn't exactly a deep one and Elizabeth was one of the best swimmers in there. She was attractive, smart, obviously good with animals and small children, and she had her own business. What more was he looking for, for crying out loud?

Why couldn't she stir his blood like a certain green-eyed brunette he could name? It would be far less uncomfortable, all the way around.

"Elizabeth, this is our neighbor Lucy Drake and her sister, Crystal. They're living in Iris House."

"Oh, I love that place."

"That seems to be the general sentiment," Lucy said with a smile.

"Did you know the previous owner? I was lucky enough to be invited to one of her Christmas parties shortly after I moved to Hope's Crossing and absolutely fell in love with the house and with her."

For just a moment, Lucy's expression turned stark with grief before she quickly contained it. He was struck again by her fragile beauty, so at odds with her take-no-prisoners personality. "Yes. She was my great-aunt."

"Oh. I'm so sorry for your loss. She seemed to be a fascinating woman. Someone I would have liked to know better."

"Thank you."

Elizabeth turned back to the situation at hand. "So I understand you all found a couple of abandoned puppies."

"Somebody threw them away." Faith still couldn't seem to comprehend the magnitude of the crime.

"That's terrible. How lucky that you discovered them, before it was too late."

"Yes. Wasn't it?" Brendan said. He did his best to keep the dryness out of his tone. He *was* glad they found the puppies in time to save them. He just didn't particularly want to take one home.

"Why don't you all come on back to our exam room and we'll take a look at them."

When they were all squeezed into the small room that looked as modern and comfortable as his own doctor's office, Elizabeth set both puppies in an open-topped crate that had been set up on the exam table to contain them.

"They look like they're a mix of some kind of small terrier and a miniature poodle, with maybe some Chihuahua thrown in somewhere. Because of the Chihuahua element, I wouldn't call them a true Yorkie Poo—if there's such a thing, since it's a boutique breed. I can tell you, they're going to be small, really cute and probably very smart."

One of the puppies yipped as if in agreement.

"They appear to be about three to four weeks old," she went on. "Not quite ready to be completely weaned but in a better place than they might have been a week or two ago. They seem to be fairly healthy."

"What about fleas?" Lucy asked.

"I can't see any. I can give you some shampoo for that, though." She looked at both of them. "Are you keeping the dogs?"

"Temporarily," he and Lucy said at the exact same moment. At their perfectly synchronized answer that sounded as if they had rehearsed, Lucy met his gaze with an amused look, a little dimple flitting in her cheek before it disappeared.

How had he never noticed that there before?

"This is strictly a foster-care situation," Lucy said. "Just for a few weeks."

"How kind of you," Elizabeth said. "I can get in touch with the people at the animal shelter and see if they know of anybody who might be interested in adopting them. Mixed-breed dogs can be pretty hard to place sometimes, but these guys are pretty cute and they'll be small. Maybe seven, eight pounds, max. They should find permanent homes pretty easily when word gets out."

Faith made a little sound of distress that made his heart sink. Like it or not, he had a feeling he had just made a lifetime commitment.

He wanted the hassle and headache of a puppy about as much as he wanted a raging case of appendicitis, but prying the dog out of his children's hearts was likely to prove impossible.

Again, how had his life gone so completely crazy? Kissing a woman he had no business even looking at one minute, taking in an abandoned puppy the next. He wasn't sure he wanted to know what kind of mistake he would make next.

"What would you suggest we feed them?" Lucy asked.

"Canine milk replacement is used in cases like this when the puppies are too young to be completely transitioned to puppy chow. I can get you some. You'll have to feed them about every two hours and burp them, too."

"Just like a baby," Crystal said.

"Very much like it. The good news is, they'll probably be ready to start the weaning process in a week or so and we can start switching them to regular puppy chow. I'll print out some instructions for you on how to do that and a few other guidelines for raising very young puppies. Puppies this age who don't have a mother around will need you to teach them proper behavior. For instance, if they nip at you, you need to make a whining sound and stop playing with them for a while. That teaches them not to bite."

Yeah, that was going to happen. He could just see

what the guys at the fire station would say if they heard him whining because of a little puppy nip.

He glanced over at Lucy and saw she looked completely overwhelmed.

It was one more thread of connection between the two of them, and he wasn't sure he liked it very much.

"Do you think they would be better off together?" Lucy asked.

"I really don't think it's a problem if you split them up, but you're going to want to get them together often for playdates. I can't stress the importance of that socialization factor."

"We see each other all the time," Faith assured her. "Lucy is kind of our aunt."

"Kind of?" Dr. Lynde asked. Brendan could see she was looking curiously between her and Lucy, trying to figure out their relationship. He could feel himself flush a little.

"Their mother was my cousin and dear friend," she answered, not looking in his direction.

"Ah."

"I guess that makes me kind of your aunt, too, since Lucy is my sister," Crystal said. For a troubled teenager, she seemed delighted at the idea of acquiring an instant niece and nephew. "You can call me Aunt Crystal if you want."

"Okay, Aunt Crystal." Faith giggled, obviously fascinated by this wild-looking creature with the piercings and tight clothes. Great. Another thing he needed.

"While you all work out those details, I'm going to print out a couple of puppy guides and some website references and find a couple cases of formula for you.

When you run out, you can find them at the pet store or we can order more for you."

"Thank you for your help," Lucy said. "You've really been wonderful."

"Glad to help. If it's okay with you, I would like to take a couple of pictures of these little darlings and send them to Riley McKnight at the police station so he can start looking into leads about where they came from. Whoever left them in that Dumpster could be facing animal cruelty charges."

"Of course," Lucy answered. "I didn't even think about that."

"Riley will probably want to take statements from both of you."

Considering he talked to the Hope's Crossing chief of police just about every day in connection with work, Brendan didn't think that would be a problem.

After Elizabeth left, Lucy's sister and Faith pulled the puppies out of the crate.

"Is our puppy a boy or a girl?" Faith asked.

He wanted to tell her there was no "our puppy" but he didn't see the point. He couldn't imagine yanking the puppy out of Faith's arms and handing her over to some stranger. Not when it was obvious his kids were already attached.

Maybe it wouldn't be such a terrible thing. Yes, it would add to the general chaos, especially for the next few months while the puppy was so young, but they were all in a much better place than they had been even six months earlier. They had picked up the pieces of their shattered world and were moving on with life.

Faith was almost eight. The responsibility would be

good for her and might help her take on all those new challenges she had been avoiding since Jessie died.

"She's a girl, if that's the one you wanted," Lucy said.

"What are you going to call her while you're taking care of her?" Crystal asked.

"I don't know. I've always wanted a dog named Princess."

He tried to imagine standing at the door calling for Princess to come get her supper and just couldn't wrap his head around it.

"What about you?" Faith asked.

"Max," the girl said promptly, as if she'd been thinking about it since the minute they opened that Dumpster to the little rat-squeak sounds.

"I like the name Max," Carter said. "I have a friend at school named Max. He has really stinky farts."

"Carter!" Brendan exclaimed.

"What? He does!"

"You don't need to tell everyone about it, especially when there are ladies present."

The particular ladies in question were both hiding their laughs, Crystal behind the little dog and Lucy by turning her face away.

"Sorry," Brendan muttered in an aside to Lucy.

"I love that kid," she answered in the same low voice.

"Let's just hope this Max doesn't take after the other Max," Crystal said as Elizabeth came back in carrying two packets of information and two cases of formula.

They scheduled follow-up appointments in two weeks to begin the process of giving the puppies their necessary shots and then Brendan carried both cases of formula out to the vehicles.

"You never made it to the grocery store," Lucy said. "Would you like us to pick up your list?"

Drat. He had completely forgotten that—along with dinner. How was he going to drag two kids and a tiny puppy to the grocery store now?

"That would be great."

"Let me see if I remember," she said. "Milk, eggs and bread. Is that right, Carter?"

"Yep." His son beamed at her, and Brendan felt a weird little tug in his chest.

He needed to stop this right now. Lucy wasn't at all the woman for him. That was the reason he hadn't pursued their fledgling attraction more than a decade ago, and as far as he could see, nothing had changed.

Yes, maybe he had been contemplating dating again; maybe the time was right to start dipping his toe in that dating pool he'd been thinking about earlier.

He missed having a woman in his life. It wasn't just the sex—though Lord knows, he missed that. He sometimes sat in his empty house in the middle of the night aching for the softness of a woman's curves next to his, for the sweet sound of feminine laughter, for a tender touch and a loving smile.

Lucy Drake wasn't that woman. Life might have temporarily derailed her career train, but he knew it was only a matter of time before she yanked all the cars back on the tracks and took off again.

"What do *you* think we should name her, Dad?" Faith asked from the backseat, distracting him from his grim thoughts.

"I don't know. How about Agnes or Gertrude? Or maybe Prudence?"

"Hmm. Those might work," she said after a long pause, too softhearted to laugh at his tongue-in-cheek suggestions.

He felt extraordinarily lucky to have this girl for a daughter, who had definitely inherited her sweetness from her mother's side.

"What else did you like besides Princess?"

"I like Iron Man," Carter said. "Or what about Darth Vader?"

"Those are boy names," Faith answered. "We could name her Hermione or Princess Leia."

Again, with the princess. "We don't really have to decide tonight."

"We have to call her *something*." Faith's brow furrowed as she studied the little creature in her arms.

"How about Stinky?" he suggested.

"Dad. Be serious!"

"Okay. Okay."

In all his life, he had never named a dog, he realized with a start. During his childhood, his family always had at least one or two dogs around the house, but it seemed his siblings had generally taken over naming rights. He was the third oldest and Drew and Patrick had always seemed to win the naming lottery.

"What about, uh—" he glanced in the rearview mirror and saw the flowers adorning the neckline of Faith's favorite shirt "—Daisy."

"Oh! It's perfect! I *love* it. We'll call her Daisy! Hi, Daisy. Do you like your new name?"

The dog made its little mewling sound that wasn't quite a bark yet, as if in agreement.

"She likes it," Carter exclaimed. "Hi, Daisy. Hi, girl. You're such a cute puppy. Yes, you are."

Brendan sighed as he pulled into the driveway. Yeah. Like it or not, he wasn't getting rid of this dog anytime soon.

"First order of business is finding her a bed and some old towels to sleep in, then let's see if we can get her to eat some of this food."

They were in the middle of it all twenty minutes later when the doorbell rang.

He answered and found Lucy on the other side of the door, her arms loaded down with bags. He smelled something delicious—besides Lucy—and his stomach rumbled at the reminder that they *still* hadn't eaten dinner.

"What's this? I thought I told you I only needed milk, bread and eggs."

"I know that's what you said. But since we hadn't had time to fix dinner yet, we figured you hadn't, either. We picked up an extra rotisserie chicken for you and some pasta salad from the deli. If you've already grabbed something tonight, you can always save it for tomorrow. I'm sure you're well aware that rotisserie chicken can be repurposed in casseroles or chicken salad sandwiches or enchiladas or whatever."

She carried the bags inside and to the kitchen, setting them down on the counter and started pulling items out to put in the refrigerator.

"Thank you," he managed through his shock. He couldn't figure out this woman. Every time he thought he had her pegged, she surprised him again.

He had always figured she was tough, driven, ambitious, but then she had these moments of nurturing kindness that seemed at odds to that other image.

Maybe she was all of those things. Why did one have to exclude the other?

"You're a lifesaver," he said. "Carter, in particular, is about ready to gnaw through the kitchen cabinets."

She smiled as she extracted the chicken from the grocery bag. "I'm sorry you were dragged into the whole puppy thing. I know it wasn't on your radar right now."

"Same goes. We were both unwilling victims."

"They *are* cute. You have to admit."

She was cute, with those dark curls and the warm green eyes he wanted to sink into.

"I guess," he muttered. "If you like little fur-faced, big-eyed, shaggy-eared puppies."

She smiled. "You're right. Who would? I guess we'd better take our ugly puppy home and see how much damage he can do to a historic home."

Out of nowhere, he wanted to kiss her again—just reach right out, wrap her softness in his arms and hold on tight. The need burned through him and he had to grip the kitchen counter instead. He was going to have to work a hell of a lot harder to keep himself under control or he was going to find himself in big trouble here.

"Good night," he said, his voice gruff. "Thanks for the chicken. I guess we'll have to arrange a few dates now."

She gave him a startled look.

"For the puppies, I mean," he said quickly. "You know. Playdates."

"Right. Yes. Dr Lynde said they need to socialize with each other, didn't she? Well, you know where I live. Any time you want Crystal or me to babysit, either the puppy or the kids, just call."

"Thanks."

She waved and headed for the door, leaving him to breathe in the scent of her that lingered in the air.

What would Lucy think if she knew he was beginning to weave some fairly inappropriate fantasies about her? She would probably want to rip his head off. She didn't like him, right? She had only spent a decade proving it.

On the other hand, she *had* kissed him back. Pretty passionately, as he recalled—which he did, all too frequently.

What was he supposed to do with *that?*

"Dad!" Faith called in a panic-stricken voice. "Daisy just peed on the floor! Help!"

He sighed. This was real life. His kids, his job, the chaos he called life, and now a pee-happy puppy.

"Let me grab some paper towels. I'll be right there."

He yanked a big wad off the roll and headed out to deal with the latest mess in a life that suddenly seemed full of them.

CHAPTER THIRTEEN

THE PUPPY'S ARRIVAL heralded a monumental shift in Crystal's attitude.

The day after they found Max, Lucy returned from a quick sunrise run through the quiet back street of Hope's Crossing to find her sister in the kitchen flipping pancakes while Max played in a box near her feet.

"Good morning." Lucy reached into the refrigerator for a water bottle. "I'm surprised to see you awake."

"Morning. Max woke me like an hour ago, yipping like crazy. He wouldn't go back to sleep so I finally decided to get up and feed him and make breakfast for us."

"Wow. Thanks. It looks delicious."

Who knew Crystal had any skills whatsoever in the kitchen? Lucy certainly hadn't had a clue.

"You're welcome. I've got a ton of pancakes. I really hope you're hungry."

Lucy thought of the brutal, hilly run she had just finished. She didn't enjoy running much but she did enjoy the endorphin high she found from having done it and she was much more productive and happy when she was fit.

Her plan had been to have a banana and a Greek yogurt for breakfast—why add more calories after she had just killed herself to burn a bunch?—but she didn't want to disappoint her sister, who had gone to a great deal of effort for her.

"I'm starving," she lied. "It all smells delicious."

"Great! If you want to sit down, it's almost ready."

Lucy pulled the yogurt out of the fridge—at least she could have a little protein with her empty carbs—and sat at the big oak kitchen table.

A moment later, Crystal slid a plate loaded with more pancakes than Lucy could eat in a month in front of her and then sat down across the table from her.

"Mmm. Smells good," she said. She tried a bite and just about fell off her chair.

"Oh, my word," she exclaimed. "These are *fantastic*. That can't be from a mix."

They were light, fluffy, with a little hint of something tropical that melded perfectly with the maple syrup.

"I couldn't find any mix in the pantry so I used a recipe I've tried before. They've got a little bit of coconut and almond extract in them. Those are the secret ingredients."

"These are fantastic. Seriously good. I'm not just saying that, Crys. You could get a job at the Center of Hope."

Her sister looked pleased and flattered. "What's the Center of Hope?"

"The restaurant Brendan's dad owns downtown. It's sort of the town gathering spot. Everybody goes there for the great food and all the best gossip in Hope's Crossing."

"Gossip in Hope's Crossing? Like who stole somebody's newspaper or who else died of boredom this week?"

"You'd be surprised. This town has seen its share of juicy scandals. And you can find out about all of them at the Center of Hope Café."

"I think I saw that. Is it kind of near the bookstore where we went last night?"

"Across the street and down a little." She took another bite of the pancakes that melted in her mouth. She could eat these every single day of her life—and probably wouldn't be able to fit through the door if she did, forget about jogging up and down the foothills around Hope's Crossing.

"I mean it. Dermot would love this recipe. You should give it to him."

Instead of the sullen expression she had worn since her arrival, Crystal seemed to glow at the praise. "It's no big deal. They're only pancakes."

"You should let Dermot be the judge of that. Type it down and we can email it to him."

"Assuming I get to have the Wi-Fi password today."

Lucy smiled. She wasn't naive enough to think all her troubles with Crystal were over because of one good morning and a cute puppy, but she was going to enjoy the peace while she had it. "I think we don't have to worry about that today. What's on your agenda, besides totally rocking the cakes?"

Crystal shrugged. "Nothing, really. I was going to play with Max for a while and then maybe Skype my friend Devin, and then I remembered she's in school until this afternoon. I never thought being expelled would turn out to be so boring."

"We've got to come up with a working schedule. It's time we start working on your schoolwork."

"Schoolwork? I was expelled! I can't go back."

"You can't go back *this* school year. Your father has directed all your teachers to email me with your assignments and lesson plans so you can keep up with your classes, that way you won't have to repeat the tenth grade next year. You don't want that, do you?"

"I guess not. But I don't want to do schoolwork, either."

"Life is full of hard decisions, kid. Sometimes you just have to deal. After we're done with your studies, I would appreciate your help. I've got a lot of work to do around here."

"What kind of work?" Crystal asked warily.

"I have to clear out a lot of the old clutter in the rooms so we can start remodeling them for the bed and breakfast. Who knows? We might find some fun treasures. Will you help me?"

"Do I have a choice?" Crystal asked.

"Not really."

"In that case, sure. I'd love to help you."

Lucy laughed, appreciating her sister's dry sense of humor. They shared that, at least.

"I can't tell you how much I'm looking forward to having my own minion to help me out. Especially one who cooks me delicious breakfasts."

"Yeah, well, don't get used to it."

The puppy whined at that moment and Crystal picked him up and went to fetch the supplies to feed him the formula.

The morning served as a vivid contrast to the first few days after her sister's arrival. Crystal complained a little about the homework Lucy set out for her, but it seemed halfhearted and more because she thought it was expected of her.

After the initial muttering, her sister hurried through the work in less than an hour. When Lucy checked it, she found the algebra equations impressively neat and precise—and correct—and the short essay she wrote insightful and well-done.

She had a sneaking suspicion her sister's failing grades were simply another act of rebellion against her parents' expectations. She and Crystal were apparently alike in this, too. At some point during their remaining days together, she would have to sit down and have a good talk with Crystal about all the time Lucy had wasted in high school trying to hide her intelligence.

Not today, however. They had a schedule. With Max tucked into his box under Crystal's arm, they headed up to the third floor to begin work on clearing out the house.

They started with a good-size bedroom facing east that Annabelle had always used as a craft room. It was filled to the brim with yarn, folded fabric swatches, boxes of beads.

"Some of this stuff is really retro," Crystal said, after they started digging into the drawers of the storage units around the walls.

"Annabelle has probably been collecting her whole life. Most of it is probably older than I am."

"Maybe you could use some of the fabric and notions for pillows and curtains and stuff around the house."

Oh, Annabelle would have loved that! "What a good idea! Let's box it all up and we'll take it over to Genevieve Beaumont. She's the designer helping me with the house. She might be able to look through it and find some possibilities."

"What happened to your job at NexGen?"

They were carrying yet another load of boxes down the stairs—why, again, had she bothered with an early-morning workout?—when Crystal sprang the question at her.

She tensed, that sense of failure and loss pressing down on her again. "Why do you ask?"

"I know why *I'm* here—because Dad is pissed at me and wants me out of the house. I just don't know why *you're* here. Did you quit?"

She was tempted to make some kind of excuse and change the subject. She really didn't want to talk about it. While success had always been important to her sense of herself, the failure still gnawed at her.

But she and Crystal were just beginning to foster a sense of trust between them. To her mind, that meant sharing the bad, too. She couldn't shake the memory of how her father had completely refused to discuss anything with her when Betsy started growing increasingly unstable.

"I'm here because I lost my job."

"Why? Because of the economy?"

"No. Over the last few months, I made some mistakes. The biggest was not speaking up when I should have about whether a software program was really ready to hit the market. Turns out, it wasn't."

"Why were you blamed?"

Lucy told her sister the entire story, about the disastrous marketing campaign and the PR nightmare resulting from it.

"It was a huge mistake, from start to finish, but I

have to say, it's been a hard but valuable learning opportunity for me."

The biggest lesson was the realization that had trickled over her slowly while she had been back in Hope's Crossing.

She hadn't been happy for some time, but she had been too busy to even notice. For the first time, she wondered if being fired might have been one of those proverbial blessings in disguise.

"So what are you going to do now?" her sister asked.

Ah, there was the question. "Because I worked hard all these years and saved my money, I have a few options. I'm trying to figure out what I really enjoyed about my work. Maybe I can find something new that focuses on those strengths."

She had loved the creativity and challenge of coming up with marketing strategies. Struggling with personnel issues and corporate tap dancing, on the other hand, had sucked her dry.

"For now, the plan is to focus on the house. You can see now that I have plenty to do."

"Well, I'm glad you're here. Military school would have seriously sucked."

"Your dad hasn't ruled it out," she warned.

"I know."

Max whined a little, and Crystal glanced out the window. "It looks nice out there. Would it be okay if I take him out on the grass to play for a little bit?"

"Yes. Let's take a break. I'm going to need to run these boxes of fabric over to Genevieve, anyway. You can hang out here or come with me. Your choice."

"We'll come," Crystal decided, scooping up the puppy.

She might not have been excited about taking on the challenge of an orphaned puppy, but right now Lucy wanted to take the little dog from her sister and smooch him all over his furry little face for bringing about this miraculous change.

THAT DAY SEEMED to set the pattern for the next several. She and Crystal would work on homework for a few hours in the morning and then pick a room in Aunt Annabelle's house to clear out in the afternoon.

Along the way, they discovered a storehouse of treasures, many of them delightful period items that would work nicely with the plans she had worked out with Genevieve for Iris House.

If the weather was nice, Crystal and Max would play in the sunshine of the early evening while Lucy fumbled her way through caring for Annabelle's garden.

By the end of the week, she was astonished at how much they had accomplished, on all counts.

"We have kicked butt this week," she said to her sister early Friday evening as they sat on the grass watching Max chew a stick. In a week, he had already gained weight and was looking more solid and sturdy, much less like the fragile, helpless little wisp they had found in that Dumpster.

On the veterinarian's instructions, they had started weaning him off the replacement formula and he was doing well with mushy puppy chow mixed with some of it.

He looked healthier and was definitely happier, though Crystal was still getting up several times a night to feed him. He was starting to be curious about the world and give them a little inkling into what a mischievous troublemaker he might be turning into.

"We should celebrate all our hard work," Crystal said.

"Great idea. What would you like to do? After we're done grilling, we could go catch a movie."

They had a couple of chicken breasts marinating in the refrigerator and Lucy had started the charcoal briquettes in Annabelle's old barbecue ten minutes earlier. The smoky scent was already wafting across the yard.

"Going to the movies could be fun. I don't even know what's out."

They were discussing the possible genre of movie they wanted to see—Lucy was in the mood for an action thriller while Crystal wanted a romantic comedy—when she suddenly heard an excited voice outside the iron fence.

"Hi, Aunt Lucy! Hi, Crystal. Hi, Max!"

"Hey, Faith!" Crystal called as the girl climbed down off her bike and opened the gate.

"What are you guys doing?"

"Just sitting out here, enjoying the evening. What about you?"

"Oh, we just went on a bike ride. Guess what? I finished *Anne of Avonlea,* and now I'm starting *Anne of the Island.*"

"Already? My word, you're a fast reader."

"Because I love to do it," she said simply. "Max is getting soooo big. So is Daisy. You should see her! She's so cute! I can feed her by myself now. I do it in the night when my dad is at the fire station. Mrs. Madison doesn't like dogs that much."

"Is she eating puppy chow yet?" Crystal asked.

"She started a few days ago. She really liked it. How about Max?"

"He likes it, too. He's a little piglet, aren't you, buddy?"

The puppy yipped and stumbled over his feet and both girls giggled just as Carter and Brendan rode up, Brendan on a mountain bike and Carter on his cute little BMX bike.

Lucy's stomach did a long, slow roll. How had she forgotten in less than a week how outrageously gorgeous the man was, with those rugged features, the broad shoulders, those vivid blue eyes?

It really wasn't fair.

"There you are," he called to Faith. "How did you get so far ahead of us?"

She giggled. "Because you're slowpokes, I guess."

"I guess." He and Carter both parked their bikes and walked toward them, and Lucy suddenly wished she had time to run inside and throw on some lipstick or something.

"Where did you go on your bike ride?" she asked Carter.

"We rode all the way to Aunt Charlotte's house, but she wasn't home."

"It was still a gorgeous evening for a ride, wasn't it?" she said.

"Beautiful," Brendan answered, an odd light in his eyes as he looked at her.

Carter dropped to his knees in the grass, heedless of stains on his jeans. "Hi, Max. Hi, buddy!"

He giggled as the puppy yipped and scampered to him.

"How are things on the puppy front? Faith was just telling us Daisy is transitioning to puppy chow."

"What can I say? We have a gifted dog."

"Max is clearly superior. He's been eating puppy chow for days now."

He laughed. "Oh, is that how this is going to go? A puppy throwdown?"

"You can't throw down the puppies," Carter said, alarmed. "They might get hurt."

"Just a figure of speech, honey," Brendan said. "Nobody's throwing anything."

He met Lucy's gaze, and she caught her breath at the warm amusement there. She had rarely seen him lighthearted like this, and she suddenly wanted more.

"You must not be working tonight."

"No. I finished four twelves this morning. I've got the weekend off."

"Lucky."

"You didn't bring Daisy with you?" Crystal asked.

"No. She was sleeping soundly in her crate when we left."

"I could go get her," Faith offered. "Remember, we were supposed to have playdates with the dogs, and we haven't done that yet."

"That's right," Crystal said. "I bet they've missed each other."

"Have you eaten?" Lucy asked on impulse. "We were just getting ready to throw some chicken on the grill."

"Hey! We were going to barbecue, too!" Carter exclaimed. "Right after our bike ride. Dad took out a steak for him and hot dogs for me and Faith."

"Yum. Why don't we save some charcoal and you

can bring your dinner and your puppy up here? I'll even let your dad work the grill while I throw together a salad and some oven-baked fries."

"Wow. That's nice of you," Brendan said dryly.

She grinned. "Scientific fact. Guys like to grill."

"So I hear."

"Can we stay, Dad?" Faith asked.

He looked reluctant for just a moment, and she suddenly felt guilty for springing the invitation on him like that, in front of the children. She should have known better.

"Sure," he finally said. "I'll go grab our dinner and Daisy. You kids can stay here and play with Max."

"I should have everything you need," Lucy said.

"I guess I'll be back in a minute, then. Kids, behave yourselves."

"Okay," Carter said cheerfully.

"I always behave myself," Faith said, rather primly. To Lucy's mind, the girl needed to tumble into a little trouble once in a while.

When Brendan headed for his mountain bike, she followed him where they could speak out of earshot of the children, feeling guilty about her thoughtlessness.

"Sorry," she murmured. "I should have talked to you first before I said anything about dinner. It was unfair of me to back you into a corner like that. I can make an excuse if you want."

She couldn't read the expression in his eyes. "I don't mind," he said. "It's a nice night for a barbecue. The kids will enjoy eating at Iris House, and I will enjoy not having to think about anything but grilling."

"Next time I'll try to remember to clear any brilliant ideas with you first," she assured him.

"Thanks."

She could swear his gaze dipped to her mouth and she wondered if he was remembering that incredible kiss. Was he thinking about the slow slide of his tongue along hers? How her body seemed to fit so perfectly against his?

He cleared his throat, and she thought she saw a muscle flex in his jaw. "I'll be back in a few," he said, then rode off fast before she could even answer.

She stood for a moment trying to will down her unruly hormones before she hurried back to the children.

Faith and Carter didn't look up from playing with Max, but Crystal gave her an appraising sort of look.

"You like him," her sister said in a low voice.

Lucy felt herself blush, much to her dismay. A few weeks ago, she would have argued most vehemently about that, but things had changed since her return to Hope's Crossing. She *did* like him. Entirely too much.

"Sure, I like him. He was married to my dear friend and I adore his children."

"I'm not talking about the kids or about his late wife. I'm talking about the way you get all flustered around him."

"I do not."

Crystal gave her a pitying sort of look that had her blushing even more. "Oh, please, Luce. Don't get me wrong, I'm not saying I blame you. For an old dude, he's pretty hot."

Oh, yes. He was, indeed.

"Don't let your imagination go into overdrive or anything," she said, in what she hoped was a stern, dismissive tone—which might have held more weight if she wasn't blushing like a teenage girl over her first crush. "Brendan and I are friends. That's it."

It was true, she realized, and far more than they had been a few weeks ago.

CHAPTER FOURTEEN

FIFTEEN MINUTES LATER, Brendan headed back up the hill toward Iris House with a grocery bag in one arm and a tiny smidge of a dog named Daisy tucked in the crook of his other.

This was what he considered a perfect late-April evening in the mountains, with the air smelling of pine and fresh-cut grass and new growth.

He told himself he had no reason to feel ridiculous carrying the dog—if she could legally be considered a dog, when she was little more than a ball of fluff.

If a guy was going to have a dog, he ought to have something big, muscular. Meaty. A German shepherd or a Siberian husky or some breed like that, not a little purse pooch, who barely filled out one of his shoes. And yes, the kids thought it was hilarious to stick her in one and watch her try to escape—and Carter just about had an accident himself, laughing so hard when she peed in one of Brendan's favorite sneakers.

They were having a great time with Daisy—and, he had to admit, *he* was having a great time watching Faith and Carter get so excited about the little dog.

Faith was often far too earnest and serious for her own good. She would rather be reading a book than just about anything else in the world. He didn't necessarily consider that a bad thing, but he worried she spent more time reading about exciting places and people than actually trying to embrace life and taste a little of that excitement herself.

Since Daisy's arrival in their house and the upheaval four pounds of dog provided, Faith had been far more engaged with all of them.

Carter, on the other hand, had gone in the other direction. Brendan couldn't recall a time when his son ever voluntarily sat longer than two or three minutes at a time except at meals, but the evening before, Carter had sat on the porch steps for at least a half hour in the evening, just holding the puppy and chattering softly to her.

He had been dying to hear the conversation but hadn't been able to get close enough to catch any of it.

Yeah, Daisy added a new layer to the general craziness of his life, with the frenetic schedule of feedings and bathroom breaks and cleaning up after her. The guys at the station thought it was hilarious that he brought her to the station with him in her little crate—though he noticed all of them looked for any excuse to hold her.

He was getting into a routine now and had just about decided it wouldn't be terrible keeping her around.

The dog whined a little, probably ready to eat again.

"Hang on a minute," he told her. "We're almost there."

He passed the house of Lou and Maria Giordano, three houses down from Iris House, and waved at the retired railroad worker, who was raking the wood chips in one of his lush flower beds.

He had a soft spot for both Lou and his wife. After Jessie's death, Lou mowed his lawn all summer long so Brendan wouldn't have to worry about the job in the midst of all that pain, and Maria had brought a plate of gooey, warm chocolate chip cookies to the house every week for months, even though the two of them were elderly and didn't get around as well as they used to when he was a kid.

"Nice evening, isn't it?" Lou called.

"It is that. We live in a beautiful place, don't we?"

"You know it, son." Lou ambled over, rake in hand. "What you got there? Looks like a gerbil."

He held Daisy up a little so the man could have a better look. "Nope. It's a puppy. We're foster parents for a while, until the Humane Society can find her a new home."

"Oh, she is a cute one. Looks like, what, part Yorkie, with maybe some mini poodle and a few other things thrown in?"

"That's what the vet says. You've got a good eye for dog breeds."

"Oh, Maria and I love dogs. We watch the dog shows every chance we get. Where'd this one come from?"

"We found her and a littermate in a trash bin outside the grocery store."

"Oh, poor little thing. She is a cutie." Lou looked closer. "You know, we might be interested in a puppy. Ever since Sally--she was our mini pinscher—died last winter, the house has seemed a little lonely."

A couple of days ago, that would have been an answer to prayer. A good, loving home close enough that his kids could still visit Daisy whenever they wanted and even take her on walks so the Giordanos didn't have to.

At this point, he didn't see any way of extricating her from their lives without breaking the kids' hearts.

"To tell you the truth, the kids are already pretty attached to her. I wasn't in the market for a dog right now, but I don't think I'm going to be able to rip her away from them."

Lou chuckled. "I hear you. Well, if you change your mind, you know where to find me."

Brendan inclined his head toward Iris House. "Daisy here has a brother who's staying up at Iris House with Annabelle's great-niece. Lucy might have an easier time giving Max up than my kids will with Daisy. I can't make any promises. I'm heading there. I can talk to her for you if you want."

"Thanks. I'd appreciate that. I've seen her out and about since she came back to town. She seems nice as can be. Yesterday, she stopped and helped me clean up some branches after that big wind we had."

"That was kind of her."

"Yes. And she's a good-looking one, too. You could do a lot worse."

"Oh, we're not—" he started to say, but decided he would sound stupid if he protested too much. Anyway, Daisy was currently nibbling on the inside of his elbow and he wasn't in the mood to start whining at her like the vet recommended, right in front of his seventy-two-year-old neighbor.

"Night, Lou. Give my best to Maria."

"Same to you, son. Same to you."

He really did enjoy living here. After Jess died, he had thought about picking up the kids and starting over somewhere else, where people didn't whisper, "Oh, that poor man" when they saw him around town.

He hated being the object of pity, the widower whose lovely wife had died so tragically.

Now that two years had passed, he didn't notice those sympathetic looks as much. Either he'd grown impervious to them or people had come to accept that time rolls on, like it or not. He no longer had a refrigerator full of casseroles brought over by concerned neighbors and it was only rarely that somebody would stop him in the grocery store, rest a hand on his arm and ask him how he *really* was doing.

Hope's Crossing was home, for him and for the children. His family was here, the job he loved, friends and neighbors who cared about him and about his kids. He could do a whole lot worse.

When he reached Iris House, he followed the sound of shrieking to the side of the house, where he found Lucy on her back in the grass being attacked by both Faith and Carter, who had apparently teamed up to tickle her.

Crystal sat up on the porch on the swing, grinning at the assault while Max played with a chew toy next to her.

Seeing his children so happy and light sent something curling through his insides, something sweet and warm and lovely.

Just hunger pangs, he told himself

Daisy whined and Lucy looked up at the sound. For just an instant, their gazes locked and he caught his breath. She looked happy, too, and so beautiful it was hard for him to look away.

"Oh. Hi."

She quickly disentangled from the children and

climbed to her feet, brushing off grass and leaf bits from her clothes.

"There's Daisy," Faith exclaimed. "Hi, sweetie!"

She held out her hands for the puppy and immediately set her down beside the puppy's littermate.

"Look! She remembers him!" Carter exclaimed.

The puppies brushed noses and nipped playfully at each other.

"You ready to get your grill on?" Lucy asked after a moment of watching the puppies play with each other.

"Sure."

"I started the coals a while ago. They should be all set. Come in the house and you can find whatever tools you need."

She led the way around the house to the back door, which led directly to the kitchen of Iris House. He followed, enjoying the fluid grace of her movements entirely too much.

Inside, she pointed him to a cabinet that held grilling tools and then pulled out a container from the refrigerator with a couple of chicken breasts marinating in some kind of herb-infused liquid.

"Everything else is ready to go. I already made the salad and the potato wedges have been soaking in ice water, which is the secret to good oven-baked fries."

"Good to know."

She gave a rueful laugh. "Hey, I have to savor my successes where I find them. I'm not that great in the kitchen, though I've discovered Crystal is something of a budding chef. You have to get her pancake recipe. To die for."

He was aware of the sweet seduction of being alone with her here in the kitchen, of the mouthwatering scent of her, the sway of her hips and the softness of her curves as she reached into a high cabinet for a serving plate.

After all the prep work was done, he was more than ready to escape to a little fresh air and sanity.

"Do you have everything you need?" she asked.

"Looks like."

"I'll send the kids and puppies to the backyard to keep you company while I'm in here finishing up."

"I don't mind being on my own."

She sent him a searching look, and it took him a moment to realize what he'd said—and that he *was* beginning to mind it very much.

"I'll send them back," she said again.

The barbecue was a good, sturdy model he remembered using a time or two when they would come up and share a meal with Annabelle.

True to her word, Lucy sent the kids and puppies to the patio just as he was setting his steak on the grill, which took a few minutes longer than the thinner chicken breasts. The hot dogs only took about a second on the flames.

By the time he was done grilling, the sun had slid behind the mountains, though it wouldn't be full dark for another hour. With the sunset, though, the temperatures immediately began to drop so Lucy set the big kitchen table for their meal.

Dinner was noisy, chaotic, delicious—and the most enjoyable evening he'd had in a long time. Lucy, Crystal and Faith talked about books while Carter interjected the occasional knock-knock joke.

"How's the house coming?" he asked during one

of the rare conversational lulls, when everyone was nearly finished eating.

"Ugh. Don't remind us," Lucy's sister said with a groan. "We have hauled so much stuff out of here and we have tons more to do."

"Big house, big job."

"You're telling me," Crystal said.

"Everything seems to be moving along nicely. Dylan and Sam Delgado are coming next week to do a little work for me. Fortunately, the structural changes we need are minor. Bumping a wall out here, expanding a closet there. Genevieve and I have just about agreed on the design schemes for most of the bedrooms."

"Hey, maybe Brendan can help us in the green bedroom," Crystal suggested.

Lucy gave him a speculative look. "You know, that's not a bad idea," she said.

"Help you with what in the green bedroom?" he asked, not a little uneasy at that look.

"It's a job that takes someone with muscle."

"I've got a couple."

She cast him a sidelong look, and he thought he saw a hint of color brushing her cheekbones.

"Yes. Yes, you do." She cleared her throat. "I need somebody to help me move a bed. It's in a room that was hardly ever used. I think Annabelle just tossed all the furniture in there she didn't want to throw away, and one of the beds is blocking access to a closet. We need to clean out said closet but, hard as we tried, we couldn't budge the thing this afternoon."

"I can try as soon as we're done."

"I'm finished now," Faith said. "That was really good, Aunt Lucy."

"Thank you, honey, but your dad did most of the work."

"Thanks, Dad," she said with her sweet smile.

"You're welcome."

"Can I have another hot dog?" Carter asked.

"You already had two, kid," Brendan said. "I didn't grill any more."

His son's face fell.

"Oh, wait. I have dessert," he suddenly remembered. He rose and headed to the counter where he'd left the reusable grocery bag he had brought from his house. He reached inside and pulled out the pie tin and carried it back to the table.

"Now *that* is an impressive trick." Lucy grinned. "How can I get a magic pie bag?"

"Sorry, but you have to have a father like mine who drops them off at your house for no discernible reason."

Crystal snorted. "Like *that's* ever going to happen."

Lucy and Crystal shared a rueful look, and he felt a wave of sympathy for them. Really, he felt bad for everyone who didn't have a father like Dermot.

"This is one of Pop's specialties. Caramel apple."

"Ooh, that sounds delicious," Crystal said.

He sliced pieces for everyone. Lucy ate hers with a deep enjoyment he found both amusing and uncomfortably arousing.

He was entirely too aware of every movement she made, each breath, each swallow. How was he supposed to handle this?

"Look at how cute the puppies look," Faith exclaimed when they were nearly done with the pie. "They're sleeping."

The puppies were cuddled together, chin to rump.

"We should probably feed Max again," Crystal said.

Lucy checked the clock above the stove. "You're right. It's about time."

"The kids and I can do that and clear up in here," Crystal said. "You two go see if you can move the bed."

Okay, his imagination went off into all kinds of twisting directions with that innocent statement. He tried to tamp down the images as he followed Lucy up the curving staircase of the house. Up and up they went to the very top floor of the house, an area he didn't remember ever seeing.

"These were the servants' quarters originally," she told him. "I'm going to have Dylan and Sam knock out a wall and make the four small rooms into two larger spaces."

"They'll do good work for you."

"Well, the closet has to go, so I have to clean it out before they get here."

She opened the door to a room dominated by a massive four-poster bed that was entirely too large for the space. It wasn't completely blocking the closet, just limiting access, so the door wouldn't open all the way.

"Wow. That's a big bed."

"I love it and want to use it in here once we have a room of the proper proportions. If you can help me move it three or four inches to the left, that should be enough to open the door."

He figured it wouldn't be that tough, but on his first try, the thing wouldn't budge.

"Wow! What's it made of? Lead? Don't be surprised one day if it falls through all three floors below while you're entertaining guests in the parlor."

"Don't even joke about that!" she exclaimed with an

expression of horror at the very idea. "With my luck, it would probably fall just as my father walked in and sat down."

"I guess you and your dad don't have the greatest of relationships," he said, pausing the muscle-straining work of moving the bed to take advantage of the opening she had just handed him.

"That's a mild way of putting it, yes."

"So you came to live with Annabelle when you were in high school. Where did your mom fit into the picture?"

She looked startled by the question, as if she hadn't expected it, but she slumped against the bed and seemed to choose her words carefully. "She…wasn't well through much of my childhood. Looking back, I think she was clinically depressed and self-medicated with alcohol and drugs and anything else that made her forget her pain a little. That's a little easier to see when you're thirty-one than it is when you're twelve."

"I'm sorry."

She shrugged. "Everybody's got stuff, don't they? My dad got tired of it and left us when I was about thirteen and moved in with Pam—that's Crystal's mom—about five minutes later. She was twenty-one, not all that much older than I was. I lived with my mom but the situation there got worse and worse. She took one too many valiums a couple years later, and they couldn't get her stomach pumped in time, so I moved in with my dad and Pam."

He knew some of this. Jessie had told him Lucy had had a rough break in the parent department—but he had also had the impression Jess wasn't completely sympathetic to her cousin.

Lucy still had her father, a wealthy and successful attorney, while Jess's dad had left her and her mother destitute when he died unexpectedly, which is why she and her mother had come to Iris House to live with Annabelle.

"So you rebelled."

"In just about every conceivable way," she said, gazing up at the old-fashioned brass chandelier in the room. "The last thing Pam wanted to deal with was a moody, unpredictable, troublemaker of a stepdaughter, so one day my dad brought me here to Annabelle. She gave me a home and a stable center."

"Just like you are giving Crystal."

She made a face. "Except Annabelle knew what she was doing while I'm completely floundering."

He wasn't sure how she could be so confident about some things but so self-deprecating about others. He supposed it was part of what made her such a fascinating puzzle.

"From my perspective, you're doing okay. Your sister seemed happy enough tonight. Very different, in fact, from that day at the grocery store, when she looked like the chip on her shoulder was going to fall off and crush half of downtown. You're doing fine," he said. "Better than fine. Give yourself a break, for once, why don't you?"

She raised an eyebrow. "You know, I do believe that's the nicest thing you've ever said to me."

Yeah, probably. He hadn't been exactly warm to her over the years when he knew how much she disliked him.

"Don't let it freak you out. I'm sure I'll go back to being an ass as soon as we leave the room."

"I don't think you're an ass," she said, her voice low. "No?"

She shook her head slightly, that tantalizing brush of color on her cheekbones again. She looked at him, eyes huge and impossibly green, and he saw that mysterious *something* in her expression again, there and then gone again.

It wasn't quite an invitation, more like a simple acknowledgment of the currents simmering between them. They were alone with that awareness of each other in a small room dominated by a huge bed. The realization sent heat surging through him and a deep aching hunger.

She swallowed and that color rose higher. He saw a wild little pulse flare in her throat suddenly, and with a sense of inevitability, he reached a thumb out to cover it and lowered his mouth to hers.

CHAPTER FIFTEEN

LUCY CAUGHT HER breath, frozen in place as his mouth brushed against hers once then twice, ever so gently.

Oh. Oh, yes.

Some part of her had been waiting in glittery anticipation for exactly this since the instant she had looked up from her spot on the grass with Crystal to see Brendan riding past with the children earlier.

All evening long, her mind had been whirling, replaying their last heady kiss over and over until she couldn't seem to think about anything else.

It seemed inevitable, somehow, as if both of them had only been preparing for this moment.

Those first soft kisses were only a teasing prelude. He came back for more, his mouth firm and insistent this time, and she sighed as he deepened the kiss, tugging her against him.

She curled her fingers against his chest, soaking in the impact of all those hard muscles.

He smelled delicious—some kind of outdoorsy soap with notes of sage and leather and some other indefinable masculine scent she guessed was simply him. She wanted to bury her face in the crook of his neck and just inhale.

That would mean sliding her mouth away from his,

however, and why in the world would she do that, when his kiss tasted even better than he smelled?

He slid his tongue along hers and everything inside her shivered with delight.

She wrapped her arms around his neck to pull him closer, and he took that as an invitation to lower her onto the bed as he continued those fierce kisses that consumed all reason.

She didn't want this moment to ever end. Why couldn't they just lock the door and stay right here, while the old house settled around them and dust motes floated in the air?

They couldn't. Some tiny bit of common sense tried to push itself to the forefront of her mind, but she was a little busy at the moment and didn't pay it much mind.

"Lucy," he murmured, his voice ragged and sexy as his hand teased her skin just above her hip bone.

How could she have ever thought him taciturn, distant, cold? He was all fire and flame, heat and hunger. She kissed him, her tongue tangling with his as a slow, steady ache burned through her.

That little corner of her mind picked up a distant sound, the slam of a door somewhere several floors below them, but it seemed to echo through her head.

They couldn't do this. Not here. Not now.

Crystal was down there with two children and two puppies and any moment now, any one of them might decide to come up here to see what was taking them so long to, um, move a bed.

It was the hardest thing she had ever done, but she finally wrenched her mouth away. "Brendan. You have to stop."

He stared at her, and the hazy arousal in his gaze sent little sparks shooting through her. "What?"

"The kids," she murmured. "Crystal. They're going to come looking for us in a minute."

As she watched, the arousal on his expression slowly gave way to reality. After a moment, he eased away from her and sat on the edge of the bed, his shoulders tense and his expression twisted into one of stunned disbelief.

"What is *wrong* with me?" he growled. "I touch you and I completely lose control."

She sat up, as well, rearranging clothing and trying hard to return her breathing to something that didn't sound as if she'd just finished a half marathon into the mountains.

"Losing control means something's wrong with you?"

His jaw flexed. "With you? Yes. Isn't this a little weird to you? The way we ignite when we're together?"

"Weird?"

"Yeah. You were Jess's cousin. Her best friend. You loved her."

Of all the things she might have expected him to say, that hadn't been on the list. He was upset because of her relationship with Jessica? If she hadn't been Jess's friend, would he be more enthusiastic about this heat between them?

"Both of us loved her," she said, choosing her words carefully. "Nothing will ever change that. She's inside each of us. Why does that necessarily mean it's weird if we are, er, attracted to each other? Especially considering we had a little history together before you ever met Jess?"

He stared at her and for one terrible instant, she wondered if he had forgotten. In all the years since, they had never referred to it. She had never seen the point in telling Jessie about it and she had to wonder if Brendan ever had.

How humiliating would it be if he didn't know what on earth she was talking about?

But after a moment, he shrugged. "We shared one night. One kiss."

Did she tell him that for her, that one kiss had always been simmering between them? "A pretty intense kiss," she finally said. "After which you completely brushed me off and started dating my best friend."

"Is that why you despised me? Why you told Jess she could do better than a washed-up jock with more muscles than brains?"

She gaped at him and then felt color soak her cheeks as she remembered that heated conversation with Jess on the eve of their wedding, when she had tried one last time to convince her not to marry a man Lucy worried would just break Jessie's heart. Like he had broken her own.

"She told you that?"

"Why shouldn't she? You said it, didn't you?"

"Ye-es," she said slowly, wishing she could sneak into that closet and just slam the door closed behind her so she didn't have to face him right now.

Wasn't it bad enough that she couldn't seem to control herself around the man? Now he had to dredge up some of her most embarrassing moments and toss them out into the middle of the room between them.

"Okay, I admit, I was a…a jerk after you and Jess started dating. My feelings were hurt, okay? I liked you. A lot. I know we only spent the one evening together, but I'd never really dated anybody seriously, especially not…somebody like you."

"Somebody like me? You mean a big dumb jock?"

She felt uncomfortably exposed, all her insecurities laid bare in front of him.

"You were never that. You were…gorgeous and fun and sweet. Or at least I thought so. This is corny, but it felt like you saw me in a way that no one else ever had. I don't know how else to describe it, I just know I liked you a lot and I wanted to see where things between us might go."

She shrugged, inordinately fascinated with the chevron pattern of the parquet floor. "But you never called me and the next thing I know, Jess starts bubbling over about the great guy she was seeing. Imagine how I felt when the great guy turns out to be you. It stung my pride more than a little. My best friend and the first guy I ever really liked seriously. It didn't bring out the best in me. I wanted to think you were just a jerk who went around breaking as many hearts as you could."

"That wasn't who I was. You know that, right? You were an…anomaly."

"An anomaly."

"And I was the jerk," he muttered with a pained expression. "I should have called you to explain, especially after I found out you were Jessie's friend."

"What would you have explained?" she asked, suddenly desperate to know he hadn't set out to break her heart just as a joke or something.

He sighed. "This is really awkward, Lucy."

"You're telling me," she muttered.

"Okay. Here it is. I've always had this idea of what

I wanted out of life. What my parents had. After my mom died, I guess I idealized my childhood probably more than I should have. What I had as a kid seemed... perfect to me. After I left the NFL, all I could think about was having the same thing. Living in Hope's Crossing, settling down, raising a couple of kids here."

"White picket fence and all."

"Something like that." He made a face. "I liked you, too, for what it's worth. I wasn't just messing around. But that night, as I listened to you talk about your goals and your dreams and all the hills you wanted to conquer, I couldn't quite make those two pictures gel in my mind. I figured it wasn't worth wasting either of our time when we wanted different things and we'd only shared a few kisses."

"And then you met Jess," she said quietly. "And she *did* want that white picket fence and everything that came with it."

"Or at least she said she did," he said darkly.

"Why would you say that?"

He eased away and went to sit on the window ledge. "Do you remember when she was pregnant with Faith and came up to Seattle for a week?"

She smiled at the memory, even as her heart ached a little. "We had a great time. We went to every single baby clothing boutique in three counties, bought way too much, ate even more, stayed up all night and laughed."

His jaw tightened. "After she came home, she cried herself to sleep for the first three nights she was back, and she could barely look at me."

Lucy stared. "You think she was unhappy being married to you?"

"I think some part of her saw you in your element, this exciting world filled with travel to exotic places, a challenging career, interesting friends, while she was now pregnant and facing a lifetime stuck in the same small town. All she talked about was the shopping, the fantastic restaurants, the parties you went to."

That was so far removed from the long, hard corporate days that made up her usual life in Seattle that she almost laughed.

"The truth is," she said, with stark, uncomfortable honesty, "maybe I went a little over-the-top on the trip trying to prove to her what a perfect life I had created for myself. Maybe I wanted her to be envious of *me,* for a change."

She wanted to recall the revealing words as soon as she spoke them, especially after he gave her a searching look that made her flush.

"I'm pretty sure it worked. She was envious of you and your success. She didn't begrudge it. I think she just contrasted it to her world of facing dirty diapers and the terrible twos and oatmeal ground into the carpet. Even after that, whenever she talked to you, she would be in a difficult mood for at least a day or two before she snapped out of it."

No wonder he resented her, if he blamed her for causing Jessie even a moment's discontent.

She meant what she said to him, *she* had always been the one envying her cousin her great marriage, adorable children, a community that cherished her.

"She loved you, Brendan, with her whole heart. She loved you, she loved the kids, she loved your life together here in Hope's Crossing."

"I know she did," he said, his voice low. "That doesn't mean she didn't have regrets."

The ache in his voice arrowed straight to her heart. She couldn't imagine how difficult it would be to love someone so deeply and then lose her. Second-guessing his wife's happiness and commitment to the life they had created together was a futile, heartbreaking exercise, and she couldn't bear knowing she might have contributed to some of his uncertainty out of some stupid effort to protect her ego.

"Regret and curiosity are not at all the same thing, Brendan. Here's the thing about women. Sometimes even when we have everything we ever dreamed, we wonder about the road we didn't take, the choice we didn't make. We wonder who we might have become, even when we absolutely, positively would still make the same choices again, a hundred times over. If Jess ever seemed unhappy, I'm sure it was only for a moment and only because she was curious about the person she might have been if her life had gone in a different direction. It wasn't because she ever regretted loving you."

He gazed at her and she wondered what he was thinking. Why did the man have to be so blasted inscrutable?

"And just so you know," she was compelled to add, "I believe Jess made the best possible choice with her life. I'm the one who always envied her."

Okay, that was enough true confession for this evening's program. She jumped off the bed. "We'd better go check on the kids. Thanks for helping me move the bed and for…everything."

She hurried from the room before he could answer.

"I'M GOING TO have to take a break pretty soon or my arm is going to fall off," Crystal declared.

A week later, the two of them were painting one of the bedrooms on the second floor. This one was a lovely soft lavender that would look magnificent with the deep oak moldings and the pale marble fireplace mantel.

"Let's see if we can finish this wall and then we'll wrap things up for the day. Maybe we can take a walk or something. It looks like a gorgeous evening out there."

Between the puppy, Crystal's schoolwork and the fast-progressing work on Iris House, they had been insanely busy the past week, but everything was moving along nicely.

"We should have another barbecue," Crystal said. "That was fun last week, and Max has only played with Daisy one time, when we met the kids and their babysitter at the park."

Lucy forced a smile, even though her insides felt a little hollow every time she thought about Brendan and the last time she had seen him. That fierce, intense kiss haunted her every time she walked into that bedroom—okay, let's face it, every time she closed her eyes—and the conversation afterward had been even more troubling.

She had basically told him that she'd been crushing on him for years, that she had been cold to him all this time because her feelings had been hurt that he'd picked her best friend over her.

She was such an idiot.

She hadn't seen him in a week, so he obviously had

been too embarrassed to face her after that humiliating revelation.

The playdate with the kids and their kindly babysitter had been a coincidental thing that had only come about after Crystal happened to be walking past their house with Max and had bumped into Faith and Carter, out walking Daisy.

"There. That's it for me," she said as she set down the cutting brush Genevieve had taught her to use to get a clean, crisp line between colors.

"I'll be done with the rolling in a minute, then I'm *so* ready to be done."

She was just cleaning off her brush in the adjacent bathroom when she heard the chime of the doorbell.

"I'll get it," Lucy said. "It's probably Genevieve. She mentioned she was going to drop off the curtains she sewed for this room today so we can hang them as soon as we're done painting. You stay here. I'll grab it."

The puppy, chunky and adorable, yipped when she passed the tall-sided box where they had restrained him while they painted.

"You're probably due to go out, aren't you?" Max wasn't anywhere close to being trained but they were doing their best to reinforce the basic concept with him.

She scooped him up and headed for the door and down the stairs as the doorbell rang again.

"I'm coming," she called.

A quick glance in the ornately carved mirror hanging in the front hall revealed the damages were worse than she imagined. Her hair was falling from its braid and she had a small smear of lavender paint on her cheekbone. She scrubbed at it with the rag from her back pocket, which left her cheek reddened but at least removed the paint.

She was a far cry from the polished, perfectly groomed professional who rushed out the door every morning with a go-cup in one hand and a laptop case in the other.

At random moments, she missed a few things from her previous life but mostly she was too busy to think about it.

The bell rang a third time—Genevieve wasn't always the most patient of people—and she hastily headed over and yanked it open. "Sorry. We're in the middle of painting the lavender room…"

The words caught in her throat, and her heart did a happy little jump when she realized her visitor wasn't her designer and friend after all, but the big, gorgeous fire chief of Hope's Crossing.

She drew in a breath, telling her heart to simmer down. That scene upstairs seemed burned in her brain suddenly, and she knew her face must be suddenly bright red.

"Brendan. Hi. This is a surprise."

Too embarrassed to meet his gaze, she focused on his left earlobe—which, naturally, was perfectly shaped, just like the rest of him. If an earlobe could be perfectly shaped, anyway.

"Hi," he said, his voice gruff.

"Hi, Aunt Lucy!"

Ah. Here was a person she wasn't afraid to face. She had been so busy stewing in her own embarrassment and trying to avoid making direct eye contact with Brendan, she hadn't noticed Carter standing next to his father.

"Why, if it isn't my favorite almost-six-year-old!"

"I know. That's me."

She smiled and leaned down for a kiss, deeply grateful for the buffer.

"Come in. Excuse the mess. We're in renovation mode."

"Looks like you've had a busy week."

"Yes. Things are progressing nicely. Can I get you guys something? I've got soda, juice or water."

He shook his head, but Carter tugged her hand eagerly. "Hey, can I have a juice box?"

"Sure, kiddo. You know where they are, right? Same place as last time."

"Yep."

He left, and she suddenly realized what a strategic error that had been as she and Brendan were now alone in the foyer except for one four-pound puppy.

"Wow. Max is growing. Hey, dude."

He reached out to take the puppy from her. Their fingers brushed as she handed Max over, and she felt a corresponding tug in her gut. It seemed grossly unfair that a simple touch could leave her insides quivering.

He didn't help matters when he held Max to eye level and started talking to him, nonsense about how much he was growing and how he hoped Max was behaving himself and using good manners.

Unfair, she thought again. How on earth was any woman supposed to resist a big, tough firefighter who could talk sweetly to a tiny puffball of a puppy—and even more sweetly to his children?

"How's Daisy?" she asked.

"Growing a ton. Just like Max. Her new favorite

game is hide-and-seek. She loves to hide under the sofa and jump out and scare you."

"You're so keeping her, aren't you?"

He made a face. "You knew we were goners from the beginning. How can I rip her out of my kids' arms?"

"Softie."

"The writing was on the wall for us the minute Faith held her."

She relaxed enough to smile a little at his disgruntled tone, which didn't fool her for a second. "Yeah. Same here. Crystal is in love. She's working hard on her parents to convince them if they let her keep Max when she goes back home, she'll never cause them another moment's grief."

"She still leaving this week? This is the end of her two-week's grace period, isn't it?"

"I'm a sucker for puppies *and* teenage girls, apparently. Things have been going so well, I've agreed to let her stay another few weeks. We'll see what happens. So far, everything seems to be working out."

"Have you heard they found the guy who dumped the puppies?"

"No," she exclaimed.

"Chief McKnight probably hasn't had a chance to call you yet. He updated me this morning. Turns out, he traced evidence he found on the box markings to an idiot twenty-year-old half-stoned ski bum, Andy Barfuss, who left town the day before we found the puppies. It turns out, Max and Daisy's mother was a stray Andy's roommate had been taking care of over the winter. When the roommate took off after the ski season ended, he dumped the responsibility on Andy, who claims the mother was run over by a car the night before he was supposed to leave for another job at some resort up in Jackson Hole. He says he was desperate and didn't know what else to do."

"So he just dumped them in a garbage bin? It never occurred to him to call the Humane Society?"

"He figured they would die, anyway, without their mother. I get the impression from Riley that Barfuss is a few peas short of a casserole."

"I guess it was lucky we found the puppies when we did."

"For them, anyway," he muttered, not fooling her for a moment. He might complain about having a dog, but she couldn't see anything but affection as he held Max—and this puppy wasn't even the one his children adored most.

"I was just going to take him out," she said.

"I'll do it," he said, and headed out the front door just as Carter returned from the kitchen poking the straw through the top of his juice box.

"I found an apple one. That's my favorite."

"Good job."

"Hey, where's my dad?"

She pointed out the door. "He took Max out to the grass."

"Oh."

The boy headed out onto the porch. "Did you give it to her, Dad?" he called to his father, who stood on a little patch of grass waiting for Max, who seemed to be more interested in sniffing Brendan's shoes than taking care of business.

"No. That was your job, remember? I guess you got distracted by Lucy's goodies."

Brendan aimed a quick look in her direction then

glanced away again, making her wonder if he was also distracted by her…goodies.

"You have it, though, right?" Carter pressed, heading down the steps. Lucy followed out of curiosity.

"Right here." Brendan pulled an envelope out of the breast pocket of his shirt and handed it to Carter, who in turn delivered it to Lucy with an elaborate flourish.

"Wow. What's this?"

"It's an invitation! I want you to come to my party!" Carter beamed at her.

"A party? Wow! What kind of party?"

"Birthday, silly! In five more days, I'm going to be six years old. And guess what? I'm having two parties. One is just my friends. We're having pizza and going swimming."

"That sounds fun, but I might have to go buy a new swimsuit."

He giggled. "You can come swimming if you want to. It's at the recreation center on Saturday. Then Sunday night, on my real birthday, we're having a party at Grandpop Caine's house, and my dad said I could invite you and Crystal if I wanted. We're having hot dogs and cake and chocolate ice cream."

"Three of my very favorite things. Thank you! We would be honored to celebrate your birthday with you."

"Does that mean you'll come?"

"Yes. We'll be there."

"You can bring Max, too. He and Daisy can play with Tucker and Tina. That's my uncle Andrew's dog."

"Are they having their own party?"

"It's a dog party. A big dog party!" Carter chortled. "I love that book. I always laugh so hard at the page with all the dogs in the tree wearing funny hats."

She had read him the classic *Big Dog...Little Dog* one of the times she had stayed with the children and remembered that particular laugh-inducing page.

"What can we bring?"

"A present," Carter said promptly. "A good one. I would really like a LEGO Star Wars set. The one with the real X-wing fighter."

"Carter," Brendan chided, rolling his eyes—at the specificity or the cupidity, she wasn't sure.

"I'll see what I can do."

"You don't have to bring a present. Just yourselves," Brendan said pointedly. "Isn't that right, Car?"

When his son was disgruntled, he looked remarkably like his father. "I guess," he said in a long-suffering voice. "Hey, can I tell Crystal about the party?"

"She would love to hear about it, I'm sure. We're painting one of the bedrooms upstairs. Follow the sound of the music to find her."

He rushed off with his usual energy, leaving her and Brendan alone with the puppy, who was now exploring the wonders of a dandelion puff.

"You don't really have to get him a LEGO set," Brendan said, his voice embarrassed. "Man. The kid is ruthless."

"He's just a kid. You know I think he's adorable, right?"

"That's part of the problem. Everyone thinks he's adorable."

"I'm sure it's a curse," she said with a smile. "Funny, this must be my day for invitations."

"Oh?"

"I'm officially invited to a bridal shower being held

by Claire McKnight and Katherine Thorne for Genevieve and Charlotte. It's a week from Friday."

He looked faintly amused. "Good luck with that one."

"Oh, no. What am I in for? With those two as hostesses, I figured it would be tasteful and safe. No male strippers or condoms on cucumbers."

"Good Lord, no."

She had to smile a little at his horrified expression. "Then why wish me luck?"

"They're just a fairly terrifying group of women as a whole. I do my best to stay out of their way. Oh, and go along with whatever they ask me. It's safer that way."

She had the rather sobering realization that she found Brendan every bit as adorable as his son.

She was developing feelings for him, she realized. Seeing him again after a week made her realize how very much she had missed him. This was far more complex and layered than the slightly ridiculous crush she'd had on him so long ago.

She pushed away the shock of that as Crystal walked outside with Carter's hand in hers.

"I understand someone's having a birthday party next weekend. And he apparently would like a Matchbox pickup truck, red not blue. If it's not too much trouble, anyway."

"Carter!" Brendan's long-suffering tone made her laugh and want to kiss both of them.

"What?" his son said, genuinely confused.

"You have to admire a guy who knows what he wants and isn't afraid to let people know," Crystal said.

Lucy wondered why that made a muscle flex in Brendan's jaw.

"Now that we've raided your juice boxes and left the birthday wish list, I guess our work here is done," he said. "Come on, kid. Let's go before you ask for a green pony with purple polka dots."

"Ponies don't have polka dots, Dad," Carter said. "But I wouldn't mind having a regular one. A black one, though. Not green."

"See you next week," Brendan said.

She knew perfectly well that shouldn't fill her with this giddy sense of anticipation.

CHAPTER SIXTEEN

WHEN HIS ENTIRE family gathered, the volume usually shook the walls of Dermot's big rambling house on Winterberry Road. This time, most of the party had moved outside to take advantage of the lovely May Sunday afternoon.

Five of his six siblings were there—even Aidan, much to his shock. He hadn't known his brother was flying in from the Bay Area until they pulled into Pop's driveway and found him driving up in the car he kept garaged at the Hope's Crossing airport for his frequent trips home.

Even when a guy had his own private jet, it was kind of a big deal for him to fly over a thousand miles for a nephew's birthday party.

Of his six siblings, only Jamie hadn't made it, but since he was currently stationed in Alaska, that was completely understandable.

Brendan stood at the kitchen sink wishing he was outside where all the men seemed to be gathered around the grassy area off the patio to listen to Charlotte's fiancé, Smokin' Hot Spence Gregory, give batting tips to his nephews.

For once, it was an unusually stereotypical gender division in the kitchen, with all the men outside and the women—and him—in the kitchen.

The Caine family was far from a chauvinistic patriarchy, where the women always cooked the meal and the men sat around watching sports and drinking beer.

Pop was usually the one running things in his kitchen and his big mantra was, *if you don't work, you don't eat.*

Still, Brendan was happy to see him out there in the middle of the baseball chatter. Pop didn't take enough time to relax.

He could see Faith sitting in the grass not far away with Daisy on her lap and Dylan's big coonhound, Tucker, bigger than she was, snuggled up against her leg. The birthday boy, Carter, was right in the middle of the action, of course, running from group to group.

He would much rather be out there in the soft evening sunlight than stuck here in the kitchen prepping his famous burgers, heavy on the diced onion and the Worcestershire sauce.

That would teach him not to volunteer to take care of the grilling duties for the party, though he imagined once he actually started things up he would have any number of volunteers standing around with tongs, trying to pretend they were helping.

For now, instead of talking baseball, he had to listen to Charlotte and Genevieve and his sisters-in-law Erin and Allison discuss flowers and dresses and other wedding-related topics.

"Only six weeks. Are you both just going crazy?" Erin asked. "I remember how stressful that last month was leading up to our wedding."

"I can't tell you how many times I wailed to Patrick that I just wanted to jump in the car and run to Lake Tahoe and be done with the whole thing," Allison said.

"I'm not nervous at all," Charlotte said. "But then, Spence happens to be very, very good at stress relief."

The women all gave throaty, knowing laughs that made Brendan clear his own throat.

"I'm still here, just in case you all forgot."

Damn, he missed, er, stress relief.

"Sorry," Charlotte said with a grin, looking not at all repentant.

He didn't begrudge her joy. Charlotte deserved a great guy like Spence, who plainly adored her. It was about time she found somebody worthy of her, and he knew she had loved Spence most of her life.

As for Genevieve, he could admit now that he had been wary when Dylan started seeing her, worried his brother was only setting himself up for more pain in a lifetime that had already held too much, but it only took a few weeks for him to want to pick up Genevieve and smooch her right on her perfectly made-up lips for somehow working a miracle and helping Dylan begin to heal his battle scars.

She might have been the pampered princess daughter of the Hope's Crossing mayor, who had spent the past two years hobnobbing with the hoity-toity in Paris, but somehow she fit right in with the rest of the crazy Caines.

Dylan loved her, and she adored him right back, and that was all Brendan cared about.

"I thought you and Carter invited guests," Charlotte said.

He glanced at the clock above the refrigerator. The invitation had been for a half hour earlier. Yeah, he was running behind on the burgers and needed to step it up to keep the hungry masses happy.

"I guess Lucy and Crystal couldn't make it," he said. He told himself the disappointment in his gut was only for Carter, whose feelings would be hurt.

"Maybe they're just running late," Genevieve offered. "I can text her and see."

He didn't need his sisters-in-law—prospective or otherwise—to feel as if they had to jump in, nor did he want Lucy to feel pressured in any way to come if something else had come up.

"No. It's not necessary," he began, but Genevieve had already pulled out her phone.

Before she could finish the text, the doorbell ring.

"That's so funny!" Gen exclaimed. "I bet that's her."

"I'll get it!" Peyton Gregory, Spence's daughter, called out from the living room, where she was hanging out with Ava and Maggie, Patrick's daughters.

A moment later, he heard Lucy's voice as she and Crystal talked to the girls. Something churned inside him, something warm and sweet.

When she walked into the kitchen carrying a deli bag and looking lovely and casual in jeans, a white cotton shirt and chunky multicolored beads, the strange feeling bubbled up, making his chest feel tight with something.

Happiness.

It had been so long since he'd felt truly happy, it took a moment for the feeling to register.

He was happy.

Seeing her there with her hair up in a loose, casual style, her toes peeking out of strappy sandals and her cheekbones edged with an appealing pink filled him with bright, incandescent joy.

"Hi," she said, sounding breathless.

Her gaze met his and he wondered how the hell he had stayed away from her for a week. He was crazy. He should have been up at Iris House every single spare minute.

He suddenly remembered that kiss—the strawberries-and-cream taste of her, the silky slide of her hair through his fingers, the luxurious softness of her skin.

Raw craving left his knees weak. How could he get all these women out of the kitchen *now* so he could do it again? Would an impromptu fire drill do the trick? Surely he had the authority for that...

Her gaze met his. For long moments, they just gazed at each other while the color on her cheekbones seemed to rise.

"Sorry we're late. It's all my fault." Crystal had followed her sister, and he was in such a bad way, he hadn't even noticed.

Lucy seemed to gather herself. "It's not," she protested, her voice a little husky. "I was the one who decided to go into Denver today to find a certain LEGO set for a certain young man's birthday present."

"But I was the one who wanted to stop and pick up a few things at my house, where we ended up stuck talking to my parents for two hours."

"Neither one of us had anything to do with the flat tire, though."

"You had a flat tire?" Genevieve asked, wide-eyed. "Did you call roadside assistance?"

"No. I taught Crystal how to change it the old-fashioned way, just like Annabelle taught me."

He had to smile at the pride in her voice. Out of the corner of his gaze he caught Charlotte looking at him with surprise and spotted the speculative look she sent back to Lucy.

"You're here now," Charlotte said. "That's the important thing. Anyway, we haven't eaten yet. Bren is still throwing together the hamburger patties while he listens to all our boring chatter about caterers and flowers and such."

"And our favorite stress relief," Genevieve added cheerfully, which made all the women laugh.

"I'm prone to Hatha Yoga," Lucy offered. "Something about the downward-facing dog just makes me completely loose."

"An oldie but a goodie," Erin said with a straight face, which sent all the women busting up again.

Brendan could feel his face heat and was really grateful Lucy didn't know the subtext of the conversation.

"Okay, I think I'm done here," he said. In more ways than one. "I'm just going to check on the coals to see if they're ready yet. I'm glad you made it, Lucy. Carter will be happy to see you."

He told himself his son's happiness was the important thing—and that he didn't have any business feeling the same.

He wasn't completely surprised that Lucy managed to charm his entire family within a few moments of walking outside with the other women.

His father obviously already had a soft spot for her, but within minutes, Drew and Patrick were deep in conversation with her, though he was too far away to hear the subject matter.

He had noticed the skill of hers before, something

he wasn't sure she fully recognized. He got the impression from a few things she'd said to him that she considered herself fairly humorless, all-business. She was certainly focused and driven, but she also had the rare ability to fit into any situation and make whomever she was talking to feel as if he had her undivided attention.

"Did I ever tell you how Jamie and I both tried to hit on Lucy at your wedding?"

He glanced over at Dylan, who had ambled over to the barbecue grill so he could pretend to help him. This was a very different version of his brother than the man he had been six months ago, mostly because of Genevieve Beaumont and her stubbornness.

He was glad his brother had lost all those hard edges, but he still didn't think he wanted to hear the story Dylan was obviously itching to tell. "I missed that, I guess. I was a little busy. You know. Getting married and all."

"Trust me when I tell you she was, by far, the hottest thing there. Really hot. All those long dark curls and those big green eyes. She was great-looking, and we were two just two lonely soldiers with a few days' leave, trying to get la— Um, find a little company," he amended quickly.

He suddenly wanted to punch his brother, which wouldn't be the first time. For so long after his near-death injuries in Afghanistan and then the demons he had battled after he returned, they had all walked so gingerly around Dylan, Brendan sometimes forgot what a pain in the ass he could be.

"Did you?" he asked, trying not to grit his teeth.

Dylan snorted. "With Lucy? Hell, no. Not for lack of trying, you can be sure. I believe we may have even

wagered about it." His gaze narrowed. "And if you tell
Pop that, I'll deny it to my dying breath. He would still
box our ears over it, even though it was a decade ago.
Didn't matter, though. Wager or not, neither of us had
the stuff to collect on it. She shut us both down tighter
than The Speckled Lizard on Sunday morning."

"Nice to know she has that much good taste, anyway."

Dylan shrugged. "We figured maybe she played for
the other team."

He raised an eyebrow. "Just because a woman's not
interested in a couple of horny military dogs, you think
she must be a lesbian? How arrogant is that? Maybe
she just didn't like either of you idiots."

Dylan shrugged. "That was Jamie's hypothesis, anyway, after none of his usually fail-proof helicopter-
pilot-mojo techniques yielded anything more than mild
amusement on her part. Though I do think he was a
little drunk when he said it."

"She's not a lesbian," he said, with a little more force
than he intended.

"And you know this, how?" Dylan asked with a
smirk.

Brendan's grip tightened on the tongs to keep from
reaching out and wrapping them around that smirk and
twisting it right off. "None of your damn business."

His brother only chuckled, with an affectionate
amusement that made Brendan want to growl when
he realized he'd just been played. Dylan's intention
by starting up the conversation about Lucy in the first
place had only been to dig a little and try to get a reaction out of him.

For all he knew, Dylan had made up the whole damn

thing about a competition between him and Jamie over
Lucy, just to tease out some information from him
about what she was doing here and what their relationship might be.

The man was an army ranger, trained in interrogation methods, for crying out loud. When would he ever
learn? He was thirty-six frickin' years old. At what
point in a man's life did he decide to stop letting his
brothers goad him?

Now that Dylan had the information he apparently
had been seeking, Brendan had to give his brother
points for not gloating. In fact, he seemed actually
happy. "Good for you, man. Lucy is great. I've always
thought so."

A few weeks ago, he might have argued, but he was
beginning to see things very differently. Amazing how
a man's perspective could shift so abruptly.

"She is."

"It's time, don't you think?"

"Time for what?"

Dylan brushed away a fly that had landed on his
arm above his prosthetic hand. "After I was injured,"
he said after a long moment, "I thought that was it. I
was done. Even after I started to heal, I didn't want
to. I couldn't understand why I survived that ambush
when everybody else didn't and I didn't see the point
in going on when I had lost so much."

He met Brendan's gaze, and the raw sympathy there
from his brother who had fought more wars than he
could imagine made his stomach cramp.

"I would never dare to equate losing an arm to losing
your wife," Dylan said quietly. "They're not anywhere
near the same level. But one of the things I've learned

from working at A Warrior's Hope is that whenever anybody has been through something hard—losing a spouse, losing a dream, losing an ability—there eventually comes a point when everyone comes to a crossroads. Life rolls on, no matter what. Like a convoy of Humvees, you know? You can either be squashed beneath the treads or jump on and grab tight and enjoy the ride."

Trust his brother the former army ranger to come up with a military analogy that somehow managed to fit the situation.

"Turning into quite the philosopher, aren't you?"

"I'm full of all kinds of BS. You know that by now."

Except this had been remarkably insightful of him. "I appreciate the advice," he said. "I don't want to leave you with the wrong idea, though. As great as Lucy might be, she's a friend. That's all."

The first part of that statement was absolutely true. Lucy had become a good friend these past few weeks, someone he cared about, liked talking to, enjoyed spending time with. She made him laugh and she loved his kids.

The second—that she was *only* a friend—was a little more of a hazy area when a big part of him wanted her to be much, much more.

"Just keep your options open," Dylan said. "That's all I'm saying."

To his relief, Dermot wandered over to the grill before Brendan had to come up with an answer to that.

"How are those burgers coming?" Pop asked. "We've got starving children here."

"Just about ready," he answered, and turned back to something he knew he could do well.

FOR THE REST of the evening, he couldn't seem to stop watching her.

He tried to check himself, but he would inevitably find his attention returning to her again and again.

He watched as she enjoyed her dinner, deep in conversation with Genevieve, Dylan and Drew. As she helped Charlotte light the candles on Carter's cake. As she grinned over Car's obvious delight at the presents he had basically hand-selected for himself.

A few times, she would catch him watching her, and both of them would quickly look away from each other. He felt as if he was back in junior high school.

Despite the awkwardness, the steady simmering awareness between them, it was an enjoyable evening. After dinner, he was in the middle of conversation with Charlotte and Spence about the latest group of veterans coming to A Warrior's Hope in a few days when his phone beeped.

His sister's face fell. "Oh, no. Don't tell me you have to go out on a call right in the middle of a birthday party."

He shook his head. "That's not the pager, just an alarm on my phone. I have to feed Daisy. If I can find her, anyway."

"Faith had her last I saw," Charlotte offered. "I think they were enjoying some quiet time on the porch swing."

"Thanks."

He headed through the crowd in that direction and found Faith sitting by herself on the swing.

"Hey there. You got room for one more?"

To his surprise, Faith hesitated for a moment before she finally slid over.

He sat down beside her, chains rattling with his weight. "Sure is a pretty night, isn't it? Your mom used to love these May evenings. Sweet as sugar pie, she used to called them. I think she got that saying from your Great-Aunt Annabelle."

She didn't answer, and he peered into the darkness and saw she looked even more pensive than usual.

"Something wrong, bug?"

She continued petting Daisy, who appeared to be asleep on her lap.

"Is Lucy your girlfriend?" she finally asked, completely out of the blue.

He froze, making the swing come to a rattly stop. "What? Where did that come from?"

"I heard Aunt Charlotte talking to Aunt Allison. Aunt Allison asked if the reason you're smiling again had anything to do with the pretty brunette. Aunt Charlotte said she suspected as much but didn't know for sure, and she said if you have half a brain, you won't let her move back to Seattle because she's the best thing to happen to you in two years."

Curse his daughter's photographic memory. He was pretty sure the conversation went exactly like that.

He pushed the swing off again with his foot while he took his time trying to come up with a satisfying answer for her. They moved together there in the quiet porch while the sun slid behind the mountains in a blaze of dusky yellows, reds and oranges.

"I like Lucy, but she's not my girlfriend. We're friends. That's all."

Was he going to have to offer that explanation to every single person in his family? He vowed to have a serious conversation with his son next time Carter

wanted to invite any non-Caines to the family birthday party.

"So she still might leave us and go back to Seattle?"

Was Faith worried that Lucy *was* his girlfriend or
that she *wasn't?* He had no idea. This was way too complicated a conversation for him on a sweet-as-sugar-
pie May evening.

"Maybe. I don't know the answer to that. She still
has a house there."

"She has a house here, too," Miss Logical pointed
out. "Why can't she just stay here?"

"That's going to have to be Lucy's decision. It's been
fun having her in Hope's Crossing, but you have to accept that she might be returning to her home in Seattle
sometime. Or she might take a job somewhere else.
Whatever happens, you know you can still Skype her
and email and talk on the phone as much as you want."

Daisy woke up and started making her hungry little
snuffly noise. Faith lifted her up and rubbed noses with
the puppy. "Aunt Charlotte told Aunt Allison that you
shouldn't let her leave."

"I can't control that, honey, no matter what your
aunts say." Apparently he would have to talk with the
women of his family, too.

"You just don't want to," she accused.

That wasn't necessarily true. He didn't want Lucy to
leave, he suddenly realized. Just thinking about it left
a sour taste in his mouth, which made him uneasy. It
shouldn't matter to him what she did, should it?

How had everything changed so drastically?

And what the hell was he supposed to do with this
ball of nerves that seemed to have burst in his gut?

"It's not up to me, Faith. Lucy makes her own decisions."

"You *have* been smiling more since she came here," she said in a matter-of-fact tone. "I like it."

"I have a lot to smile about. You. Carter. Even Daisy," he said as the dog climbed from Faith's lap to his, obviously knowing on which side her kibble was buttered.

"Lucy makes you smile, too," Faith pressed. "I've seen it."

Oh, this was turning into a mess. He didn't want Faith spinning all sorts of romantic daydreams about something that wasn't meant to be.

"Lucy is my friend. I like being with her but that's it."

Part of being a parent was taking opportunities when they presented themselves to talk about things that needed to be said, no matter how uncomfortable. He decided this was too rich a chance to pass up. "But you know, even though Lucy isn't my girlfriend right now, I probably will eventually start dating again."

Yeah. He really, really missed stress relief.

"I might even have a girlfriend someday. What would you think about that?"

She let out a sigh. "I don't know. Weird, I guess."

He remembered how he had used that very word to Lucy the other night in that bedroom at Iris House. He was beginning to wonder if maybe he was just looking for excuses not to let her any closer.

Yes, she had been Jessie's best friend. The maid of honor at their wedding. He still had a tough time working through the complexities of that. But she was so very different from Jess, it wasn't as if he could some-how substitute one for the other.

His family apparently didn't think it weird, if all the subtle conversations flowing around them were anything to go by. And if they didn't, why should he?

The fact remained that he was beginning to care about Lucy, to feel things for her he hadn't thought he would for any other woman. It scared the hell out of him, but there it was.

"It would be weird. But if she made you happy and smile and laugh like you do with Aunt Lucy," Faith went on, "I guess it would be okay. As long as she was nice to Carter. He can be a pain sometimes."

He closed his eyes, profoundly touched and humbled that his sweet little girl was worried about her brother first. "I could never like somebody who wasn't nice to you and to Carter. I promise."

Lucy certainly fit that particular qualification, he couldn't help thinking. She loved his children with all her heart.

"If you fell in love and married somebody else, you wouldn't forget Mom, would you?" Faith asked, worry in her voice.

"Never," he vowed, smoothing a hand over her hair. "I would never want to, and I couldn't, anyway. Not when you look just like her."

She nodded as the dog began to wiggle around with a little more energy.

"I think she's hungry," Faith said.

"That's exactly the reason I came to find you two. We'd better take care of that."

He stopped the swing and reached a hand to help Faith off the swing. With her hand in his, they headed into Pop's house. Just before they reached the door, Peyton raced up to them.

"Faith! There you are. We've been looking for you. We're playing Capture the Flag, and you're the fastest runner in the family. We need you on our team."

Faith looked conflicted until he smiled at her. "Go on. I can take care of Daisy here."

"Thanks, Daddy," she said, throwing her arms around him for a quick hug that brought another lump to his throat.

He missed Jessie every single day. It wasn't the raw crushing pain of the first few months after her death, more like a hollow emptiness that was never quite filled. There had been random times during the past two years when he didn't know how he would survive that aching black void.

But he had come to see that even if he'd known from the beginning he would lose her, the pain in store down the road, he wasn't sure he would have been able to make a different choice.

He had thought about that conversation with Lucy a lot, about choices made and paths followed. If not for Jessie, he wouldn't have these two amazing children, who loved him despite his many weaknesses.

How could he ever regret that?

CHAPTER SEVENTEEN

"COME ON, DAISY. Guess it's just you and me."

He carried the puppy into the kitchen and set her down on Pop's tile floor while he found the bag containing the puppy chow and bowl he'd brought along for this purpose.

The outside door opened and he turned, expecting Pop or maybe Charlotte. When he spotted Lucy walking through the door with Max tucked under her arm, his pulse ratcheted up as if he was heading out on a dicey ambulance call.

She looked fresh and sweet and so beautiful, he almost couldn't breathe.

He was *so* pathetic.

She, on the other hand, stopped dead when she saw him as if she'd just discovered a den of particularly terrifying vipers in Pop's kitchen.

"Oh. Hi."

He gave a one-fingered wave. "Looks like we're on the same feeding schedule."

"Looks like." She pulled a sandwich bag full of puppy chow out of her purse, along with a small double bowl.

He leaned a hip on the counter and watched as she filled one side of the bowl with puppy chow and then mixed a little water into it, then filled the other side with straight water.

She set Max down and the puppy went to greet Daisy first before he headed back to his food as if he were starving.

After a moment Lucy joined him at the counter to watch the puppies together. The scent of her seemed to swirl around them, sweet and enticing and Lucy.

Despite the chaos and complication she stirred in him, he still found a tender, unexpected peace in standing here with her listening to the little dogs snuffle their food.

When Daisy finished her meal, she headed over to help herself to Max's, who didn't particularly appreciate the culinary poaching and butted her away while he finished up.

As soon as he licked the last bit, the two started wrestling. Lucy smiled, watching their antics, while Brendan couldn't help watching *her*.

"I never thought I would admit this, but I'm really going to miss Max when Crystal takes him back to Denver next month," she said.

"So it's official?"

"Dad agreed. That was part of our agenda in the city today. I can't quite believe that. He would never let me have a pet when I was a kid. They were just one more thing to upset the perfect order of his world."

Her childhood seemed so very different from his own. This kitchen—and the entire house, for that matter—had always been a source of strength, support, encouragement. Thinking of her trying to grow and blossom in such a rigid household made his throat ache.

"News flash, Luce," he said after a moment. "You're

an adult now. If you want to get a dozen dogs, there's nothing to stop you except the kennel licensing laws of the great state of Colorado."

She laughed, as he had intended. "Now there's a thought for a new career direction."

"Are you looking for a new career direction? Isn't opening a bed and breakfast enough challenge for you right now?"

She gave a heavy sigh. "It was always going to be a temporary plan. I never intended to stay and run the place."

Even though he had just told Faith the same thing, that Lucy probably wasn't going to be around Hope's Crossing forever, the idea of her leaving left a cold knot lodged under his breastbone. "Then why put all this time and effort into fixing it up?"

"Excellent question." She gave a smile that appeared strained. "Right about now, I'm asking myself the same thing."

He didn't miss the way she avoided answering, but he decided not to press her about it.

"Thanks for Carter's gift. He loved it. I'm only sorry you drove all the way to Denver for it. Sometimes a boy needs to learn he can't always have what he wants."

She flashed him a searching look then looked back down at the puppies. "It was no big deal. I wanted to get it for him, and we had to talk to Robert and Pam about Max, anyway."

"Well, I'm sure he will enjoy it."

"Good. That's kind of the point of a birthday present. Thanks for inviting us to the party, by the way. Your family's great."

"It was Carter's idea," he said, then immediately wished he hadn't when she gave him a long look.

"I know. Don't worry, Brendan. I won't forget who wanted me here."

Why did he always feel like a stupid, overgrown jock around her? It was ridiculous, especially when he hadn't played football in a decade.

"What's that supposed to mean?"

She looked down at the puppies. "Just that I'm getting a definite vibe that your family is trying to read more into me coming to Carter's birthday party than either of us would like. I'm sorry. I didn't mean to complicate things for you."

"Screw my family."

She laughed roughly. "You would be lost without them, and you know it."

"Yeah. I would. But they do tend to butt in where they're not welcome. My love life—or lack thereof—is nobody's business."

He saw startled awareness flit across her expression and her gaze shifted to his mouth and then back up, that hint of alluring color on her cheekbones again. "Is that what you call this?"

"I don't know what to call it," he growled. And then he couldn't help himself. He pulled her into his arms.

REALLY? HE WAS going to kiss her *now* when his family was just outside the walls of the house and somebody could come racing into the kitchen at any moment?

At least they were out of sight of the backyard, in the corner of the kitchen that couldn't be glimpsed through the window…but why couldn't he pick a time when they could be assured of a little more privacy?

Maybe he chose these moments on purpose so that they couldn't get too carried away by these wild, churning emotions that always seemed to flare between them.

Or maybe he just couldn't help himself, bad timing or not.

As usual, he smelled delicious—of charcoal and barbecue sauce and sexy male—and within seconds of his mouth tangling with hers, she forgot all about the circumstances and the birthday party going on outside and the distinct possibility that somebody might walk in at any moment.

She wrapped her arms around his strength and heat and simply gave herself up to the moment.

"You always taste so good. Strawberries."

The raw hunger in his voice sizzled down her spine, her thighs, the hollow behind her knees.

"Oh."

Even as she sighed against his mouth and savored each sensation, she was aware of a slow, sweet tenderness seeping through her.

Along with it came a grim realization. Yes, she would miss Max, with his funny face and his curious nature. A corner of her heart would always bear a little frayed edge after she took the puppy to Denver to live with Crystal and Robert and Pam.

But huge chunks of her heart would go missing when she had to leave Brendan and the children and Hope's Crossing.

She—the woman with the reputation at NexGen as having nerves of steel—suddenly felt the ache of tears in her throat, behind her eyes.

She was so *stupid.* How could she have let things go

so far? She closed her eyes against the pain she knew was headed her way.

"We have to stop," she whispered.

He ignored her, deepening the kiss, and she gave in to the weakness for a long moment before the sound of shouts and laughter from the children's game outside wended its way through her subconscious.

"Brendan. Stop. Somebody could come in any minute and find us here. You don't want that. Trust me."

He froze for a moment, his forehead pressed against hers and his breathing ragged. After a moment he stepped back.

"The minute I touch you, it's like my brains start leaking out my ears. I can't think about anything but how good you taste and how right you feel against me."

She knew she shouldn't feel the little thrill of joy at that confession—not when the only outcome to this was heartbreak for her.

"What am I supposed to say to that? I'm sorry?"

"It's a start," he muttered.

She tried to muster a smile but couldn't quite manage it.

"I would be lying," she said, her voice barely a vibration in the silent kitchen.

He stared at her with a raw intensity that stole her breath all over again.

"Lucy, I—"

She didn't want to hear him tell her all the reasons this *thing* between them was crazy, impossible, unfathomable, so she cut him off.

"I need to take Max outside." She scooped up the little dog.

"Now?"

"Yes. He usually pees about five minutes after he eats, which was about ten minutes ago."

"Don't you think we need to talk about this?"

"What's to talk about? We go a little crazy when we touch each other. The answer to that is pretty simple. We just have to stop touching each other."

"That seems to be easier said than done."

"Most things are," she muttered, and rushed out the door with Max before he could argue with her.

She couldn't face anyone else right now when her emotions were so raw and battered so she quickly made her way to the side yard of Dermot's big house. It was quiet there and lit only by the light shining from one of the upstairs windows and a slice of moonlight from the trees. Someone had situated a little bench here to take advantage of the pretty side garden and she slid down on it and let Max down on the mower-width grass pathway that wound through the gardens.

She pressed a hand to the tightness in her chest as she watched the little puppy dance through blotches of moonlight.

She was in love with Brendan.

How could she not have realized? She had been for a long, long time, maybe since that very first night they met at The Speckled Lizard.

The whole time that he had been married to her best friend, that they had built a life together and brought two children into the world, she had loved him without even being aware of it.

What was she supposed to do now?

Max waddled over to her and started nibbling at the strap on her sandal. She picked him up and held the sweet, fuzzy little puppy to her heart that felt as fragile as crackled glass.

He didn't want her love now any more than he did a decade ago.

Oh, he might be attracted to her. *The minute I touch you, it's like my brains start leaking out my ears. I can't think about anything but how good you taste and how right you feel against me.*

She let out a shaky breath. They had heat between them, but it was bound to burn itself out quickly and then what would she be left with? Ashes and scars.

Brendan would never see her as someone with whom he could build a life. He had told her as much, that their goals and dreams were too different.

The only trouble was, she didn't know *what* she wanted anymore. Everything she thought about herself had been shaken up in the past month and tossed into the air. The pieces were still falling all around her.

She loved him.

Suddenly she couldn't seem to catch her breath and her heart started to race. No. Not now. She couldn't have a panic attack now. She sank into the grass, holding on to the little puppy and did all the relaxation techniques she could manage for several long moments.

She could handle this. She could. She had done hard things before, and she could endure another heartbreak.

What choice did she have, anyway?

She couldn't stay in Hope's Crossing. She needed more out of a relationship than the occasional hot kiss, and she knew Brendan would never allow himself to want more than that from her. He would never love her. As much as she loved the children, she just wasn't strong enough to endure watching him pick up the pieces of his life and move on with someone else.

She had suffered rejection from him before and it had taken her a long, long time to get over it—if she ever had. She couldn't put herself through it again.

Nor could she hide out back here forever, as much as she might want to. It was a party. People were going to wonder what had happened to her. Crystal would at least be wondering what had happened to her puppy.

Lucy picked up Max and headed around the house. Just as she almost reached the circle of light in the backyard from the outdoor lights strung through the trees, a dark shape headed for her.

She tensed, not ready to face Brendan just yet, but to her surprise it wasn't him, it was Aidan.

"Hey, Lucy! You're just the person I was coming to find."

"Oh?"

"Great to see you again. It's been a while." He leaned in and kissed her cheek, and she smiled, wishing she could fall for someone like Aidan. He was astonishingly great-looking, like all the Caine brothers but with more of a tamed, manicured sort of look than Brendan, less bulky in the shoulders, leaner features, those thin-rimmed glasses he wore sometimes.

On paper, the man should be perfect for her. They both lived and breathed high tech, knew many of the same people, shared a similar work ethic.

Why couldn't she feel even the tiniest of sparks for him?

"What are you doing in Hope's Crossing?" Aidan asked, with that way he had of focusing with laser-beam precision on a person. "I was assuming you were in town only for a visit, that maybe you scheduled a trip around the same time as Carter's party. But Charlotte was just telling me you've been here living at Iris House for nearly a month."

"That's right."

"You've left NexGen? I hadn't heard!"

"If by *left* you mean I was fired, then yes."

He pulled off his glasses and stared at her. "Fired? Seriously? Damn. I thought their board of directors was smarter than that."

She found his reaction rather gratifying, even though she really didn't want to have this conversation under these circumstances, while she was still reeling from discovering she was in love with his brother.

"It wasn't without reason," she finally said. "I was ultimately responsible for their latest PR nightmare. You know. The one where NexGen's ad campaign urged hackers to take their best shot at breaking through the firewalls of their new software."

"Right. At the same time the software had a security flaw big enough to fly a jumbo jet through. You didn't create the security flaw."

"No. Only the campaign that ended up making them a laughingstock in the industry."

"I had assumed some heads rolled over that. I just never expected one of those to be yours, after all the good work you've done there."

She shrugged. "One huge failure can obliterate a thousand small successes. That's the way it goes."

"So what are your plans?" he asked.

He was always on point, one of the many things she admired about him. Brass tacks with very little small talk. Aidan Caine had a reputation as someone aggressive but fair. She had enjoyed watching him take Caine Tech in amazing directions over the years.

"Right now I think I might go out and grab a piece of your father's huckleberry pie."

"You know that's not what I mean."

She sighed. "I know. The truth is, I have no idea. At the moment, I'm working to renovate Annabelle's house. I plan to turn it into a bed and breakfast."

"Going into the hospitality industry? I wouldn't have expected that from you."

"I plan to hire someone to run it for me. I know my own strengths, and I don't think I've ever been particularly, er, hospitable. But Jess and Annabelle always talked about turning the house into a small inn someday. It seems only right that I make that dream come true for them, even though they're not here to enjoy it."

He studied her for just a moment and then gave a considering sort of nod and that elusive, sexy smile of his.

"Would you have any interest in coming to work for me?"

She stared at him, not sure her emotions could take another jolt right now. "You're serious?"

"Jessica used to brag about you endlessly at every family party, long before you and I ever met. It made me curious, and I've tried to keep an eye on you over the years. I have to tell you, I've been very impressed with what I've seen and I've been planning to approach you about a career move for some time now. A guy never knows when he's going to need a marketing genius in his corner."

He had been watching her career? She wasn't quite sure how she was supposed to feel about that.

"I've got to tell you, Aidan, that's a little creepy."

He gave a full-fledged laugh that drew the attention of several others at the party—including Brendan, who turned in their direction and suddenly glowered.

"Professional curiosity only," he corrected. "No creepster intentions whatsoever."

Okay, this was turning into one of the strangest evenings of her life. She couldn't believe she was having this conversation with sexy gazillionaire tech geek Aidan Caine at Carter's sixth birthday party.

"I'm serious about the job offer. I would love to have you on board at Caine Tech."

"I got fired. You heard that part, right? I screwed up and lost NexGen millions of dollars."

"I'm completely confident your responsibility in that fiasco was minimal, and I've never been of the let's-find-a-scapegoat mentality." He pulled out a business card and handed it to her. "That's my private cell number. Think about it, Lucy. I can have my people throw together a very enticing package. The only catch is, you would have to consider relocating. I've got a new endeavor in the Portland area that might be perfect for your skill set."

"I'll think about it," she said, tucking the card into her pocket.

"Good." He gave her that full-fledged smile again that shattered geek-girl hearts around the world and returned to the party.

She stared after him for several seconds, unable to believe what had just happened.

The fact that Aidan had made this offer now, tonight, just fifteen minutes after she had reached the heartbreaking decision that she would have to leave Hope's Crossing seemed an eerie coincidence.

This could be the answer to all her worries. She could sell Iris House, move on with her life and leave Brendan to move on with his.

"Hey! Aunt Lucy!" Carter raced up to her. He had been running nonstop all evening, she could tell, his face flushed with the excitement of being the center of attention at his party. When this was over, he was going to drop like a rock.

"Hi, bud."

"Can I play with Max?"

"Sure," she answered. "Just be careful. Not too rough."

She watched him go with Max in the crook of his arm, even as her heart started to ache all over again. The job offer from Aidan might have come at a perfect time, but she had no idea how she could endure leaving Carter and Faith—and their father—behind.

CHAPTER EIGHTEEN

LUCY DECIDED THE mark of a truly great gardener was someone who coordinated her plantings so perfectly that it could still look stunning months after the gardener wasn't around, when somebody else with no green thumb took over caring for the spot.

Two weeks after Carter's party, Lucy sat on the arbor bench that had become her favorite spot at Iris House, savoring the perfection of an early June morning after her run.

A light breeze stirred the plantings, making the flower heads bob and dance as bees buzzed from bud to bud. All around her, the garden bloomed with rich, verdant life.

In the soft, rosy morning light, it looked like a showplace—even though she had barely touched the garden, only weeded a little and cleared out the dead heads.

Though it was early days yet in the short Hope's Crossing growing season, she thought the yard was shaping up to be particularly beautiful this year. Maybe it was their early spring or the perfect level of moisture the area had received through the winter—or maybe the mulch and fertilizer she had added on the advice of Annabelle's neighbor Lou—but everything was green and lush.

Lucy gazed at the home whose care had fallen to her. Iris House looked truly beautiful, warm and inviting.

Would her great-aunt have been happy with what Lucy had accomplished here?

The work inside was nearly done. Dylan and Sam had wrapped up the major construction work the week before and the crew of painters she had hired for the rest of the house had finished two days earlier.

Genevieve only had to do her part, moving the furniture and making all the small decorating changes that would infuse glowing life into the house.

Leaving would be so difficult, especially after all the work she had poured into it.

She would miss so many things about this place. The creaky stairs, the softly blooming garden.

The inescapable sense of Annabelle's presence.

She had to go, though. She had no choice. Her decision had been made, the die cast.

Two weeks from now, Iris House would officially open for business as a bed and breakfast. She was close to hiring a great retired couple to run the place for her, and she knew it would be a huge success. Already, she had taken reservations several weeks out.

She wouldn't be here to see it, though. A week from Monday, she would be moving to Portland to take over as marketing director of one of Aidan Caine's new companies.

A vehicle engine broke the silence of the summer morning as it drove past, and her pulse jumped.

Brendan. She recognized his SUV and was grateful for the arbor that concealed her from view.

He had likely just finished an overnight shift at the fire station and was heading home for a few hours' sleep. He slowed down as he passed Iris House and she drew herself farther into the arbor.

She wasn't sure which one of them was doing the better job of avoiding the other, but she hadn't seen him in two weeks.

She was painfully aware that she tended to finish her run at the same time each morning and always spent a little extra time sitting out here in the garden, wondering if she would see him returning home when he was on the overnight shift.

Yes. She was ridiculous.

She sighed. She didn't have time to indulge this today. In a few hours, she needed to leave for the town's Giving Hope day, when everyone in town gathered to help each other clean yards, build sheds, paint fences and otherwise do what they could to make Hope's Crossing a better place.

When she walked into the kitchen, she found Crystal dipping her spoon into a bowl of cereal at the table, Max playing at her feet. Her hair was pulled back in a ponytail and she looked sweet and young, bubbling with excitement.

She still couldn't believe this was the same sullen girl who had shown up at her doorstep weeks ago.

"Morning," her half sister said. "Want some cereal? I'm happy to pour you a bowl."

"I had some toast earlier. I need protein." She grabbed a Greek yogurt out of the refrigerator and slid into the chair across from Crystal.

"How was your run?" Crystal asked.

How was it ever? A necessary evil if she wanted to stay in any kind of shape.

"Okay. Are you ready for today?" she asked.

"Yes! It's going to be so fun. I'm meeting up with Peyton and Ava and their friend Molly."

Crystal had become good friends with Spencer Gregory's daughter, Peyton, and Brendan's niece Ava. "That should be fun."

"They're a blast," Crystal agreed. "I really wish I could stay in Hope's Crossing for the summer."

"I'm sure your friends in Denver will be happy to have you back. And now you have friends here, too. It shouldn't be hard to stay in touch, with all the options at your disposal."

"I guess," Crystal said. "Maxie! Cut it out."

The puppy had one of the laces of her sneaker in his mouth and was tugging it. The little poodle-terrier mix was still tiny and still far too cute for his own good.

"Are you sure we can't we take him with us today?" Crystal asked. "He's going to be lonely. We should have arranged a playdate with Daisy. He hasn't seen her in *forever*. The two of them could have kept each other company. Do you think it's too late to call Brendan?"

"Yes. Far too late." In more ways than one. "Max will be okay. Don't worry. We'll put him outside in the play yard and he'll have a great time sniffing around in the grass or sleeping in his crate. If I can swing it, I'll try to come back here during the day to play with him a little, then later you can take him for a walk."

"Okay."

Lucy finished her yogurt and glanced at the clock. The morning was already slipping away. "I still need to take a shower or we'll miss the whole day."

"Hurry, then," Crystal said. "I've been looking forward to this for weeks."

Lucy tossed her yogurt carton into the trash and

headed for her bedroom, wondering how she was going to get through the last week of her stay in Hope's Crossing—and how she would possibly leave.

"Did you have something to do with this?" she hissed to Genevieve Beaumont as she looked at her volunteer assignment for the day.

"What?" Gen asked with deceptive innocence.

Lucy frowned and held out the paper. "Assigning me to work with Brendan Caine all day clearing the Wild Iris Ridge trail."

She would have thought her friend had entirely too much on her plate right now to bother with a little matchmaking. She was in charge of decorating for that evening's gala and charity auction, she was finishing the work at Iris House *and* her wedding was only a week away.

Lucy had agreed to stay until that weekend so she didn't have to miss the wedding, which was one more thing she wasn't sure how she would endure.

"I didn't have anything to do with the assignments other than to hand them out," Genevieve protested now. "Claire McKnight and Charlotte figured out all the details this year."

Charlotte. She should have known.

"Is there a problem?" Gen asked innocently. "You and Brendan are friends, right?"

Right. Friends who happened to ignite whenever they found themselves in the same room.

"It's going to be fun," Genevieve said. "In fact, maybe I'll trade you. I would much rather be outside enjoying this beautiful June day than spending all day decorating for the gala."

Under other circumstances, she might have been thrilled at the chance to spend the day in the mountains. Her time in Hope's Crossing was giving her a definite appreciation for the Colorado landscape.

Being assigned to work in the mountains all day with the man she had been doing her best to avoid was a different matter.

"What will we have to do?" she asked.

"Oh, you know. Cut back the overgrown branches, pick up litter. That sort of thing. It shouldn't be too hard," Genevieve said. "It's really beautiful up there. Dylan and I were just up there the other day walking with Tucker. It's not very steep, and once you reach the overlook, you have some great views down into the valley, almost as good as the Woodrose Mountain trail. It's a shame more people don't use it."

"It sounds lovely."

"I do think you'll enjoy spending the day there. But we can switch things around if you would rather not tackle that assignment. I'm sure we can find someone else to help Brendan. The whole point of the Giving Hope day is to have fun helping each other. You shouldn't be stuck doing something you would rather not."

She didn't know how to tell Genevieve the problem wasn't the assignment itself but the person who was to share it with her.

Anything she said now would sound ridiculous. She would just have to deal. They were assigned a mile section of trail. She could see no reason they had to work cheek to jowl. She probably wouldn't even see him all day.

"No. I don't need a new assignment. It should be

fine." She spoke the words so stiffly it made her jaw ache a little.

"Oh, perfect. And look. Here's Brendan now. Maybe you can ride to the trailhead together!"

She really liked Genevieve and considered her a good friend and a fantastic decorator. But in that moment, she wanted to pick up one of those water bottles they were handing out to the volunteers and dump the whole thing on the other woman's perfectly styled hair.

Apparently she hadn't completely shed her juvenile delinquent ways.

She could do this. Lucy manufactured a polite smile from somewhere and turned to face him for the first time in two weeks.

"Hi," she said, hating that her voice came out breathless and a little squeaky.

Something flared in his eyes when their gazes met. "Morning," he murmured, his voice rough and a little raspy.

Her insides seemed to shiver. Those furtive little schoolgirl glances she stole as he was driving home on the occasional morning hadn't prepared her to remember how gorgeous he was—big, tough, muscular, especially in a T-shirt that molded to his pecs and low-slung cargo pants.

Amazingly, Genevieve looked wholly unaffected by so much in-your-face masculinity.

The woman had to be crazy.

"Hey, Bren." His sister-in-law-to-be beamed at him. "No kids today?"

"No. Each class at their school is working on a project together. Faith's class is sorting donated books at the library, and Carter is on playground cleanup duty."

"Oh, that's right. The teachers have been working closely with the Giving Hope committee this year to make sure the elementary school children are involved."

"That seems like a great idea," Lucy said, grateful she sounded a little less flustered now. "The earlier they learn to help others, the better."

"That's the idea," Genevieve said.

"I should probably get going," Brendan said. "Where's the rest of my crew?"

Gen pointed to Lucy with a wide smile. "You're looking at her."

Dismay spread across his features for just a moment before he returned them to a stoic mask. "Seriously?"

"You two are going to have so much fun," Genevieve said. "I don't know what supplies you brought, but if you think of anything else you might need, Chief McKnight and Brodie Thorne are handing out tools in the parking lot."

A muscle flexed in his jaw—the same jaw she had pressed her mouth to a few weeks ago.

"Do you have gloves?" he asked.

She held out her flowered cotton gardening gloves. "Will these do?"

He snorted. "Sure, if we were picking petunias. Since we're not, you're going to need a heavy-duty pair. I'll stop at the fire station and pick some up for you. If I can find a small enough pair for you."

"Um, thanks."

"You want a lift to the trailhead?"

Reluctance filtered through the question. He obviously didn't seem any more eager to spend time together in an enclosed space than she was.

"I'll meet you there, just in case you're called out on a fire or something and have to leave early."

"Smart," he said, and she tried not to be hurt at the relief she saw in his eyes.

That was her. Smart Lucy Drake, who was a braniac in just about every aspect of her life—except when it came to protecting her heart.

If he hoped the hard physical labor of cleaning up a trail would distract him from the simmering hunger for Lucy, he was doomed to disappointment.

Two hours after they started work on the Wild Iris Ridge trail, Brendan's mood still hadn't improved.

She was a hard, hard woman to ignore.

He thought he had a system figured out by sending her ahead to pick up trash along the trail—the occasional cigarette butt or water bottle left over from last summer's hiking season—while he focused on clearing the deadfall branches that blocked the path.

Out of sight should have meant out of mind, but he still couldn't seem to stop thinking about her, wondering about her, worrying about her.

He should have figured his plan wouldn't work, after the past two weeks. He hadn't seen her once in that time but every single day he had to fight the fierce temptation to go up to Iris House.

The kids hadn't stopped nagging him about it. They were getting a little tired of his excuses and Faith had even asked him if he and Lucy had had a fight.

He had made up some kind of answer to her about how they were all really busy right now. It wasn't a lie. His life was a constant juggling act. Homework, shopping, school pickup, not to mention his actual job as fire chief responsible for fifty volunteer firefighters and EMTs.

As the kids wrapped up their school year, he had the added fun of trying to figure out day care for the summer and making sure they were enrolled in art camps, baseball clinics, the horseback riding lessons Faith had been begging to take.

He didn't find it very amusing that while all those things might fill every waking hour he still managed to fit in plenty of time to wonder about Lucy and miss her like hell.

He could have found a chance to see her. A few times late at night, he had been sitting on his favorite chair on the porch and could see the flutter of a curtain or lights going off in one room and on in another up at Iris House.

Was she having the same trouble sleeping as he was?

He could have seen her anytime these past two weeks but he had decided it wouldn't be wise.

He lost his head when he was with her. That night in Pop's kitchen, he had been so hungry for her, he would have taken her right there against the cabinets if she hadn't forced him to come to his senses.

He hadn't thought for a second about the fact that anybody could have walked in on them. *She* had been the one doing the thinking for both of them.

Afterward, he had sat out on the patio with his gut a tangled knot of emotions as he watched her with Aidan or talking to his sisters or smiling at Pop.

After two years, he had just begun to feel as if he had found steady footing again. The kids were doing well, he was coping. The battle had been hard-fought and bloody, but they had all emerged to an okay place.

How could he let Lucy into their lives to shake everything up again?

He didn't want this. The vulnerability. The need.

She would be leaving Hope's Crossing eventually. He just figured it was better for all of them if he did his best to keep her at arm's length until she finally took off.

So much for that grand plan. It was a little tough to keep a person at a distance when he was forced by circumstances—or meddling friends and relations, he wasn't sure which—to spend several hours alone with her in the backcountry.

He finished running his chainsaw through a deadfall tree that blocked the trail and tossed the cut logs into the thick undergrowth beside it just as Lucy headed toward him through the trail carrying another bag of trash to the four-wheeler.

She looked fresh and beautiful and young out here with the sun on her face and her hair pulled back into a ponytail. He wanted to yank off her gloves, pull off those sunglasses and tangle his mouth with hers for about three or four hours.

How was he going to get through this? And why couldn't she have been assigned to some other project today?

Lucy hefted the bag into the wagon hooked up to the four-wheeler. "I went all the way up to the overlook and back. That's as far as we were supposed to go, right?"

"Yes. Beyond that, it's the U.S. Forest Service's responsibility."

"That's three bags of garbage in only a mile of trail. I had no idea the hikers of Hope's Crossing were such slobs."

"It's been a few years since this area has had attention," he said tersely. "Hope's Crossing has a large trail system. It's impossible to clean every inch of it annually."

"Well, I cleaned every inch of this one this year. What can I do now?"

Leave me alone. Take your curls and your green eyes and that delicious mouth and just head back down the mountain.

"Hydrate. Take a break. Your water bottle is still on the four-wheeler."

"Are *you* taking a break?" she asked.

He knew he shouldn't. What he *ought* to do was send her back down to Hope's Crossing but he was weak when it came to her.

He *was* thirsty from running the chainsaw. Might as well quench at least one of his needs.

He set the chainsaw in the wagon of the four-wheeler and grabbed two water bottles for them. Lucy took hers and headed for a sunny boulder alongside the trail that offered a nice view of town through the trees.

After a pause, he followed her. Though he knew it was a mistake, he couldn't seem to stop himself from sitting next to her on the boulder, feeling the heat of her skin that warmed him more than the June sunshine.

A couple of squirrels chased each other up an aspen trunk, chattering the whole way, which sent a nuthatch flitting from branch to branch.

The air was cool and smelled of pine and the wildflowers just beginning to burst out along the trail. This area was spectacular when all the flowers were out, an explosion of color from blue-and-pink columbine, vivid red Indian paintbrush, the pale lavender plump-petaled wild irises that gave the trail its name.

He needed to spend more time outdoors with the kids. When he was younger, Pop was always taking him and his brothers—and then Charlotte, after she came along—up into the mountains for fishing trips.

Sometimes he wondered if those trips were intended more to give their mother a break from them all than to actually catch fish, but some of his best childhood memories had to do with a mountain setting like this, a fishing rod and a slow-moving creek.

"Genevieve was right," she murmured. "It *is* peaceful up here. I don't think most people in town realize how lucky they are to have this within a ten-minute walk of their house."

"Probably not."

He certainly didn't take advantage of all the recreational offerings around Hope's Crossing, though now that Faith had conquered the two-wheeler challenge, maybe he could take the kids mountain biking this summer.

"Are you going to the gala tonight?" she asked.

She was trying to make polite conversation. He couldn't see the point in being rude in response.

"Not by choice. Galas aren't really my thing, but I promised Claire McKnight I would represent the fire department and handle any first aid needs. You never know when a fistfight might break out during the silent auction, especially if Gen is involved."

She frowned. "What are you talking about?"

"You haven't heard the story of how she and Dylan first connected? She started a bar fight at The Speckled Lizard last year at Christmas and Dylan stepped in to protect her. They were both arrested and ended up serving community service at A Warrior's Hope. The rest, as they say, is history."

She looked as if she couldn't quite grasp the concept. "Genevieve Beaumont? Are we talking about the same person?"

"One and the same. The mayor's daughter. Your interior decorator. My elegant lovely future sister-in-law. From what I hear, she's got a nasty right hook and she's really good at pulling hair. I'm sorry to say, I missed the whole thing. Who knows? Tonight might be a repeat performance. A guy can always hope. You're going, aren't you?"

"I don't know. I still haven't decided. Like you, grand galas aren't really my thing and, well, I don't have a date, which makes it that much more awkward."

Color the same shade as the wild roses blooming behind them burst over her cheekbones. Did she worry he would construe her words as a hint that he should take her to the gala?

If he were any kind of decent, he would. But how could he possibly spend several hours with her making small talk, brushing against her, maybe even dancing?

Sitting here alone with her on a sun-warmed rock was tough enough on a guy's self-control. Holding her soft, lithe form in his arms even for a five-minute fox-trot would be torture.

"Half the people there won't have dates," he said curtly. "You'll be fine."

He felt like a jerk when she pressed her lips together and he thought he saw a trace of hurt in her eyes.

"I still have a few hours to decide. The auction is really the only reason I might go. I'm intrigued by all the items I've heard are up for bid. I mean, a couple of original Sarah Colvilles! I would kill to have one of those, especially when all the proceeds go to a good cause, I understand."

"Yeah. The money from the silent auction goes to fund college scholarships for deserving students. It's in honor of Layla Parker, Maura Lange's daughter. She was killed in a car accident a few years ago. The whole Giving Hope day was started in honor of her. Over the last few years, it's become something much more than a celebration of one girl's life, though."

"I think it's wonderful," she said softly. "The volunteer work, the auction, the gala. All of it."

He loved how his town reached out and helped others. It was one of the reasons he couldn't imagine living anywhere else.

"Crystal loves it here," Lucy went on. "She doesn't want to leave."

"When does she go?"

"Tomorrow. Dad and Pam are taking her and Max back to Denver. She has to start summer school on Monday to make up for everything she's missed if she's going to start her junior year on track. I'm going to miss them."

"I'm sorry. But you did a good thing, having her here, Lucy."

"I know. That doesn't make it any easier."

She didn't cry, even though her chin wobbled at the words. His chest felt tight and achy. He couldn't bear seeing her sad.

"I'm sorry," he said again, and then he did the one thing that seemed natural and right. He slid an arm around her and pulled her against him.

She froze for just a moment and he thought she might yank away from him and scramble off the rock. It would probably be better for both of them if she did. Instead, after a pause, she seemed to collapse against him.

She still didn't cry, simply rested her cheek for a moment against his chest, her breathing a little ragged. He had been married for eight years. He knew when a woman sometimes only needed a minute to compose herself so he kept his trap shut, just let her deal with her stuff in her own way while the squirrels chattered at them and some meadowlarks sang out from a nearby bush.

Finally she gave a long sigh and slid away.

"Better?" he asked.

"A little. Thanks."

She gave him a tremulous smile, and she looked so beautiful there in the sunlight, as soft and as lovely as any wildflower, he knew he had to kiss her. Even though he knew it was a mistake, even though he had been telling himself for two weeks to stay away from her, even though he knew he was only creating more trouble for himself in the long run, he reached for her and was overwhelmed when she came with a soft willingness.

Her mouth was sweet and deliciously cool from the water bottle. For two weeks, he had been dreaming of kissing her, touching her again. Now that she was finally here in his arms, he wanted to savor every taste, every sensation. The thick churn of his blood, the soft curves pressed against him, the alluring scent of strawberries and vanilla that made him want to lick every luscious inch of her.

After her initial startled reaction, she kissed him back, her mouth opening for him with an eagerness that both humbled and aroused him.

She made a soft, sexy sound, and he had no choice but to deepen the kiss as she wrapped her arms around his neck and snugged her body closer to his.

Oh, he had missed the sheer pleasure of a woman's body next to his, all those curves and enticing hollows. Even more, he had missed this sweet tenderness that seeped through him like rain on parched earth.

He loved hearing that sexy little catch in her breath when he kissed the corner of her mouth, when he lifted the edge of her T-shirt and clasped bare skin at her back.

He wanted her, right here, right now. He wanted to yank everything off, to touch that curvy body, to kiss her and listen to her cries of pleasure as she exploded in his arms....

The squirrels chattered at them from even closer than they'd been before, and the sound yanked him back to his senses.

What was he doing? They were making out on a rock on a public trail, for hell's sake, where anybody could wander past.

As usual, their timing was impeccable—and, as usual, he lost any grain of reason or sense where she was concerned.

He was furious, suddenly—at her, at himself, at the whole tangled situation.

He glared at her. "For two weeks, I've tried to stay away from you. It was working until you had to go and screw everything up."

She looked dazed, aroused, and he almost tugged her back into his arms.

"I...did? How?"

"This." He jerked his hand in a sharp gesture between the two of them and then wider, to encompass the trail. "Today. The fact that we were so conveniently assigned together on this trail project."

"Conveniently?" She gave a raw-sounding scoff.

"You probably didn't have to work too hard to convince Gen. She already thinks she's an expert matchmaker. No doubt she was over the moon at the chance to meddle in our business."

Her color rose higher. "Wait a minute. You think I engineered this whole thing to throw us together?"

"Didn't you?"

"No! Seriously? Can you possibly be such an arrogant, self-absorbed *ass?*"

The heat of her words started to filter through his frustration. She was every bit as angry as he was, and he started to wonder if he had made a mistake.

"You want the truth?" she bit out. "Okay, hotshot. Here it is. I would rather be changing bedpans at the senior care center than be here with you right now. I was *trying* to make the best of the situation. Do I think Genevieve and Charlotte are attempting a little matchmaking? Yes. Am I on board with that matchmaking plan? Absolutely not!"

She jerked to her feet. "I had nothing to do with any of this. I will also point out that, as usual, *you* kissed *me.* So before you go all high-and-mighty, 'you screwed everything up,' blah blah blah, maybe you better think about why you apparently can't keep your hands off me."

She gave him one more glare and then started stomping down the trail.

Yeah, he was an idiot. She was right. It wasn't her fault he was so tangled up over her. He had done that all on his own.

"Lucy—"

She didn't stop, just kept on heading back the way they had come, leaving him no choice but to follow after her.

"Where are you going?"

"Home. We're done here, aren't we?"

He wasn't sure if by *done* she meant the trail cleanup or everything else between them.

It took him about three steps to catch up with her. He moved in front of her, blocking her progress on the trail.

"Lucy, stop."

"Why? So you can kiss me again and then somehow turn everything around in your head so you can blame me for it?"

He sighed, knowing he had earned every ounce of her anger. "I'm sorry. Look, you're right. I can't keep my hands off you. I could give some excuse about how it's been a long time for me and you're a beautiful woman. But we both know it's more than that. I... have feelings for you."

"And you're obviously so very thrilled about that, aren't you?" she said quietly.

He clenched his jaw. "I'm doing the best I can, Lucy. I lost my wife twenty-six months ago. My life has been a mess since then. I'm sorry if I'm not quite ready to jump into something right away with her best friend."

"No matter what your feelings are?"

His feelings.

The word seemed vague, meaningless—especially when he realized this *feeling* seeping through him was love.

He didn't know how it had happened but he loved Lucy Drake.

He couldn't believe he hadn't recognized it before. Since the moment she moved back to Hope's Crossing and he found her at Iris House, coughing and wheezing and covered in soot, he hadn't been able to get her out of his mind. These past weeks, he had come to admire so many things about her. Her sweetness with his children. The concern she showed her sister. Her passion and strength and those rare moments of vulnerability.

He loved her.

And it scared him senseless.

He thought of those hellish months after Jessie died. How could he do this again? Give another person that kind of power over him, even when he loved her?

"I care about you, Lucy. More than I ever expected. I just…I'm not sure I'm ready for this yet. Can you give me a little time?"

She swallowed and looked down at the trail at their feet. When she looked up again, her eyes shimmered with tears.

"No. I'm sorry. I can't."

CHAPTER NINETEEN

IT WOULD BE so easy to say yes.

He had feelings for her. Even if not for his endearingly awkward confession, she knew he cared about her. So why couldn't she just tell him that she would wait as long as he needed?

She pictured herself a year from now, two years from now, still hanging on, marking time until he decided he was finally ready to let himself love her.

She had spent most of her childhood fighting for her father's attention, waiting for him to love her.

Brendan had broken her heart once when she was a stupid twenty-one-year-old and he had chosen Jessie over her. In the time since, she had worked too hard to become someone she could respect to put herself through that again.

She folded her hands together, wishing she could do something about their trembling. "I could give you time to figure things out. But I won't. What would be the point? This will never work. Surely you can see that. I think that's why we've both tried so hard these last few weeks to stay away from each other, because our heads understand even if our hearts don't."

"Understand what?"

"I can't be the woman you need."

He needed someone sweet, warm, loving. Someone like Jess, not a tangled mess of a woman, who was prone to panic attacks and insecurity.

"Don't you think I should be the one to make that decision?"

"Yes. You're not ready to make it yet. I get that. But I can't put my life on hold until you do."

"So that's it?"

She gave him a long look. "What else is there to say? I'm sure you won't mind if I let you finish things up here."

"I can give you a ride," he said, his voice terse again.

She shook her head. 'No thanks. I could use the walk right now."

In reality, as soon as she was out of sight of him on the trail, she started to jog and then full-out run, needing as much distance between them as she could muster. By the time she made it to the trailhead, her breathing was ragged, her chest tight.

She blamed it on exertion but when she reached her BMW and went to unlock the door, the keys slid from her suddenly tingling fingers to fall into the rocky dirt. The panic attack roared out of nowhere like an out-of-control freight train slamming into her, and she followed the keys to the ground.

She huddled by the side of her car with her chest fluttering, her stomach roiling, praying he took his time coming down the trail after her. She couldn't bear for him to see her like this.

As always, she was afraid she was going to die. This time, though, she was also afraid of how she could possibly survive the pain that would come from being without Carter and Faith and Brendon in her life.

When the worst of it receded, she threw up in the

bushes, rinsed her mouth out with the water bottle she still somehow clutched in her hand and then climbed with aching muscles into her car.

Though every instinct urged her to go back to the safety net of Iris House after the panic attack to indulge in a big bout of tears—and maybe a hot bath and some ice cream—she refused to wallow.

That would accomplish nothing, other than leaving her feeling worse than she already did. Instead, she forced herself to drive back to the community center. This day was about Giving Hope and she would darn well do her part, even if it ripped her heart out.

The parking lot was a bustle of activity with people coming and going, picking up supplies or new assignments, dropping off trash to the big recycling bins in back.

She parked her car and headed toward the door when it opened and Claire McKnight came outside with a box that looked twice as big as the bead store owner.

"Here." Lucy stepped forward. "Let me help you with that."

Claire peered around the box and her face lit up when she spotted her. "Oh! Hi, Lucy! How did things go on the trail cleanup with Brendan? Are you guys done already?"

So very done, in every possible way. "Yes. Things went well. It's ready for the season now and looks fantastic. I came to see if there's anything else I can help you do."

"Oh, you are a lifesaver!" Claire exclaimed.

"Am I?" Right now she didn't think she could save

much of anything. She felt weak and stupid and heart-broken.

"Several boxes of decorations for the gala were accidently overlooked and left here. Genevieve called in a panic, looking for them. Any chance you could be a dear and drive them up to the resort ballroom? I've been trying to get them to her for half an hour but my cell phone won't stop ringing. I've been waylaid four times just trying to make it to my car with the first box."

She didn't want to be anywhere *near* the gala that smacked too much of hearts and flowers and romance, but she supposed she could manage a small errand for Claire. "Of course. I'm happy to help."

"Thank you!"

Claire grabbed a couple of teenage boys to help her load everything in Lucy's car and she took off again, this time driving through town toward the winding Silver Strike Canyon Road that led to the resort.

On the way, she passed many small groups working on various projects around town. A couple of teenagers were painting benches along Main Street, more were planting flowers out front of the senior center. Several family units were collecting trash along the roadways.

This evidence of people helping others seemed to soothe her battered heart. This was a good town, a place filled with kind people trying to make the world a little better wherever they could.

When she skulked into town in the dead of night nearly two months earlier, desperate for a place to lick her wounded ego, she never would have guessed she would come to love Hope's Crossing and the people who lived here.

She hadn't really hated Hope's Crossing when she lived here with Annabelle, but she hadn't felt any real burning affection for the town, either. For her, Annabelle and Iris House had always been the reason she returned.

Something had changed these past weeks. She felt part of a community, a piece of something bigger than herself. In the process, she had made lasting friendships with Genevieve and Charlotte and some of the other women in town and had created cherished memories.

She would miss it.

She put away her melancholy and the lingering effects of her panic attack as she arrived at the huge resort lodge, where she was directed to a back entrance that led straight to the resort ballroom.

Genevieve rushed out to greet her the moment she pulled up.

"I can't tell you how glad I am to see you! Claire told me you were on the way with the rest of the decorations. We can finally get this done."

A group of volunteers—most of whom she had met at the bridal shower for Claire and Genevieve— swarmed her car and carried the boxes inside. Lucy followed with the last of the supplies and stood inside the ballroom, which had been transformed into a magically elegant place of cleverly angled mirrors, fairy lights, candles.

"Oh. It looks wonderful!"

"Watch. It will be even better in about fifteen minutes when we set up the table decorations you brought us," Gen said as she rushed past with an armload of floral arrangements.

"What can I do?"

"You can help Charlotte and Evie hang the lanterns. They'll show you what to do."

This was much more her speed than clearing the trail in Wild Iris Ridge and the company much easier on her heart.

For the next hour, she was able to bury her emotions while helping do her part for the Giving Hope celebration. When every task on her extensive list had been completed, Genevieve gathered everyone into the middle of the room for one last look around.

"It looks perfect," Evie Thorne, hugely pregnant, declared.

"Absolutely wonderful," Charlotte said.

"You're brilliant," Lucy said. "Hiring you to decorate Iris House was one of the smartest things I've ever done."

Genevieve looked delighted at the praise. "It's been a thrill. I almost feel guilty letting you pay me. Don't get me wrong. I'm charging you an arm and a leg. But I can still feel guilty about it, right?"

Charlotte and Alex Delgado chuckled.

"So when do we get to see the place?" Evie asked. "I can't wait for the grand opening."

"Two weeks," Lucy said. "The couple I think I'm hiring to run the place can't start until then."

That part of the announcement was met by a stunned sort of silence.

"You mean you're not going to be running it yourself?" Katherine Thorne asked.

"No." She might as well tell them. Word would be out soon and this way she could tell everyone at once.

"I'm, um, actually leaving town next week. I've taken a new job in Portland."

"No, you're not!" Charlotte stared. "This is a joke, isn't it?"

Lucy shook her head. "I'm afraid not. Aidan offered me a job as marketing director at one of his new off-shoots. I start a week from Monday."

"Oh, how exciting!" Katherine exclaimed. "Exciting for you, sad for us, I should say. We'll be sorry to see you go, but Aidan is a genius. He seems to do no wrong these days."

"Who ever would have guessed that the quiet, nerdy Aidan, who always seemed to be playing around on his computer would turn into such a hot geek one day?" Alex said.

"I know, right?" Gen grinned.

"Girl, you picked the wrong Caine," Alex said to Gen. "Why would you want Dylan when you could have a Learjet and a house in San Francisco and a sexy nerd in glasses?"

Gen's grin turned soft. "I wouldn't trade Dylan for a fleet of Learjets and an entire city block in San Francisco."

"Oh, that's so sweet," Alex said.

"Nothing sweet about it," Genevieve said with a sultry look. "Aidan might be a sexy nerd who knows his way around a motherboard, but Dylan has a few serious skills of his own."

"Ew," Charlotte exclaimed. "Stop. These are my brothers you're talking about, remember?"

The women laughed, and even Lucy mustered a smile, though her emotions still felt raw and tangled.

"So you're moving to Portland?" Alex asked.

"That's a great food town. I'll send you a list of a few fantastic restaurants I know in the area."

"Thanks. I appreciate it."

The women spoke for a few more moments then everyone started dispersing to begin preparing for the evening's gala. Lucy picked up a few empty boxes and stored them in the room off the ballroom then started to head to her car.

She wasn't fast enough. Charlotte intercepted her before she could reach the door.

"Do Brendan and the children know you're leaving?"

Her heart gave a hard, sharp spasm. "No. I haven't had the chance to tell them yet."

It was a lie. She had been with Brendan for three hours that morning. She could have mentioned it at any time, and she had had two weeks to prepare the children for her departure but she hadn't yet found the courage.

"Don't you think you need to?"

She sighed. "I don't know what you think is going on between your brother and me but whatever it is, you're wrong. We're friends." Right now, they weren't even that, she thought with a pang, but she didn't mention it to his sister.

"He cares about you. We all could see it at Carter's birthday party."

She flushed. "You're imagining things."

"Really? The way you were locked together in the kitchen was just a figment, then?"

Lucy winced. "You saw that?"

"I went in to grab more chips. Neither of you even heard me open the door. You were too busy being, uh, friends, I guess. I quickly backed out and ran interference so nobody else could go inside."

"Thanks for that, at least." She narrowed her gaze at his sister. "Wait a minute. You arranged for us to be assigned to work together today, didn't you?"

Charlotte compressed her mouth into a line. "You don't know what the last two years have been like. Losing Jess like that destroyed him. He never laughed or smiled at much of anything, until you came back to Hope's Crossing. I just want him to be happy."

Oh, she did, too. Even though that wouldn't be with her.

"Charlotte, I know you love Brendan. I...I care about him, too. But he needs to work things out at his own pace. Don't push him, okay?"

"Do you really think running away to work for Aidan will help the situation?"

"It's a good opportunity for me. One I can't pass up right now, especially when Brendan can't give me any other reason to stay."

To her surprise, Charlotte reached out and wrapped her in a hug that brought those dratted tears swimming to the surface. "We'll miss you. Whatever you think, you're good for Bren and for the kids. They need you. He'll figure that out. You'll see."

"Thank you," she murmured.

"Who knows? Maybe tonight you'll dance together at the gala and he'll realize he can't live without you."

Right. And maybe Max could join a dogsled team. All five pounds of him.

Lucy forced a smile. "Who knows? Anything can happen."

Except that scenario Charlotte had just painted, of

course. Since she wasn't going to the gala, Brendan wouldn't have the chance to dance with her, forget about realizing he couldn't live without her.

"I should probably go. I have a certain puppy who's been alone too long. I'll see you later, okay?"

She hurried away through the magical wonderland of the ballroom before Charlotte could press her further.

She regretted she wouldn't be able to see it at night with the lanterns lit and the fairy lights in the trees but nothing could drag her back here for the gala.

Instead, she would go back to Iris House. Maybe she would take Max for a walk and then take a long, luxurious soak in the deep claw-foot tub in her favorite of the bathrooms.

Yes, her heart might be breaking but she would look for whatever solace she could find.

"SHE'S NOT HERE."

Brendan shifted his gaze from scanning the resort ballroom to find his father at his elbow holding a couple of drinks.

"Who's not here?" he asked with deceptive casualness.

"Miss Lucy Drake. That's the woman you're looking for, isn't it?"

"I'm not looking for Lucy," he lied. "I was just checking out the crowd, following my firm instructions from Claire McKnight. I wouldn't want to miss the signs of somebody suffering from heat exhaustion or anything."

Dermot snorted, not believing him for a second. Brendan didn't know why he bothered trying. His father had a built-in lie detector, probably from raising seven children who had each been very imaginative at trying to get out of trouble.

Before Dermot could call him on the fast-talking, Brendan cut him off by changing the subject.

"Where's your date?" he asked.

Dermot opened and closed his mouth abruptly, color flaring across his weathered face. He turned his attention to the lovely Katherine Thorne, wearing a silvery blue dress and deep in conversation with another woman.

Yes, a minor miracle had visited Hope's Crossing, more interesting than the still-secret identity of the town's Angel of Hope, someone who went around anonymously doing good deeds like paying people's bills or delivering toys to needy children.

After all these years of hemming and hawing and dragging his feet, Dermot had actually asked Katherine Thorne to be his date to the Giving Hope gala.

Brendan didn't think he was the only one who thought the two were completely adorable together.

Dermot cleared his throat and held up the flutes in his hands. "She's over speaking with Sarah Colville about her newest exhibition. I only left her side to fetch drinks for the ladies."

"Champagne. Are you toasting something special?"

"Only good times and wonderful company. You don't have a problem with that, do you?"

The question was a pointed one, as if Dermot was asking permission for something. Despite the turmoil of his emotions all day over Lucy, he felt a soft little tug at his heart for his father.

"Absolutely not," he said quietly. "No problem at

all on this front. I hope you know that. I say it's about time."

Dermot gave him an arrested sort of look. "Do you?"

"Katherine is great, Pop. I've always liked her. I like her even more because she obviously makes you happy."

Dermot sent the woman in question a rather goofy smile that sent a sharp twinge of envy through Brendan.

"I only have one question," he said after a moment.

"And that would be?"

"What took you so bloody long?"

Dermot sighed. When he spoke, the Irish brogue he had left behind on the shores of County Galway when he was a lad of six glimmered through his voice, as it tended to do when his emotions were high.

"Sometimes a man can't see past his own fear. I'm not proud of it, but there it is. I loved your mother so. She was my world, you see, along with you boys and Charlotte. She was everything to me. I didn't see how I could ever care for another. My heart couldn't possibly stretch to find room to let someone else inside."

"What changed?" Brendan asked.

The music swirled around them, some kind of romantic ballad, heavy on the strings, and Dermot sent Katherine another goofy smile. She looked up from her conversation and everything about her lovely, lined features softened as she looked at Brendan's father.

"I've spent far too much time coming up with excuses. The truth is, I was afraid to let myself care for someone else again. Of all my children, you can understand that best, can't you, son?"

A lump rose in his throat at the love and compassion in his father's blue eyes, just like his own. For a moment, Jess's image shimmered in front of him, soft and pretty.

He had been a good husband and had loved her with all her heart. But she was gone. As Pop just said, the heart could stretch and grow to make room for someone else, something he never would have believed until Lucy came to town.

"Yes," he finally answered his father. "I get it."

"I waited far too long," Dermot said. "I almost let this chance slip away from me. When Katherine told me she was thinking of moving to Arizona for most of the year, I knew the time for dragging my feet was over. I had to do something, yes? There comes a certain moment in a man's life when he realizes nothing else matters but having a certain someone in his life, no matter how much courage it takes for him to make that first step into the unknown."

The words seemed to slide through him, right to his core.

"A date to the gala is a good first step," he managed.

"A fellow has to start somewhere, doesn't he, when he decides the time has come to let go of the past."

"Indeed."

Dermot glanced at Katherine again then back at him with a sort of purposeful air.

"I don't think Lucy's coming tonight. It's a shame, that. I thought she would surely be here, if nothing else to say goodbye to us all."

His heart seemed to stop. "Goodbye?"

"Yes. Our Aidan tells me he's stealing her away from us. He's hired her to work for him at a new company he's opening in Portland. She's starting week after next, from what I understand. Surely she mentioned it to you."

He had been tackled on the football field more times than he could count. Once he'd been knocked completely out of his cleats.

That's exactly how he felt right now. He could swear his ears were even ringing.

"No," he managed through lips that suddenly felt frozen. "No, she hasn't shared that with me."

"Aidan was always a smart one. He knows a good thing when he sees it."

There was that pointed tone again, the implication that Brendan *wasn't* the smart one.

He was beginning to figure that out. He was the dumb football player jock. Everybody knew that, right? Even Lucy had said so.

Lucy and Aidan.

They would be perfect for each other. Aidan was brilliant, driven, ambitious, just like she was.

And if his brother turned all that brilliant geeky ambition Lucy's way and decided to add her to one of his collections, Brendan just might have to strangle him with his wussy little glasses.

"I guess I had better deliver this champagne. Enjoy your night, son," Dermot said.

He walked away, leaving Brendan reeling.

Leaving. She was really leaving?

How could he bear it?

Why should he be surprised? He had always known she wouldn't stay in Hope's Crossing. Lucy's dreams were always bigger than a little town like this. She might stay for a while but he had known from the beginning she would leave them all behind eventually.

Wasn't that the reason he had ignored the connection between them all those years ago? Because the paths they each wanted to take led to very different destinations?

He let out a breath that seemed to burn in his chest. Damn her. Damn her for thawing all those cold and empty places inside him and then walking away and leaving him raw and exposed.

His phone suddenly rang and he recognized the dispatch ringtone.

"Yeah," he growled.

"Chief, we've got a situation you might want to know about."

He didn't want to deal with this right now, but he knew his duty to the people of Hope's Crossing. "Hang on. Let me go somewhere I can hear you."

He walked outside the ballroom and was surprised to see it had started raining, steady drops that plunked noisily on the roof. That was spring and early summer in Hope's Crossing. You could have lovely weather all day and then a blizzard by nightfall.

"Chief, we've got a possible missing person situation," Peggy Taylor said. "Somebody went for a hike this afternoon and hasn't come back. She was supposed to be back three hours ago."

A little early to be too alarmed, but the rain would complicate the situation.

"Does Chief McKnight know?"

In Hope's Crossing, search-and-rescue operations were jointly run through the police department, county sheriff and fire department.

"Not yet. The person who called it in asked specifically for you. She says the missing person is a friend of yours. I figured you might want to take point on this."

One problem with being the fire chief in a small town was that most people considered themselves his friend.

"What's the story? You got a name?"

"Yeah. I don't know her, though. Girl who called it in is a Crystal Drake. She said the missing person is her sister, Lucy."

CHAPTER TWENTY

HE PROBABLY BROKE about a thousand traffic laws on his way to Iris House. Not that he gave a single damn.

At the house, he raced up the front porch steps like he was running away from the entire Broncos defensive line.

Crystal opened the door before he could bang it down.

"Brendan! You're here!"

She burst into noisy tears and just about collapsed to the wood planks of the front porch.

"Okay, okay." Impatience burned through him as he helped her up and into the house. She was a mess, with mascara dripping down her face and her skin red and blotchy from crying. She looked scared out of her wits.

That, more than anything, ratcheted up his own anxiety.

"Take a deep breath, Crystal," a familiar female voice said, and he turned with shock to see his niece Ava—Andrew's daughter—come forward and place a comforting arm around Lucy's sister. "You have to calm down or you won't be able to help Uncle Brendan find her."

"Ava! What are you doing here?"

"We came over to watch a movie during the gala,"

she answered. "We were going to watch at our place, but—"

"But Lucy just had the den turned into a surround-sound theater room for the B&B and we thought it would be way more cool here," Crystal said, wiping at her eyes with a mangled tissue. "I called Lucy to see if it was okay and she said it was because she was going to be home soon."

"Do you remember what time you talked to her?"

The two teens looked at each other and shrugged. "Maybe six or so. Was it before we went to McDonald's or after?" Crystal asked.

Ava shrugged. "Wasn't it just when we were going inside? Because, remember, you were on the phone when that jerk in the Rockies hat bumped you on the way out."

He just wanted a timeline, not every freaking detail. "So six, you think?"

"Yes. Around six or six-thirty."

More than three hours ago. Again, not a terribly long time, except for the rain.

"And what did she say in the phone call? Where was she going?"

"She said she left her sunglasses somewhere. She thought she knew where they might be. She was going to take Max for a little walk to see if she could find them. It wasn't far, she said, and she would be back before we got here. But she's not here. Neither is Max, and now it's raining. He hates the rain. Do you think they'll be okay?"

A hazard of his job: he could think of a hundred things that could have happened to her, none of them details he wanted to share with Crystal yet.

"She didn't tell you where she was going to look for the sunglasses?"

Crystal frowned. "No. But she said she lost them this afternoon. Where was she this afternoon?"

With him. In his arms on a sun-warmed rock in the mountains. He closed his eyes, trying to remember if she had been wearing sunglasses. He remembered her having them that morning when they started work on the trail. She certainly hadn't been wearing them when he kissed her. He could clearly picture those lovely green eyes going murky and dark with need....

He jerked his mind back to the situation at hand. Had she left her sunglasses on the trail somewhere? At least this could give him a possible place to start.

"I think I know where she might be."

"You do?" Crystal exclaimed.

"I'll start there, see if her car is at the trailhead. If it's not, we'll start over."

"You have to find her. Please, Brendan. And Maxie, too. He's so little."

He hugged her and then Ava, too, grateful Crystal wasn't alone here. His niece had brains and common sense, huge assets in this situation.

"I want you both to stay here, in case she comes back. Ava, I'm going to call your mom to come stay with you two. She didn't go to the gala, did she?"

His niece shook her head. "She has a cold. Since Dad had to go to a conference in Denver, she decided to stay home and rest."

"Okay. Well, she can sneeze here just as well as at home. Ava, you've got my cell number. I want you to call me if you hear something. Anything at all, got it?"

He had to change out of the suit and dress shoes he

had worn for the party or he would be of no use on a rain-slicked trail. He would run to his house for five minutes and at least grab his rescue pack and his hiking boots.

He was already taking off his tie and unbuttoning his shirt as he trotted down the stairs.

"She's going to be okay, isn't she? You'll find her and everything will be fine, won't it?"

He turned around to face Crystal standing on the porch, twisting her hands. He didn't have time to pat her head and give her empty platitudes. Lucy was out there somewhere, cold, possibly hurt, and he had to find her.

He *would* find her. He refused to consider any other alternative.

All those dark, ugly possibilities pressed in on him, just about making his knees crumple. He knew all the things that could happen to somebody unprepared in the backcountry. Rock slides, falls, drowning—not to mention the danger of exposure whenever the temperature dropped.

Please God. Not again. He had done this once already. He couldn't survive it again.

Somehow he found the strength to give Crystal a small, tight, completely bullshit smile.

"I'll find her," he promised. "I swear I will. I know it's tough but try not to worry."

"Thank you."

He nodded and hurried to his SUV, knowing he wouldn't be able to heed his own advice. He was sick with worry and wouldn't be able to breathe again until she was safe and sound and back where she belonged.

In his arms.

"This is another fine mess you've gotten us into, Maxie."

The dog who had started the whole trouble just gave a tiny yip, his whole body vibrating with his shivers. Or maybe those were her own. At this point, after three hours in the cold, wet wind with an ankle that screamed at her every time she moved, she didn't know.

Lucy tucked him back inside her T-shirt, all the protection either of them had against the cold. He added another layer of wet and cold to her general misery.

They were in serious trouble, and she didn't have the first idea how she could possibly extricate them both from it.

The panic attack that had been prowling around the perimeter of her consciousness like a voracious mountain lion growled suddenly, and she was so very tempted to give in to it.

For once, she had something to be panicked about.

She couldn't, though. Max was depending on her for his very survival, and she wouldn't do either of them any good if she freaked out even more.

Brendan would find them. She just had to hang on and continue trying to climb out on her own until he did—though maybe he wouldn't want to come look for her, after the mess she had made of everything.

Yeah, this was going down in the record books as the worst possible day of her life.

The worst part was knowing this was all her fault, not Max's at all.

The evening had started out fine. Okay, as fine as possible, considering her heart felt scoured raw by the events of the day.

On her drive back down the canyon from helping to

decorate the ballroom, the sun shone directly into her eyes and she realized she didn't have her sunglasses. The last time she clearly remembered having them had been while she and Brendan cleaned up the Wild Iris Ridge trail.

She must have left them somewhere up there. Yes, it was a small disaster in a day filled with much bigger problems but she loved those sunglasses. They were the best pair she had ever owned and fit her face perfectly. Finding an adequate replacement would be a challenge, especially since she had purchased them on a trip to Japan just before Annabelle died.

This, at least, was something within her control to fix.

She decided to go look for them, especially after she returned to Iris House and found Max looking bored in his outdoor play area.

A little exercise would be just the thing for him and would also provide the much-needed bonus of distracting her from the deep ache in her heart—or so she thought.

The evening had been lovely, though after only a few moments, she had been wishing she had thought to bring along a jacket. In town, it was sometimes easy to forget how quickly the temperatures could drop in the higher elevations as soon as the sun started to set.

She had been moving at a good clip, though, and that helped keep her warmer. As she expected, the puppy's energy had started to lag when they were only halfway to their destination. He was just a tiny slip of a thing and had to take about eight steps to every one of hers.

While she hadn't brought a jacket, she *did* have the foresight to bring along the padded backpack carrier

Crystal bought for Max that even had a little hole for him to stick his face out and look at his surroundings.

Lucy had plopped him into it and continued on her way, figuring she still had another hour of daylight—which should have been plenty of time to reach her destination and still make it back to the car before dark.

Finally she reached the glacier-carved boulder where she and Brendan had taken their break and had shared that devastating final kiss. She smoothed a hand over the stone, cool now that the sun had slipped behind the trees.

On some level, she hadn't really expected to find the sunglasses. As she scanned the area, though, she suddenly spotted a flash of light in the tall meadow grasses—the dying sun reflecting off one of the lenses.

Though she didn't remember doing it, she must have taken them off and set them down on the rock while they were talking. Somehow during that kiss, the sunglasses had slipped into the grass.

She picked them up now and discovered the frame was a little bent, the lenses dirty—both things she could fix. The small victory was one tiny bright spot in a day filled with sorrow and pain.

That should have been the end of it.

Now, as she huddled with the little dog whimpering against her skin and her ankle howling with pain, she wished with all her heart that she had just tossed the glasses in the pack and headed back down the trail.

If she had, she would have been home now, soaking in that claw-foot tub with a glass of wine and her broken heart.

What stupid instinct had compelled her to go up the trail a little bit higher? She remembered thinking it was going to be a spectacular sunset, especially with the clouds that had started rolling in.

She was leaving Hope's Crossing, probably for good. How many more chances would she have to watch the sunset over the town from such a spectacular vantage point as the Wild Iris Ridge overlook?

The town had been lovely, glowing in the pale peach light, like something out of a postcard. The tidy downtown, the pretty houses rising up into the foothills and the magnificent mountains that seemed to embrace the little valley.

Someone had placed a redwood bench at the overlook, angled down for the perfect viewpoint into the valley. Perhaps it was even a project from a previous Giving Hope Day.

With the wind rustling the pale green aspen leaves and moaning in the tops of the tall pines, she sank down onto the bench. Max yipped to be let out of his backpack carrier so she unzipped it and set him down to sniff around the bench.

She sat there watching the spectacular show and listening to the wind as all the emotions she had been shoving down all afternoon seemed to bubble to the surface.

This was why she wanted to come up here, she realized, the tears beginning to slide down her face. The sunglasses had only provided the excuse. She had needed the space and the privacy to mourn for the future she could never have with Brendan.

They could have made it work. She could have worked for Aidan long-distance from Hope's Crossing or she could have considered being a marketing consultant for other tech companies. She could picture the whole perfect thing with startling clarity—entwining her life with his, sharing her successes, embracing his, raising the children they both loved together.

She wanted that future fiercely but knew it was impossible for them. He might say he had feelings for her, but he wouldn't let himself completely love her, for a hundred different reasons. She had to accept it and move on, as painfully difficult as that would likely prove.

She indulged in the tears for only a few moments, figuring she had earned them. After this she would wipe her eyes, square her shoulders and go back to rebuilding her life.

When she looked around, however, she discovered she was alone there on the bench, with no Max in sight.

"It's not your fault, little guy," she said now to the puppy whose small body trembled against her. "I'm the only one to blame. I shouldn't have taken my eyes off you for a second. I'm sorry. I should have been watching."

The puppy licked her chin in complete forgiveness, adding yet another layer to her guilt. So many things could have happened to a fragile five-pound dog. This area was thick with red-tailed hawks, snakes, wildcats, anything that might decide a warm, wriggly puppy would make a delicious dinner on a rainy night.

She had been grossly negligent to let him out of the carrier pack for even a second. And she had been too absorbed, first in her own heartache and then her fear and frantic searching for Max to pay any attention to how those gathering clouds had begun to turn stormy.

She felt the first raindrop just about the time she heard a little yip from below her somewhere.

"Max!" she called and strained her ears until she heard it again.

It was a minor miracle that she heard it at all—and another that she finally located him by isolating the sound. He was downslope from the trail, roughly twenty-five feet down the steep mountainside.

She had no idea how he had made it that far, whether he had just wandered down the hill or had fallen, like a child rolling end over end down a hill.

She suspected the latter. When he saw her, he tried to scramble up and ended up sliding back down, unable to gain purchase to make it up the steep slope.

"Don't move. I'll come get you," she had called to him. It was a stupid thing to say, since she knew perfectly well he couldn't understand her, but she had to say *something*.

Right now he was safe, on a spot where the hillside flattened out into a sort of wide plateau, but just below that was a rocky talus slope that cut at least two hundred feet down the mountain.

She was afraid that if the puppy tried too hard to climb up, he would end up falling into that dangerous rock field and would slide all the way down, where she wouldn't be able to retrieve him.

With her heart pounding, she started toward him. By now, the rain was falling steadily, turning everything into a slick mess.

She made it perhaps ten feet down the steep slope by hanging on to shrubs and saplings to help her fight gravity. Grateful now for all those runs and the free weights she did on alternate days to tone, she thought she was strong enough to make it—until she grabbed hold of what she thought was a shrub and it turned out to be only a weed that she pulled out from the roots.

Just like that, she lost her purchase on the rain-slick slope, her feet slipped out from under her and she went tumbling down and down and down.

She hit her head hard during her fall on a rock or a stump, she wasn't sure, but even then she might have been fine except that momentum carried her just past the wide plateau where Max waited. The only thing stopping her was the huge boulder she slammed into, with most of the impact absorbed by her right foot.

Raw pain exploded up her leg and she thought she must have passed out—from the head injury or the leg pain, she wasn't sure.

She only knew when she woke up, Max was licking her face, she was drenched and freezing and the mountainside had gone dark.

Worst of all, her phone must have fallen out of her pocket during her tumble and continued bouncing down the slope without her. She heard it ring several times from far below them, but she couldn't see it and knew she couldn't risk trying to find it in the dark when she didn't know how far down it was or how steep the terrain.

Better to try scrambling back up to the trail, but that was much easier said than done. She had fallen at least two hours ago. In that time, she had tried to fashion a splint for her ankle out of branches and the straps of the backpack, which miraculously was still over her shoulder after the fall.

Clawing and scrambling, she had made it up about ten feet but the twenty more to the trail seemed impossible—not to mention the mile she would have to make it down the trail to her car.

Max licked at her face, and she realized she was crying again, salty tears to join the rain dripping down her face.

She didn't want to die. She closed her eyes and pictured Brendan and the children. They would be shattered to lose her. Nothing else mattered.

If she curled up here and allowed herself to wallow in her pain and her fear, she would freeze to death. She had to just push past all of it and move forward. She didn't have any other choice.

Yes. Another perfect metaphor for her life.

"Come on, Max. We can do this." The dog yipped and she grabbed the backpack, now down to one strap. She pulled him out of her shirt and tucked him into the backpack so she could use both scraped and gouged hands to climb her way up.

It was hard, strenuous, painful work. She fell back down a few feet three different times but picturing Brendan, Faith and Carter helped spur her a little farther and then a little farther still.

She was roughly ten feet below the trail when she heard it, the sound of her name in a hoarse, frantic voice she knew well.

"Bren!" she called back, sobbing with relief and exhaustion. "Brendan! I'm here."

"Where?" he yelled. "Keep yelling so I can find you."

She could see a flashlight beam over her head, bright and beautiful through the rain.

"Here. Here. Below the overlook. M-Max is here."

The dog helpfully yipped in excitement, and Lucy

clawed her way up a few more feet, calling out every ten seconds or so, until he rushed down the slope, wrapped her in his arms and carried her the rest of the way up to the safety of the trail.

He didn't let go of her, even when they were back on solid ground, just held her close, and she could feel tremors shake both of them. Were they from her, from Brendan or from Max? Probably all three of them.

"I thought I'd lost you, too," he said, and the agony in his voice made more tears drip down her cheeks.

"I'm here. You didn't l-lose me. I'm okay. So is Max."

Heat radiated off him like a beacon and she wanted to burrow into him and never move again.

He carried her to the bench where the whole thing had started, sagged onto it with her still in his arms and pulled out his radio. She clung to him, completely exhausted while he reported their location in that same hoarse, raw voice and called for one of the search-and-rescue ATVs to come up to the scene.

"It will take them about ten minutes to get here," he said. "I was supposed to wait for the rest of the team to assemble so we could start the grid, but when I saw your car at the trailhead, I couldn't do it. I knew you had to be up here somewhere, hurt, cold. I figured I would hear you better without all that engine noise on the trail, anyway."

She couldn't muster any response past the bone-deep cold and this vast, sweet relief.

"I need to let go of you for a moment. Just for a moment, sweetheart. Hang on."

She made a sound of protest as he pulled off his

backpack. From inside, he pulled out several supplies—
a survival blanket, a dry shirt, a rain poncho.

The rain seemed to have eased up to a drizzle as he
pulled off her soaking T-shirt and slipped her into the
dry shirt he pulled from the pack. He grabbed another
dry shirt out of the bag and wrapped Max into it, then
laid the puppy in her lap and pulled the poncho over
all three of them to keep out the rain.

"Can you tell me what happened? Where are you
hurt?"

"Ankle," she muttered. "I think it's broken or at least
seriously sprained."

"How?"

"Max wandered away. I should have been watching
him, every second, but I wasn't."

She let out a little sob as the adrenaline rush that had
pushed her to claw her way up that hillside began to
subside. She would have felt so horrible if something
had happened to the dog.

"He wandered down the slope or fell or something.
I don't know which. I j-just know when I tried to climb
down to get him, I slipped in the mud and my ankle
smashed into a r-rock. We've been trying to climb back
up for hours. I'm so cold."

"I know. I've got you now. You're safe. You'll warm
up in a minute and the rescue team will be bringing
more dry blankets."

She could hear his heart pounding furiously beneath
her ear, and the sound humbled her.

She *did* feel safe. Safe, sheltered. Loved.

"I knew you would find me," she murmured. "I
know that sounds like something out of a corny movie,
but it's true."

He made a strangled sort of sound and pressed his mouth to hers. The kiss was deliciously warm, tender, etched with a desperate relief she completely echoed.

"By the way, I changed my mind," she said against his mouth.

He shifted away from her, and she could barely see him, despite the glow of the flashlight he had left as a beacon to the rescuers. "About?"

"You. Us. I'll wait for you, as long as it takes. I don't care. A year, two years. Ten. The whole time I was down there, all I could think about was you. This. I knew you would find me. As I was lying there in the mud and rain and grit, I vowed that when you did, I had to tell you what you mean to me. I love you. I have loved you forever. You asked me to wait and I will. Take as long as necessary. I don't care. I just… I need you."

"Lucy." He said her name like a hoarse prayer and then he kissed her again with fierce emotion, his big hands cupping her face.

"I love you," he rasped. "From the moment I found you were missing, I've been sick with fear, thinking I was too late, that I was going to lose you, too, before I ever had the chance to tell you how very much I love you."

The cold, the rain, the pain that still screeched up her leg every time she took a breath. None of it mattered compared to the sweet, healing joy of hearing those words she had never expected from him.

She gave a laugh that was a sob, too, and tightened her arms around him.

From below them on the trail, she could hear the roar of engines, several of them. Headlights cut through the dark and the rain, and rescuers called out to each other and to Brendan.

As they worked around her—bundling her in blankets, splinting her ankle more adequately than her makeshift effort, tucking her into an all-terrain vehicle that held four people then driving down to the trailhead—he stayed close to her.

She held Max closely, wondering how she could shift in only a few moments from the depths of fear and sorrow to this brilliant, incandescent joy.

She was safe and loved. What more could she possibly need?

He had almost lost her.

As Brendan rode with Lucy down to the waiting ambulance at the trailhead, that truth kept rumbling through his brain.

If she had tumbled a little farther down the slope, if he hadn't found her, if she had struck her head on that rock a little harder, this situation could have gone far differently.

He couldn't bear thinking about it. It seemed a rare and precious gift, somehow, that they were here together, that she held his hand as they bumped along in the back of the little four-seater Ranger all-terrain vehicle.

Some part of him was still shaking inside, consumed with memories of that nightmare time after Jessie's death. How could he do this to himself again? Open himself up to that kind of soul-crushing pain again?

The rest of him realized he had no choice. He loved her too much. Pop was right. He couldn't give up a future filled with joy and love because he was afraid something might happen to her.

The love would just have to be stronger than the fear.

He closed his eyes and let it wash over him, all his relief that she was okay and the sweet peace he found sitting beside her.

At the parking lot, the guys brought over a stretcher and he lifted her into it, which was totally against protocol but he didn't care.

"I'm riding in the ambulance," he said.

Since he was the fire chief, nobody argued with him. Sometimes a little authority came in handy.

"What about the dog?" Mike Chen, who was driving the ambulance, asked him.

Lucy cuddled Max closer. He thought about letting her keep the dog, but he would only get in the way at the hospital.

"He'll be okay. I'll have somebody take him to Iris House. Crystal's going to be out of her head with worry for you and for him."

"Take care of him. He's a good, brave puppy," she said, obviously already feeling the effects of the pain medication his guys had given her first thing.

"So what happens now?" she asked after they were on their way and he had relayed her vitals to the waiting emergency department.

"You're probably going to have to stay overnight," he said as he cleaned up some of the scrapes on her hands she had earned climbing up that slope, an image that chilled his blood. "I'm going to take a guess here and say you probably broke your ankle. You might be looking at surgery, but that will be up to the ortho doc.

I would recommend Jeff Bradford. He can be a bit of a jerk but he's the best bone guy in town."

"Thanks. But I meant with us."

That trace of insecurity in her voice tugged at his heart. He brought one of her battered hands to his mouth. "You're flying high from the pain meds right now. You will be for a while. Maybe we should wait to talk about this."

"I don't want to wait. I've waited long enough."

So much had happened that day, his head was spinning as if *he* were the one who had taken the pain meds. "We'll have to figure that out. In the short-term, I imagine we'll do a lot of flying back and forth. In the long term, I suppose they need firefighters in Portland, too."

She twisted around to stare at him, and after a moment her eyes began to fill. "You…you would leave Hope's Crossing for me? Your family, your life, Faith and Carter's whole world?"

He smoothed back her hair, careful not to touch the ugly bruise blooming just to the left of her temple. "Not their *whole* world. You're a huge part of that. They love you as much as I do."

She sobbed out a ragged-sounding laugh, sniffling so hard now she ended up using the corner of the sheet as a handkerchief.

"Everything okay back there?" Chen called.

"Yeah," he growled. "Keep driving."

Brendan picked up her hand again. "I didn't mean to make you cry. You're not in any shape to talk about this now. We have all the time in the world."

She shook her head.

"I don't want to go to Portland," she admitted. "I

never did. I just knew I couldn't stay here, the way things were between us."

That set him back a bit. "What do you want?"

"To stay here with you and Carter and Faith," she said softly, almost shyly. "I want to stay in Hope's Crossing and make Iris House the most amazing bed and breakfast in Colorado."

"What about your career?"

"I loved my career and I was good at it. I used to love the challenge of it, but lately something has been missing. I never had the kind of peace I've found here these last few weeks."

She sniffled again. "I don't know. I don't want to throw all my experience away. Maybe I can open a consulting business on the side."

"Aidan's going to be pissed," he warned. "He likes getting his own way. Always has."

"Must be a family trait," she answered with a loopy sort of smile as the pain meds continued to be metabolized.

"Must be."

"I like Aidan," she said, "but I'm not sure I could have worked for him, anyway. One Caine brother is enough for me, I think."

"This one's yours," he said solemnly.

She gave him a soft, tender smile, and he almost had to close his eyes again as the wonder of second chances seemed to seep through him, healing all the shattered pieces of his heart.

For a long time, he didn't think he could ever be happy again. But here he was, tangled up in love for this smart, beautiful, amazing woman.

He suddenly remembered what Dylan had said to

him the night of Carter's party. *Life rolls on, no matter what. You can either be squashed beneath the treads or jump on and grab tight and enjoy the ride.*

That was exactly what he planned to do—hold on tight to Lucy and enjoy the ride. The good and the bad, the hard and the sweet. Birthdays and anniversaries, baseball games, movie nights.

And stress relief. Lots and lots of stress relief.

He felt as if he had just been handed an unbelievably miraculous gift, and he couldn't wait to spend the rest of their lives unwrapping it together.

EPILOGUE

THE GREGORY-CAINE and Caine-Beaumont combined wedding reception would forever go down in the annals of Hope's Crossing history as one of the wildest, biggest, most over-the-top celebrations ever.

Genevieve had really outdone herself on the venue. Brendan didn't know the first thing about wedding décor, but if somebody asked him to describe the Silver Strike ballroom right now, he would have called it simple elegance, with little twinkly lights, spears of fake trees, candles everywhere.

The food, the music, the decorations—everything was perfect. If it didn't sound too corny, he would have said the whole ballroom seemed to vibrate with happiness.

As he swayed to the music with his pint-size partner, Brendan could see his sister and his new sister-in-law on the fringes of the dance floor, each of them breathtaking in her own way.

Genevieve and Charlotte seemed happy enough to share this reception after their individual ceremonies. Charlotte and Spencer had married the night before at the charming little church in town where the Caines always attended, and Genevieve and Dylan wed that morning in a stirring sunrise ceremony in a wildflower-covered meadow in Snowflake Canyon.

Brendan was proud of himself that he hadn't even ribbed Dylan about the dazzled look on his face every time he caught sight of his bride. As for Spence? Smokin' Hot Spencer Gregory—who had been on magazine covers around the world and had once been married to a supermodel—actually had tears in his eyes when he married their sweet Charlotte.

All in all, a perfect weekend, Brendan thought. But when it came to happiness bubbling over, Brendan figured he had both Dylan and Spence beat. He had one of his favorite girls in his arms as they spun around the dance floor, and his other one was currently sitting at a table nearby with her broken ankle elevated on a pillow while Carter leaned against her other leg and chattered a mile a minute, as usual.

"Aunt Charlotte and Genevieve are the prettiest brides ever, don't you think?"

"Definitely," he answered Faith, smiling as he spun her around on the dance floor with a complicated flourish that made her giggle.

"I like Spence," she announced. "He said I should call him Uncle Spence now. And Genevieve said I can call her Aunt Gen or Aunt Genevieve. Except Uncle Dylan heard her say that and told me to call her something fancy like they would in Paris. He had me practice it over and over. Listen. *Tante Jahn-Vi-Ev.* Isn't that pretty?"

He never would have figured Dylan for a guy who knew any French whatsoever, but then, nothing his little brother did surprised him anymore. That included marrying the town's spoiled rich girl, who was turning out to be far more than everyone in Hope's Crossing ever thought.

Now that Faith reminded him of it, he remembered hearing Dylan say Gen's name with an exaggerated French accent a time or two in a teasing tone. It was kind of sweet coming from a big, tough army ranger, especially the way she would blush and give him a soft, secret smile.

He had been the recipient of a few of those secret smiles himself the past few weeks. Unable to help himself, he glanced over toward Lucy's table and had to glower a little when he found Aidan now sitting next to her, deep in conversation.

Carter had left her, and a quick glance around revealed his son had been grabbed by his niece Ava and Peyton Gregory, Spence's daughter, who were now trying to teach him how to foxtrot—much to Carter's loud and obvious displeasure.

Oh, how he loved that kid—and the rest of his loud, crazy, wonderful family.

A moment later—just as Brendan and his partner passed Mary Ellen and Harry Lange on the dance floor—the music stopped and his son gave an extremely audible sigh of relief and raced toward the refreshment stand.

"Thanks for the dance, bug," he told his daughter.

"You're welcome, Daddy. I told Uncle Jamie I would dance with him. Is that okay?"

She gave him a worried look, as if afraid she would hurt his feelings by casting him aside for his younger and infinitely more charming brother.

"Of course it's okay. He's among my five favorite brothers."

She frowned in puzzlement for just a moment then made a face. "You only have five brothers!"

Brendan had never before heard anybody use the word "only" with that particular phrase. "Why, so I do. And Jamie is certainly one of them. One of the better dancers among us, for what it's worth. But are you sure you wouldn't rather go dance with Uncle Aidan? He looks like he could use a little exercise and he loves to dance."

It was a blatant lie but then, he figured Aidan had been monopolizing Lucy long enough.

"After Uncle Jamie. I did promise him."

With the proper manners instilled in him by Pop, he led his daughter off the dance floor to the corner, where Jamie was sending out all his helicopter-pilot mojo with a couple of Genevieve's friends who had flown over from Paris for the wedding.

To Jamie's credit, he didn't seem at all bothered to be interrupted in mid-flirt by his seven-year-old niece and quickly swooped her back out to the dance floor.

Brendan, in turn, headed toward the nearest waiter, intending to nab a couple flutes of champagne and return to Lucy's side. Just as he reached the guy, Dermot approached from the other direction.

"Great party, Pop." It had to be said.

Dermot beamed at him, glowing as brightly as either of the brides. "It certainly is. A blessed time for the Caine family, isn't it? Overnight, I've gained a son and a daughter. And, of course, a new granddaughter in our Peyton. Oh, how your mother would have loved to see this. She always loved weddings and she would be bursting at the seams with joy."

"She is," he said, with perfect certainty.

Pop squeezed his arm, his blue eyes suddenly watery. "True enough, son. True enough. No doubt we had two angels these last few days, joining in our celebrations."

Jessie and Charlotte had been close friends. She would have loved this, too.

"It's a good thought, isn't it?"

"That it is." Dermot nodded back at the table across the way where a certain lovely woman with dark curls sat in conversation with Aidan. "And here's another beautiful thought. Lucy. She's a true delight, son, so full of love and heart."

Carter was back with her now, he saw. He was sitting at the table beside her eating yet another piece of cake. As he watched, Lucy reached out with a napkin to wipe a little smudge of frosting from the corner of his mouth.

"She is indeed," he answered.

"There," Dermot said softly. "That smile. I thought for certain you'd lost it forever. I can't begin to tell you how thrilled I am to see you happy again, my boy."

The past few weeks had been amazing, filled with more laughter and joy than he believed possible.

"Same goes, Pop. You and Katherine are enough to make the worst cynic want to write a love song."

Pop blushed as he sipped at his champagne. "She's... amazing. That's all there is to it. You and the other boys and Charlotte probably think I'm an old fool, don't you?"

"Never. We think you're finally showing a little good sense when it comes to Councilwoman Thorne. We're all happy for you." He gave his father a sidelong look. "Just one question. When will we all be dancing at your wedding?"

To his great amusement, Pop's blush intensified and

he cleared his throat with a surreptitious look around. "How would September work for you?"

Brendan stared. "I was only joking. Really, Pop?"

"Nothing's official yet. I would ask you not to say a word to any of the others until we're ready."

"Of course. Of course." He considered it a great honor that his father trusted him enough to confide in him, no doubt because of the unique bond created between them over the past few years. Each of them had endured the raw, devastating pain of losing the woman he loved. And both of them were slowly coming to see that the world hadn't stopped spinning because of it.

"Do you think it's too soon?" Dermot asked, edgy nerves in his voice.

"Are you kidding? You and Katherine have been a thing for years. Everybody saw it except the two of you."

He suddenly couldn't contain a grin. He found it hilarious that his father, who had been so cautious that he hadn't asked out the woman he loved for years and years, was now talking about marriage just a few weeks into making their unspoken relationship official.

"Neither of us wants to wait. We've both been alone so long and don't want to stay that way a minute longer than we have to. Besides, we're seasoned enough to know our own minds by now, don't you think?"

He found the whole thing sweetly wonderful. "It's great, Dad. We all love Katherine. You know we do. Most of all, we just want you to be happy."

Dermot inclined his head back toward Lucy. "And do you have any similar plans in that direction?"

He could feel his own features heat. The idea of taking that huge step again should fill him with panic. Instead, whenever he thought about Lucy and the future, a warm, tender peace seeped through him. For the past two years after losing Jess, each day had been a battle of endurance, just trying to make it through and doing his best to give his children some kind of normalcy.

For the first time, he looked toward the future with eager anticipation. He couldn't wait to see what life had in store for them—but mostly he was learning to simply savor right this moment.

He wasn't ready to talk about any of it with his father just yet. The love he had for Lucy was too new, too precious.

"Maybe," he conceded. "But why don't we focus on the weddings we're celebrating tonight before we start looking down the road?"

Dermot smiled "Good idea, my boy. Good idea. Let's party. Isn't that what you kids say?"

He hadn't been a kid in a long time but he got the general idea. "Close enough," he said, nodding to Pop and heading back to Lucy.

When he reached the table, Lucy smiled up at him, eyes shining with joy and love and a hundred other emotions that just about laid him flat on the dance floor.

Aidan at least had the good sense to rise and surrender his chair as soon as Brendan approached.

"I'll be in town until Tuesday," his brother said. "Why don't we meet at Pop's place Monday morning for French toast and we can go over all the details?"

"Perfect. I'm excited about this. Thanks, Aidan."

"Don't thank me. You're the one with all the good ideas. Bren, I hope you know you're one lucky son of a gun."

He thought of the dark place that had been his home the past two years. He felt as if he had been walking alone through that thorny, rocky, miserable place and was just now emerging back into a place filled with light and joy and hope.

"Yeah. I know."

He reached for Lucy's hand and she tangled her fingers through his with that soft smile that always made his heart pound. He wanted to kiss her, but Carter still got a little grossed out by it—something his son was just going to have to get over pretty darn quickly.

Aidan—the original cynic, who wouldn't be writing anybody love songs anytime soon—watched them both with an unreadable look for just a moment then smiled. He started to turn away but before he could make it far, Faith skipped to their table with her pink skirts twirling.

"Uncle Aidan, will you dance with me?"

The man a Bay Area magazine had called one of its 100 most eligible bachelors looked thoroughly delighted. "Why, Faith, my dear, that's the best invitation I've had all night."

He pulled his niece's hand through his arm and headed toward the dance floor.

"He seems to be taking your change in plans amazingly well. Very unlike the Aidan we all know and love," he said to Lucy.

She shrugged. "You know, I really don't think he will mind having his own private marketing consultant on speed dial."

"Just as long he remembers that you're my private marketing consultant," he growled.

She gave a throaty laugh and squeezed his fingers.

Too bad for Carter, Brendan couldn't resist leaning in and giving her a light kiss.

His son only rolled his eyes and finished off his cake. He must be adjusting to the new situation—not that he or Faith had a problem with him dating Lucy. Both of them had privately told him they were thrilled about it.

After Spence and Charlotte's wedding the night before, Faith had asked him a similar question to the one Dermot just had, if he planned to marry Lucy. She expressed in no uncertain terms that she would love, love, love it if Lucy came to live with them.

Since Carter didn't have many memories of his mother, he just wasn't used to seeing his dad kissing anybody. They would all figure it out.

Lucy had slipped effortlessly into the current of life in Hope's Crossing. The open house the night before the inn opened had been filled with friends, new and old. She was loving the challenge of it, and had already been contacted by a dozen tech companies who had heard she was moving into consulting from this little Colorado town.

"I'm all done with my cake. Can I go talk to my friend Ethan?" Carter asked.

He saw Sam Delgado, his wife, Alex, and their son, Ethan, at a nearby table. "Sure. Just don't go farther than that."

As soon as Carter left, he reached out and kissed Lucy again, not caring who saw them.

"I'm crazy about you. You know that, right?"

"Yes," she said, her voice soft and a little dazed. "Aidan's wrong, by the way. I'm the lucky one."

He didn't agree but he also didn't want to argue in the middle of a wedding reception. "How's the ankle?"

She shrugged. "A little sore. It's been a long couple of days, on top of the craziness of the last week at the inn. I'm fine, though. Wishing I could be out there dancing. You know you don't have to sit here by me all night, right?"

He took her hand again, his heart overflowing with happiness that flooded all the dark corners with light.

"Get used to it, Lucy. Right here, next to you, is exactly where I want to be."

* * * * *

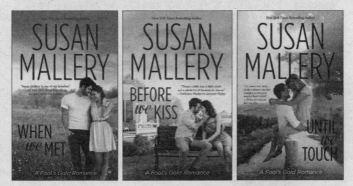

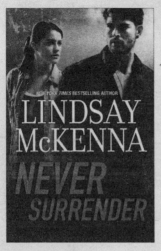

Don't miss these dangerously addictive contemporary romances that will have you begging for more...

Maggie Carpenter is ready for a change—to leave her ordinary life in South Carolina behind and accept a scholarship and enter the lavish lifestyle at an International School in London. Torn between her dream guy and the boy haunting her dreams, she might get more than she bargained for....

Charlie and his brother, A-list movie star Cato, have been rivals for years, and have buried one huge family secret. With Cato's unexpected return, Charlie knows his life at Usherwood will be in jeopardy...

Carmen Shelby wants what's been left to her—the valuable estate that she once called home. The heir to Burlington Manor is Rex Carruthers, a ruthless playboy who enjoys playing games, and all he wants is for Carmen to surrender....

Available now wherever ebooks are sold!

REQUEST YOUR FREE BOOKS!

2 FREE NOVELS
FROM THE ROMANCE COLLECTION
PLUS 2 FREE GIFTS!

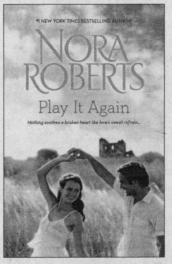

RaeAnne Thayne

77769	WILLOWLEAF LANE	__ $7.99 U.S.	__ $9.99 CAN.
77747	CURRANT CREEK VALLEY	__ $7.99 U.S.	__ $9.99 CAN.
77670	SWEET LAUREL FALLS	__ $7.99 U.S.	__ $9.99 CAN.
77593	BLACKBERRY SUMMER	__ $7.99 U.S.	__ $9.99 CAN.

(limited quantities available)

TOTAL AMOUNT	$ _____
POSTAGE & HANDLING	$ _____
($1.00 FOR 1 BOOK, 50¢ for each additional)	
APPLICABLE TAXES*	$ _____
TOTAL PAYABLE	$ _____

(check or money order—please do not send cash)

To order, complete this form and send it, along with a check or money order for the total above, payable to Harlequin HQN, to: **In the U.S.:** 3010 Walden Avenue, P.O. Box 9077, Buffalo, NY 14269-9077; **In Canada:** P.O. Box 636, Fort Erie, Ontario, L2A 5X3.

Name: _____
Address: _____ City: _____
State/Prov.: _____ Zip/Postal Code: _____
Account Number (if applicable): _____

075 CSAS

*New York residents remit applicable sales taxes.
*Canadian residents remit applicable GST and provincial taxes.

HARLEQUIN® HQN™
www.Harlequin.com

PHRAT0714BL